Escape to Polker

Cass Grafton began her writing life in Regency England, enlisted Jane Austen's help to time-travel between then and the present day and is now happily ensconced in 21st-century Cornwall. Well, in her imagination and soul; her heart and physical presence reside in northern England with her ever-patient husband and Tig and Tag, their cute but exceptionally demanding moggies.

A bit of a nomad, Cass has called three countries home, as well as six different English counties, but her aspiration is to one day reunite with her beloved West Country. In the meantime, she writes feel-good contemporary romances set in Cornwall and, in doing so, manages to live there vicariously through her characters and settings.

An Ambassador for the Jane Austen Literacy Foundation, Cass is also a member of the Romantic Novelists' Association, the Jane Austen Society UK and the Society of Authors.

Also by Cass Grafton

The Austen Adventures (with Ada Bright)

The Particular Charm of Miss Jane Austen
The Unexpected Past of Miss Jane Austen

The Little Cornish Cove series

New Dreams at Polkerran Point
Escape to Polkerran Point

Escape to Polkerran Point

Cass Grafton

CANELO

First published in the United Kingdom in 2024 by

Canelo
Unit 9, 5th Floor
Cargo Works, 1–2 Hatfields
London SE1 9PG
United Kingdom

A CIP catalogue record for this book is available from the British Library.

Print ISBN 978 1 80436 601 1
Ebook ISBN 978 1 80436 602 8

Cover design by Head Design

Cover images © Shutterstock

Look for more great books at www.canelo.co

Printed and bound in Great Britain by Clays Ltd, Elcograf S.p.A.

1

To my beautiful daughter, Rachel – my very own unexpected bundle of adventure.

(Tom, you're not being overlooked, but there was a bit more planning involved with you, so here's advance warning of you receiving the next book's dedication!)

Chapter One

Parking Meet-her

Lauren Kirkham sensibly ignored the satnav instruction to 'proceed straight ahead' and drive off the short pier. Charming as the bay was, with its small harbour filled with bobbing boats and the clusters of quaint cottages clinging to the surrounding hillsides, she had no desire to become intimately acquainted with its watery depths.

Pulling over, conscious of the double yellow lines, she peered around. It was a dull early-April day, and the few people venturing out scurried to and fro without raising their heads. Lauren wiped her glasses and popped them back on her nose, relieved to spot a familiar blue 'P' sign. She eased the car along a short street lined with whitewashed cottages and pulled into one of two free spaces in the tiny car park.

Lauren picked up her phone from the passenger seat – no signal. Well, she had been warned.

'It's as though the village has a shield of protection over it, repelling all such modern idiocies,' Anna Redding, her best friend, had cautioned.

Getting out of the car, Lauren wrinkled her nose at the salty air. Gulls wheeled overhead against a steel grey sky, their cries mingling with the sound of hammering from the nearby boatyard. A stiff breeze toyed with Lauren's cropped blonde hair as she looked around, then set off, holding her phone up and angling it now and again in hopes of a signal.

A 'cliff path' sign directed Lauren to the right, and she sprinted up the steadily rising slope, emerging onto a viewing spot which afforded a stunning vista across Polkerran Point, a charming Cornish fishing village. Sitting on a conveniently placed bench bearing a dedication – *In memory of Grumpy Dave, who sat here so no one else could* – Lauren was relieved to pick up a weak signal.

She put in a call to Anna, who gave her precise directions to Westerleigh Cottage, and Lauren retraced her steps, keen to end the journey. It had been a long drive from North Yorkshire.

'Oh, for goodness sake!'

Back at the car park, Lauren stared in disbelief at the mud-spattered Jeep parked so close to her car, there was no chance of getting in on the driver's side. To add insult to injury, it began to rain. Her umbrella and coat were inside, and she'd parked too close to the wall to open the passenger door.

Lauren looked around for the driver, but there was no one in sight, and she glared at the heavens. The rain's intensity increased as the heavens glared back. She'd have to take shelter.

Brushing damp tendrils of hair off her forehead, Lauren spotted a teashop on the corner and hurried to open the door. A bell jangled jauntily in a very old-fashioned way, but what the place looked like, she couldn't say, her glasses had steamed up.

'Yes, my lovely? What can I get 'ee?'

Lauren whipped off her specs. A grey-haired lady in a spotted apron eyed her with curiosity from behind the counter.

'I – er – nothing, thanks. At least,' Lauren glanced around the small tearoom. Three of the four tables had occupants: someone half-hidden by a newspaper, a young couple with their heads together as they studied a tourist leaflet and an old dear, pausing her knitting needles to watch on with interest.

Before Lauren could explain, a door labelled 'WC' opened and another elderly woman emerged, trying to peer over her shoulder as she joined the knitting lady.

'Is me dress tucked in me knickers again?'

'No, you'm done up proper this time, Cleggie.'

Lauren turned back to the counter. 'It's my car. Some idiot has parked so close, I can't open the door.'

The aproned lady's mouth opened, but the response came from behind the paper.

'Perhaps you should check if you're parking in a reserved bay before you do so.'

Lauren frowned. Had she? The newspaper lowered to reveal its owner: a man in paint-smeared overalls, with a smudge of dirt on his cheek above a short-cropped beard. His dark blond hair stuck up in a quiff above his right eye, as if he'd been resting his head in his hand at some point.

'Seen enough?'

Lauren lowered her gaze to meet a pair of brown eyes. They weren't any more obliging.

Turning back to the lady behind the counter, Lauren smiled. 'Please can you help me? I'm stranded until I find the owner. It's a Jeep – green and very dirty.'

'Oh yes, love. That belongs to—'

'Me. The village idiot, apparently.'

Feeling dreadful, Lauren met the unpromising look of the man with the paper. 'I'm so sorry. I shouldn't have said that. I've had a long drive and parked up to make a call for directions but with no signal had to walk to find one.'

The man made a faint sound. 'You're from up country, then.'

The tone wasn't unpleasant, but the lady behind the counter came round to stand beside Lauren.

'Now, now, young'un. No need to take an ill humour out on an emmet.' She frowned as she eyed the man. 'Wasson, lad? This isn't like 'ee, being so teasy?'

Anticipating a sharp retort, Lauren was astounded when the man smiled warmly at the lady.

'Sorry, Morwenna. Got out the wrong side of the bath.'

Encouraged by this flash of humanity, Lauren tried again. 'Please could you move your car? I'm sorry I messed up.'

The man winked at the lady who headed back to the counter with a satisfied air. Tossing the paper aside, he grabbed a set of keys from the table and stood.

'Come on,' he urged Lauren as he passed her.

With a vague smile round the room, she hurried after him. The man reversed the Jeep, waiting with the engine running, and Lauren hurriedly unlocked her car and slipped inside, only then noticing the small wall plaque: No Parking – Reserved.

Oh well. She'd know in future.

Waving a hand at the grubby Jeep, Lauren emerged once more by the harbour, then headed towards the small bridge spanning the river flowing into the bay, driving slowly along the lane as Anna had instructed.

'Turn right. Turn right now.'

'No, I won't. It's a straight drop into the water. Shut up.' Lauren switched the satnav off. Heavens, the lane was narrow! Good job she was in her Mini Cooper and not Kit's Audi...

Lauren's insides clenched involuntarily, and a hand went instinctively to her midriff.

'Let it go,' she murmured as the lane ahead rose.

She could see Anna before she reached the house, standing beside the wooden sign proclaiming Westerleigh Cottage as a B&B, and for some reason, Lauren's eyes prickled. What was *this* all about? Tears weren't her thing.

Easing the car through the open gates into the driveway, Lauren swallowed hard against a sudden rigidity to her throat.

'I can't believe you're here!' Anna opened the door and beamed at her. 'I thought you'd never take enough time off. It's a shame Kit couldn't come with you.'

A frisson of guilt shot through Lauren as she tossed her driving glasses onto the passenger seat and got out of the car. She didn't normally keep secrets from Anna, but somehow, with everything that had happened, she felt she wanted to be with her friend when she fessed up.

'I can't believe it either. Didn't think I'd ever find you.'

Anna laughed as they hugged, and she led Lauren into the house.

'Oliver will join us later. He's busy writing.'

Lauren looked around appreciatively as they walked down the wide hallway and emerged into a fabulous open-plan room filled with light, despite the grey day outside: a well-equipped but old-fashioned kitchen, a massive log burner throwing out a comforting glow, with sofas nearby and, in the large bay window, a long, scrubbed pine table and—

'Wow!'

Lauren fetched up by the table, taking in the sweep of sea as it met the waters of the harbour, both arms of land protecting the bay, one reaching further out in a diminishing rocky outcrop, on top of which was a small lighthouse. Even with spring rain falling, it was a stunning view.

'Isn't it wonderful?' The contentment in Anna's voice was obvious, and Lauren pushed aside her own worries.

'I'm so happy for you. The photos you sent didn't do it justice.' She pointed across the water. 'Is that where Oliver lived? Harbourside, was it?'

'Harbourwatch. Yes, the owner came back last September. Funnily enough, it doesn't hold my attention in such a way anymore.'

Lauren eyed her friend affectionately, knowing just how devoted she was to her fiancé, Oliver Seymour – a much sought after social historian and successful author. So far, he and Lauren had only ever met via Zoom.

Anna patted the back of a chair. 'You enjoy the scenery, and I'll pop the kettle on. I've made your favourite cupcakes.'

Feeling a tremor of happiness for the first time in ages, Lauren smiled gratefully. 'I'm parched.'

Anna pulled out plates and mugs. 'And how was the journey?'

'Long! I'm amazed how often you managed to get down to see your Aunt Meg.'

Aunt Meg had passed away the year before, and although not a true relative, Lauren knew Anna had cherished the memories she had made as a child, passing her summer holidays with the elderly lady here at Westerleigh Cottage.

She took in the charming space, with its nautical themed cushions, thick throws on the sofa backs and a wicker trough planted with spring bulbs on the coffee table, then sank into the chair, suddenly overcome with weariness.

'I see Heathcliff is still very much at home.' Lauren nodded towards the dog basket to one side of the hearth, where Anna's formerly stray black cat lay sleeping.

'Dougal usually spends the time between walks with Oliver in his den, but decided to give all his attention to Heathcliff yesterday, wore her out.'

'Heathcliff's a trans cat? Since when?'

'When Oliver moved in last year, he derived far too much pleasure informing me of my mistake. Too late to rename her, though, so Heathcliff she is.'

'I'm looking forward to finally meeting your man properly.'

Anna placed the plate of lemon drizzle cupcakes on the table and fetched the mugs of tea before taking the chair next to Lauren. 'Oliver'll be a few hours yet. There's so much to catch up on. Thank goodness you were able to take a fortnight off – you've been so elusive. Is work manic again? What's happened with the culling restructure? Did you get the role you wanted?'

Lauren's executive career with a large multi-national had been on an upward trajectory ever since she joined as a graduate, but where to begin explaining now? She took a sip of tea, then placed the mug on the table and met Anna's gaze solemnly.

'Yes and no. Accepted it, but then had to back out.'

Her friend's expression mirrored that of Lauren's former boss just weeks ago, as well it might.

'Why?' Anna's confusion was evident. 'Wasn't a supply chain director's role the dream?'

Lauren's mind flew to all the broken aspirations of the past few months. She had to forge new ones now. Again, her hand went to her midriff.

'It was in the US.'

Frowning, Anna selected a cup cake. 'Wasn't that one of your preferred locations?'

Her gaze drifting to the window, Lauren watched the waves crashing against the rocks beneath Harbourwatch, the white tips splintering into the air and dissipating, much as her career had shattered, along with her relationship with Kit, and all because—

'Hey, where have you gone?' Anna drew Lauren's attention with a gentle prod of her arm. 'This isn't like you. What's up?'

Lauren took another sip of tea. 'Sorry, love. Head's a bit mashed lately, and it's hard to know where to begin.' She laughed, aware it sounded forced. 'Probably at the end. I'm pregnant.' She shook her head as Anna went to speak. 'There's more. Kit and I split up because of it. I wanted to tell you in person.'

Anna stared at her friend, brow furrowed in concern. Then, she reached out a hand and took Lauren's, giving it a squeeze. 'I'm so sorry. You only moved in with him in February.'

'And you know how long it took me to make *that* decision!' Lauren had been Harrogate's favourite party girl – happily living a casual dating lifestyle, her emotions intact. Until Kit, that was. She summoned a faint smile for Anna, who was waiting patiently for more. 'Anyway, it all but never happened. I'd barely finished unpacking when the bomb dropped. Put being late down to the stress of the move, the restructure.' Lauren shrugged, despite feeling far from nonchalant. 'I'd have gone back to the house-share, but there's such a shortage of rentals, the room was snapped up the moment I gave notice. I've been with the parents back in Pateley Bridge.'

'And how's that going? How did they take the news?'

'Claustrophobic and a little nonplussed. I'm grateful to them, but Mum won't stop fussing over me. Hasn't had a child at home for years. Besides,' Lauren rolled her eyes, 'she's convinced Kit will change his mind, realise he can't live without me and come charging after me, diamond solitaire in outstretched hand. Think she's been watching too many of those Hallmark films.'

'If she has, she'd know that's not how it pans out. I'm confused, I mean how can they fire you if you're pregnant?' Anna's tone was indignant.

'It wasn't like that. I'd accepted the offer but the timeline didn't pan out. I'd be giving birth just around the time the visa came through. They'd already filled any vacant UK roles in the restructure, including my old one, so...' She shrugged. 'I made it easy for them, and my boss negotiated a generous package.'

'You can stay here as long as you like.'

Comforted, Lauren blew Anna a kiss. 'You're so sweet, but I have to make a new life now, and I can't see that working out in Cornwall.' She nodded her head towards the window. 'And I suspect Polkerran isn't much different in size to Pateley Bridge.'

'How did it...' Anna pulled a face. 'Sorry. I mean, I know *how* but...'

Lauren reflected on the many times she and Anna had discussed contraception when they'd shared a house, when they were both living it up as young, unattached women with few cares in the world.

'A classic case of unsafe sex. You remember I went to Manila with the team at the end of November, and once there, how procurement asked for a volunteer from supply chain to go to Thailand to visit a local supplier?'

'Yes, of course. You said your hand went up before they'd finished speaking.'

'Exactly. I was the only one on the team with no pressure to get home to Christmas present-shop or prep for descending family.' Lauren forcibly quashed the regret swirling through her. 'I hadn't taken enough pills with me for a prolonged stay. When I got back, I warned Kit we'd best be careful until it was back in my system. I mean,' she smirked at Anna, 'it's not like there aren't other things you can do.'

'Very wise. But…?'

Lauren sighed. Wisdom hadn't come into it. 'Way too much wine and a few shots of passion over the festive season got the better of us.'

'What about Kit?'

Feeling slightly nauseous, Lauren sipped at her tea. 'It was going really well. We'd been getting used to each other's foibles.' Trying not to remember how fun it had all been, Lauren summoned a smile. 'Guess this was a more extreme curveball than leaving the top off the ketchup. Kit assumed I'd have a termination. North America was a target location for us both, and he'd got irons in the fire and no intention of changing his plans.'

'How could he—' Anna stopped. 'Sorry. It's none of my business.'

'It was me minus the baby or nothing.' The leaden weight Lauren had borne since the split felt heavier for a moment.

'And...' Anna hesitated. 'You didn't think about... you know...'

Lauren sent Anna an understanding look. 'You know me well. I've always been more likely to gush over a puppy than a newborn in a pram, but not having the baby crossed my mind for all of ten seconds.'

It was true. Lauren was full of trepidation over whether she'd be a natural at the motherhood thing, but abortion had never been an option.

Anna's gaze was full of sympathy. 'And Kit wasn't ready for a family?'

Lauren drew in a short breath. 'Although I'd never really considered when that might be, Kit clearly had – as in, never...'

In truth, Lauren was too scared to think about the responsibility right now, but she'd no intention of admitting that to Anna, who'd grown up without the love of any parents and suffered for it.

Anna held her friend's gaze for a moment, and Lauren reached out to squeeze her hand. 'Don't worry about me. I'll be fine.'

If only I believed it...

'What do you want to do? My mind would be in chaos.'

Decisive by nature, Lauren hated not having all the answers, but before she could formulate a response, the door behind them opened and, expecting Oliver, she turned in her seat.

Frozen in the doorway, his gaze moving from her friend to Lauren, was dirty-Jeep man.

'Oh Lord.' Lauren looked between Anna and the new arrival. 'Surely I haven't committed another heinous parking crime?'

Chapter Two

Mind the Gap

'Ah.' The man hesitated, his gaze on Lauren as she rose from her seat.

Anna's face lit up. 'Hey, come in stranger.'

He looked much as he had earlier, but without the streak of dirt on his cheek or the uncompromising expression.

'Daniel, this is my friend, Lauren. Lauren, I've mentioned Daniel loads of times – he's Alex's cousin.' Alex was Anna's ex.

'We've met.' The man held out his hand, and Lauren shook it firmly.

'But were not introduced.' Lauren was confused. Anna had often spoken of Daniel Tremayne, with whom she was good friends. The local DIY man, unfailingly upbeat and friendly had been the impression Lauren had gained.

'I owe you an apology.' Daniel's brown eyes were warmer than earlier, and although his hair remained stuck up in a tuft, he had an attractive face – especially now it was less sullen.

'What happened?' Anna was looking from Daniel to Lauren in confusion.

'I made the mistake of parking in a reserved bay when I stopped to call you, for which I was duly reprimanded.'

Daniel raised both hands. 'Guilty as charged. Sorry. I wasn't having the best one.' He grinned. 'If you'd said you knew Anna, I'd probably have been less snappy.'

Relieved she hadn't permanently alienated a local – and a friend of Anna's too – Lauren met Daniel's look openly.

'I was on a short fuse too, but it was no excuse for being rude. I really am sorry.'

Daniel shook his head. 'I've been called worse.'

He winked at Lauren, and she gratefully accepted a fresh mug of tea from Anna as Daniel sank into the chair opposite.

'Do you want one?' Anna waved the pot, but he shook his head.

'I had one at the plumbing centre just now, and I'm due to meet the foreman up at the site in—' he glanced at his phone '—fifteen minutes. Being pressed to book a date in for the final recording, so I'm hoping we're not far from handover. Popped in to say hi as I was passing.'

Lauren cradled her mug, tuning out the chat as Daniel went into detail about the rising costs on some build he was working on. Relief over coming clean to Anna about everything mingled with her ever-present regret over how things had ended with Kit, but she strove to push the swirling discomfort away. She *must* determine a new strategy, and that required her habitual commitment to the task in hand, not retrospection and misgivings.

Lauren was so deep in thought, she almost started as Daniel stood.

'The Canaries?' Anna frowned. 'She never mentioned it when I saw her in passing at the weekend.'

'You and me both. I got a text from Claud before she boarded her flight.' He shoved a hand into the pocket of his overalls and withdrew his keys. 'Said she needed a week away from the gloom. I'm not sure if she meant me or the weather.'

Daniel laughed, but to Lauren he didn't sound amused.

'Right.' He picked up his phone. 'Best love and leave you.'

He nodded in Lauren's direction, and bemused, she glanced at her watch as he left. That was ten minutes she wouldn't get back.

'What's up, Anna?'

Her friend's concerned gaze had remained on the boot room door as it closed behind Daniel.

'Nothing. It's just…' She shrugged. 'He's not himself lately.'

The house phone rang – a room booking for that night – and when Anna ended the call, Lauren pleaded tiredness from the journey.

'Let me show you upstairs and you can chill for a while. Dinner will be ready around seven but come down whenever you're ready and have a drink with us. Oh! You can't have wine.'

Anna's face was quite despondent as they reached the hall, and Lauren sent her a fond look. 'Sorry, my old drinking buddy. I'm on the soft stuff for the next few months, but that reminds me…' She fixed her friend with a serious eye. 'I don't want anyone here to know about… well, how things are right now.'

'Not even Oliver?'

'I'm only here for two weeks.' A pretend pout was the only response, and Lauren – used to the tactic – persisted. 'I'm not falling for that. Come on, Anna,' her tone was wheedling. 'I've barely come to terms with the pregnancy myself, I don't want to be telling people yet. This visit is an escape from reality for me – a respite before everything kicks off. For the next fortnight, I'd rather be just Lauren, not your pregnant friend. Please?'

'Of course.' Anna hugged Lauren, then stepped back. 'Does this mean you're stuck on fruit juice, then?'

Lauren reached for the designer tote sitting on top of her case at the bottom of the stairs. 'Thankfully, teetotalism is the new black.' She extracted two bottles: an alcohol-free flavoured gin and a bottle of pale pink lemonade. 'Once these are in the correct glass, no one will ever know! Got some naughty empties I can decant the contents into?'

Anna's lips curved. 'You always were inventive. I know you're going to take this in your stride.'

'Hmmph,' Lauren grunted as they made their way up the stairs with her bags. 'Some things are more challenging. I'm still adjusting to a midwife and regular urine checks being part of my routine.'

Anna showed Lauren to her room – formerly her beloved Aunt Meg's, but now with a small-but-smart en suite bathroom installed – and, overcome once more with the tiredness that had plagued her in recent weeks, she was thankful to be left alone.

Lauren began to unpack, but when she turned back from the wardrobe to the suitcase, her eye was caught anew by the view, and she was drawn to the window. The rain had passed over, the clouds parting, as rays of sun hit the dappled water of the harbour. Seagulls winged overhead, their faint call audible through the closed windows. The distant chug of a fishing boat drew her attention to the harbour entrance, a cluster of gulls circling and wheeling in its wake.

Leaning on the sill, Lauren's gaze roamed over Harbourwatch, the large, almost gothic-looking property perched on the opposite cliffs, then moved along, taking in the pastel-shaded cottages clinging to the steep hillsides and the colourful boats bobbing in the small harbour. Would a stay in Polkerran Point begin to heal her?

The village – referred to by locals as 'the cove' because of the crescent shape of the bay, nestled between its two arms of land, protecting it from the open sea – was as picturesque as Anna had said. It might not have much by way of the bars, clubs or trendy boutiques she loved to frequent, but Lauren looked forward to exploring it. Then, amused, she resumed her unpacking.

Provided she didn't run foul of any more of said locals!

–

Nocturnal by nature, Lauren had always been able to burn a chandelier at both ends and sleep like a cat in between. Usually up bright and early, she'd head to the gym or go for a run before work (although her ability to sleep in at weekends was legendary in the Harrogate house). Since discovering she was pregnant, she'd struggled to sleep as her life began to crumble around her, so it was a surprise to awaken at ten o'clock on her first morning in Cornwall, her body clearly needing the extra hours of recovery.

Stretching in the cosy mound of bedding, Lauren was tempted to curl up and go back to sleep, but the distant call of seabirds roused her, and she flopped onto her back, reflecting on the pleasures of the previous evening, back in her best friend's company, enjoying Oliver's conversation, a cat on her lap and a snoring Dougal by her feet.

Come on, Kirkham. Things to do, places to go, people to annoy.

Lauren flung the covers aside as the old phrase came to mind, once on a sign hanging in the Harrogate kitchen, something she and Anna had chanted to each other as they left for their respective jobs.

Refreshed after a cool shower, she enjoyed a mug of tea (Anna kept well-stocked hospitality trays in the rooms) as she leaned against the sill and took in the charming scene outside. It was Thursday, and usually on a week day she'd have gone for a run, and she stretched her arms and legs. She'd have to suss out the best route.

There wasn't a cloud in the sky today and the water reflected its blueness, along with the smoky grey of the cliffs and the shimmering brown trees, tipped with a hint of spring green. A small red-and-white boat bobbed and weaved as it crossed the water towards the far side of the bay, passing a trawler as it neared the harbour, and a couple of long, low wooden boats, with what looked like about six people working the oars of each, could be seen making their steady way through the water below Harbourwatch. It was a far cry from the view from her office in Leeds.

'Hey, sleepy head.' Anna greeted Lauren as she entered the kitchen. 'I've just boiled the kettle, come and join me.'

Lauren reached for a cookie from the plate in the middle of the table, sinking into a chair opposite Anna. 'I'm starving.'

'You missed breakfast, but I didn't want to disturb you. I'll make you a bacon buttie.'

'Sounds fab.' Lauren munched on the cookie as Anna prepared her late breakfast. 'You've not lost your touch with the baking.' Then she frowned, recalling something from yesterday. 'What did your builder friend mean? About the final recording?'

'Didn't I tell you? Last year, Daniel acquired a piece of land on the clifftop with planning permission, and he's fulfilling one of his ambitions, building a house there. His girlfriend,' Anna pulled a face as she handed Lauren a mug of tea, 'knows someone connected to *Dream Builds* – a regional TV programme in the style of *Grand Designs*. They've filmed a couple of times during the build and when it's finished, they'll come back once more. New series is due to start airing back end of the year, and Daniel's build will be the third episode.'

Lauren settled back in her chair, keenly interested. She loved *Grand Designs*. 'So what's it like? The house?'

Anna turned the bacon, and then leaned against the kitchen counter-top. 'Not really my taste.' She wrinkled her nose. 'It seems very modern from the plans, all open rooms downstairs with massive windows.'

Lauren eyed her friend with amusement. 'You and your love of old stuff. Oliver was always going to be a shoe-in.'

Anna burst out laughing. 'Cheeky!'

'I didn't mean that.' Lauren's lips curved. 'I meant his love of history. Anyway, this build; no beams and inglenook, then?' She waved a hand towards those features in Anna's home.

'Sort of. Daniel says there's a massive Cornish slate hearth with a log burner, and that there's plenty of natural wood in there – it sounds more reminiscent of a barn conversion. Except it's not a barn...'

'Or a conversion.'

'Neither, but I think it'll need some female touches to soften it. Mind you, it was still pretty much a building site the only time I saw it.'

Quickly cutting some slices of homemade bread, Anna checked the bacon.

'And you don't think the girlfriend can provide that? Is this the one gadding off to warmer climes at the drop of a sombrero?' Lauren inhaled deeply. 'Hmmm, that bacon smells delicious.'

'It's from the local farm shop.' Anna came over to the table, placing a plate of sandwiches in front of Lauren. 'Tuck in.'

'Have you got any brown sauce?'

'But you never—'

Lauren wagged a finger at Anna. '"Never" has taken on a whole new meaning. My taste buds are up the shoot.'

Anna returned with the sauce, and as Lauren squeezed some onto the bacon, she related the story of Daniel and Claudia.

'They've been together about eight months, I suppose. She has an annexe on her parents' farm at Pengillis – that's where the farm shop is. Daniel is semi-living with her.'

'Semi-living? Is that even a condition?'

'He's renting one of Oliver's cottages, but he spends weekends with Claudia.'

'So what's the problem. You don't like her?'

'She's okay.' Anna sent Lauren an amused look. 'Claudia exudes glamour. She's got this gorgeous glossy black hair, and she's always dressed in designer labels.'

Lauren raised a brow. 'Wow. From the little I've seen of Polkerran Point it doesn't seem the natural place for a fashionista.'

'Claudia works in Bristol, and sometimes London, so is only ever down at the weekends. I'm just not sure they're well-matched as a couple.' Anna shrugged. 'I suppose that's their business, not mine.'

Munching contentedly, Lauren eyed Anna fondly. 'This reminds me of breakfasts round the kitchen table in Harrogate.'

'Hmm.' Anna started to clear the table. 'Especially after a late night out. A bit of catch-up gossip, then you'd eat your buttie and head off to bed.'

A distant look in her eyes, Lauren's lips curved upwards. 'God, those were fun days.'

'I bet you didn't miss them when you left to move in with— oh!' A hand shot to Anna's mouth. 'I'm so sorry, Lauren. That was tactless.'

Though her stomach dipped, Lauren shook her head. 'Don't be. You made your mistake with Alex, and I made mine with Kit.'

She popped the last morsel of sandwich into her mouth as Anna headed to the dishwasher with her plate. Looking out at the view, Lauren chewed thoughtfully. Mistakes were all very well, but she needed a game plan. With a sigh, she watched the water lap and retreat from the cliffs. She would have to ebb and flow too.

'So what *are* your plans?'

Anna reclaimed her seat, and Lauren wished she had an answer.

'I'm not giving up on my career,' she said firmly. 'I see this as a… as an aberration. I've already lined up some project work on a consultancy basis, but as soon as the birth is over and I can get a permanent job, I'll be back on track.'

Anna looked uncertain. 'Where? You don't still aim to go abroad?'

To be honest, Lauren did. Living and working overseas – embracing the culture, lifestyle, and possibly the language, of another country – was a key aspiration, and she had no intention of letting it go. She didn't see why a single woman couldn't move abroad with a child in tow. Couples did it.

'I do. This is just a hiccup.'

'It could be the longest bout of hiccups anyone ever had.'

Lauren smiled. 'Okay, I'll call it another gap year.'

'You'll be coming back from this one with more than a dodgy Aussie accent and a stuffed koala.'

True, but she was reluctant to dwell on the reality right now. Then, she noted Anna's anxious expression, and Lauren's heart went out to her friend.

'Bear with me, mate. I don't mean to make light of it, and I'm also very aware none of this is the baby's fault. When he or she is born, I'll do my utmost to be the best mum I can, but I can't pretend my lack of a career isn't more on my mind right now.' Lauren met Anna's concerned gaze earnestly. 'It's just I'm in a situation I never anticipated at this stage of my life. Aside from a bit of nausea early on, I've had no symptoms other than tiredness. My priority has to be the consultancy, so there's an income stream. Then, I have to find a home for the two of us.'

With a gentle smile, Anna got to her feet. 'A home for a baby or small child is very different to a home for a high-flying exec.'

Lauren knew it, but for these two weeks, she could pretend none of this was happening – aside from the fake G&Ts she'd consumed the night before. She hadn't enjoyed the small deceit of Oliver and, although the taste was pleasant enough, it didn't quite hit the same spot.

'What do you have to do now?' Lauren joined Anna by the sink.

'Not much. Only one room is let out at the mo'. I'll do a quick whizz, make the bed and generally tidy up, replenish the tray. Clean the bathroom.' Anna wiped her hands on the tea towel. 'Did you get an app yet?'

With a frown, Lauren glanced at her phone. 'For what?'

'Pregnancy, of course. You're the app queen. I was sure you'd have downloaded one.'

Anna went to fetch what she needed, and Lauren looked at her mobile again. It had never occurred to her to search for anything baby related. The private scan and initial checks with the midwife felt as though they'd happened to someone else. Lauren's interest in apps lay more with her social life or addictive games to help pass time on a long-haul flight.

They made their way along the hall to the stairs, Anna carrying her box of cleaning supplies.

'I'll go tidy my own room.'

'Perfect.' Anna beamed as they reached the landing. 'It's so great to have you here. We can go down into the village once I'm done, have a mooch around.'

'I'd love that.'

They parted outside Lauren's room, and she sank onto the bed, the weariness all-consuming again. She didn't want to think about being pregnant. She had always been so career-driven, full of energy, clarity and determination.

Lauren's work life had been her passion since the day she'd got the graduate position at her company. The last ten years had been a whirlwind of roles which had changed every few years as she worked her way upwards. Once she'd taken on a global management job, the travel opportunities had been all she'd ever dreamed of, from visiting tea plantations in Kenya when working for the foods division, to running a team on a special project in Sydney.

Of course, in recent years, with travel budgets becoming restricted and new technology reducing the need for face-to-face meetings, there had been less, but that had only fed her thirst for a posting in another country.

For a moment, Lauren felt flattened, daunted by starting the upward climb again. Then, she put it aside. Her attention had to be on the here and now. Besides, she had an ominous feeling life wasn't done with throwing curveballs her way yet.

Chapter Three

Two Pints of Crisps and a Packet of Lager, Please

The day passed swiftly, and Lauren was surprised how much she enjoyed it. Anna introduced her to the next door neighbour, Nicki, where they had yet another cuppa before walking down the lane to the small jetty. The little red-and-white boat turned out to be the twelve-seater passenger ferry which linked both sides of the bay.

Anna's love for Polkerran shone in her eyes, throbbed in her voice, as she gave a running commentary, pausing occasionally to point something out or stop to chat with someone.

'And who was that gentleman?'

They both watched as the man Anna had just exchanged greetings with entered the chandlers near the harbour.

'Ralph. Chairman of the Gig Club.'

Lauren sent Anna a sideways look. 'Doesn't epitomise your typical raver.'

'Numpty,' Anna nudged her friend. 'It's a type of boat, as I'm sure you know perfectly well. *That* sort of gig.'

She indicated a couple of long, wooden boats, resting on trailers on the ramp leading down to the water. They were similar to the ones Lauren had seen from her window. 'Gig racing is huge down here, and there are loads of teams and competitions, all ages and abilities.'

They walked up onto the cliffs opposite Westerleigh Cottage, and Lauren took loads of photos, especially fascinated by the old lighthouse perched on its rocky outcrop. On their way back, they stopped at the small cafe on the tidal beach below Harbourwatch to pick up a hot drink, and as they made their way back up the lane, clutching their paper cups, Anna pointed out the windows of the office where she'd worked with Oliver.

Lauren eyed the Gothic-influenced property, perched as though it had simply evolved out of the rocks beneath it.

'It's huge! Oliver must have rattled around in there on his own.'

Anna led the way past Harbourwatch's iron gates.

'There's a family in there now. A couple with a young son. The chap's family has associations with Polkerran going back several decades.'

They lunched at the Lugger, a quaint old inn nestled between the few shops near the bridge on the quieter side of the cove, run by a married couple, Sebastian and Gavin, where Anna introduced Lauren to more of the locals.

'Are you serious?' Lauren muttered to Anna as they left the pub later. 'Colin the Cod runs the village fish and chip shop, but Dickie the Chippy is a carpenter, and Foxy Boxey – who looks like butter wouldn't melt in her mouth – is the local undertaker?'

Anna giggled. 'You'll get used to how it is down here. People are often defined by where they live or their voca-tion.'

They passed an elderly lady in the street, who seemed vaguely familiar to Lauren. She was disappointed, on being introduced to Mrs Lovelace, to hear no malapropisms, having heard of the lady's habit. Anna, however, assured her she wouldn't have long to wait.

After a leisurely evening meal in Oliver and Anna's company, Lauren tried to ignore the pang she felt at not being able to relive the old days and go clubbing or for drinks with her mate. Instead, she went to bed, losing herself in the latest raunchy novel on her tablet until her lids drooped, and she fell into a dreamless sleep.

The relatively early night meant Lauren woke soon after dawn broke, and she went for an invigorating run along the cliff path – quite a challenge with its steep dips, rises and uneven surface – took a refreshing shower, and was downstairs to find Anna preparing to cook breakfast for her guests.

'Shall I lay the tables?'

'It's already done,' Anna said as they headed for the dining room. 'I do it the night before.'

'Where's Oliver this morning? Is he writing?'

'Yes, but he also has a video call at ten with his agent.'

Anna tipped some freshly baked rolls into two baskets on the highly polished, old-fashioned sideboard. Resting a hand on the smooth wood, Lauren looked around appreciatively. Everything was, to be fair, very 1950s in style, but clearly well cared for.

'This is all your Aunt Meg's furniture?'

'Yes.' Anna refolded one of the linen napkins, adjusted a fork slightly and looked over at Lauren. 'Oliver and I wanted to keep it just as it is. Apparently, it's all the vogue these days, the new vintage.' She headed for the door. 'The guests seem to love it.'

It had a certain charm, but not to Lauren's taste, as she leaned towards contemporary design. She followed Anna back to the kitchen, deep in thought. Her friend had been a successful project manager for an event co-ordination company in Harrogate before she moved to Cornwall. Her life had been hectic, pressured, and her job a huge part of it. How had Anna adjusted so well to being in this quaint village, running a part-time B&B?

With a self-deprecating laugh, Lauren brushed the question aside. She and Anna were like beer and crisps. They went well together, but were entirely different in nature. Despite loving her job, all Anna really wanted was what she now had: to be happy with someone she loved and who – clearly – adored her.

Sadness consumed Lauren as she crossed the kitchen. Even the sun shining through the windows and bathing the room in warmth couldn't lift her spirits, and she sank onto the sofa by the wood burner, trying desperately to reclaim the positivity with which she had woken. She felt like she was in free-fall, lost for a direction, and—

'Hey.' Anna came to sit beside her. 'What's up? You were fine, and now you seem as though you're battling demons.'

Lauren shook her head. 'Sometimes it all crowds into my head. I need activity, to be busy. Too much time to think. You know I never do well with down time.'

'Then help me with the breakfasts.'

Not quite what she'd meant, but Lauren grasped the lifeline and, much to her surprise, quite enjoyed the process. The guests were friendly, and although Anna had to answer questions about the best place to find a local pottery or the easiest part of the South West Coast Path for someone with limited mobility, Lauren exchanged some banter over how delicious Anna's cooking was and how much weight she expected to gain during her stay.

After that, it was time to clear, clean and tidy the kitchen and, once the guests had gone out for the day, sort out the bedrooms. Anna refused any help, saying she had a routine, so Lauren opened the laptop and tried to immerse herself in sending emails to her extensive network, but her ability to concentrate seemed to have disintegrated, and she was relieved when Anna came back downstairs.

'Time for coffee, I think. Sorry yours has to be caffeine-free.' Anna was pink in the face, her brown wavy hair escaping from its ponytail.

'Ah, memories of when you'd decided to do a mega-clean back at the house-share.'

'It's a lot more energetic than you'd think.'

They had barely been in the kitchen ten minutes, with Anna taking a moment to re-tie her hair, when the door to the boot room opened and a young woman with red-gold curls came in, holding a young child by the hand.

'Morning, Anna.'

'Hi, Phee.' Anna turned to Lauren. 'This is Phoenix. And this,' she crouched down and offered her hand to the little girl, 'is Verity Blue.'

Making an attempt at shaking hands, the child threw her arms around Anna's neck as she lifted her up to hug her. 'And how is my VeeBee this morning?'

Verity Blue chuckled. 'Hungry.'

With a laugh, Anna placed her back on her feet. 'As always.'

Phoenix and Lauren shook hands. 'Take a seat. I'll bring the drinks over.'

Lauren glanced expectantly at the door to the boot room. 'Who else is coming?' She was well aware of the locals' predilection for calling at Westerleigh, seeking a cosy chat at the kitchen table.

'You never know. Daniel drops in if he's taking a break from the building site. Mrs L – you met her yesterday – is the most frequent and sometimes brings her daughter, Jean, but Jean runs the ice cream shop so in season I see less of her.'

'Nicki always pops in,' piped up Phoenix as she sat Verity Blue in the child's seat Anna had provided. 'Her kitchen overlooks the lane, which is the only way to get here, so she knows when people have arrived.'

Not quite the board meetings Lauren was used to, but it might prove entertaining. Lauren eyed the little girl across the table. She had her mother's red-gold curls and deep blue eyes.

'How old is your daughter?'

'Three going on thirteen.' Phoenix had a cheerful face, a sprinkling of freckles across her nose and a soft West Country burr. 'Starting playgroup in September, mornings only, mind. I don't envy they staff!'

Anna came over with a special cup for the little girl, along with a selection of mini cupcakes, which Verity Blue pounced on.

Within five minutes, there was a plate of assorted biscuits (all made by Anna) on the table, along with a teapot, coffee pot, milk, sugar and several mugs.

Lauren eyed Anna across the table as she poured a beaker of juice for Verity Blue. 'I can see you've done this before.' She glanced across to the kitchen. 'Don't you use that beast of a coffee machine?'

'For guests, usually. The regulars prefer a pot, so—'

Before Anna could finish, the door opened to admit Nicki, and gentle conversation soon filled the room as people's comings, goings and doings were dissected. Most of it went over Lauren's head, and she found her attention drifting back to her own concerns.

Where would be the best place to settle? She needed access to good travel, but she didn't yet know which company she'd join after the birth, or where it might be located. How could she make such a choice now? It wasn't the time to commit to a lease anywhere, and surely a city flat – Lauren's preference – wouldn't be the ideal environment for a baby? Was living with her parents going to be her immediate future? Beautiful though Nidderdale was, it was a galling thought.

The murmur of conversation and occasional laughter eventually roused her, and conscious Anna had discerned her distraction, Lauren made an effort to listen, ignoring the niggling notion she was somehow looking forward to Daniel putting in an appearance.

Ten minutes later, the visitors made to leave.

'Can Verity Blue stay for an hour?'

'Of course!' Anna smiled affectionately at Verity Blue. 'We can do some finger painting.'

'Yay!' The little girl had buttercream liberally spread around her mouth.

Barely had Phoenix left when Oliver came into the kitchen, and as Anna made him a coffee at the machine, he joined Lauren and Verity Blue at the table.

'You here again, Munster?' Oliver eyed the mess on the plate before Verity Blue. 'Never have I seen anyone so effectively destroy a cake.' The child merely looked at him from her big blue eyes, and Oliver took the mug from Anna as she came back to the table. 'Where's Phee off to this time?'

'She has an interview up at the hotel. Receptionist. Pays better than the coffee shop.'

'Hmph.' Oliver sipped the hot coffee. 'Perhaps she can then afford a childminder.'

Lauren was unsurprised by this response. Anna had told her back when she first met Oliver – for whom she had worked for several months before they became a couple – that he had no time for children, marriage or families, having not had a happy upbringing. It seemed he had mellowed a little, for he and Anna were at least engaged, but her friend had always desperately wanted a family. Having been an only child, orphaned as a baby and raised by an uncaring older cousin, Anna, unlike Oliver, longed for what she'd never had.

Anna, however, laughed. 'You always say that, and then I find you reading to her, or showing her one of your precious antiques.'

Oliver exchanged a swift amused look with Lauren. 'She has become profoundly interested in hallmarks. The subject never fails to calm her energies.'

'To the extent she falls asleep from boredom, you mean.'

'Harsh,' Oliver intoned, but Anna and Lauren laughed, until…

Splat!

The remains of Verity Blue's cupcake now adorned Oliver's tie.

''Liver like Anna's cake.' The child beamed through the buttercream and chuckling, Anna hastily removed the plate and fetched a damp cloth to wipe the little girl's face and fingers.

Oliver extracted a neatly pressed handkerchief and dabbed ineffectually at his tie.

'Is this a common occurrence?' Lauren wasn't sure whether to show her amusement. Oliver was quite hard to read.

'Less of late. We blow hot and cold.'

Lauren did laugh, and Oliver watched as Anna lifted Verity Blue into her arms.

'Anna calls it my education.'

'Tough love.'

'Indeed.'

Anna took the seat beside Oliver, Verity Blue on her lap. 'How was the call with Irinna?'

Oliver's face sobered. 'Ah. I could do with a word.'

Lauren looked from one to the other. 'I'll keep an eye on the little one. I mean, I don't have much experience but you won't be long, will you?'

As it happened, Verity Blue was ready for a nap, and settled quite happily on the sofa beside Lauren who took a colourful book from Anna, and began to point to the images as Anna and Oliver left the room.

Within minutes, Verity Blue slept, and Lauren tugged a light throw from the back of the sofa and tucked it around the little girl, then walked over to the sink to rinse the mugs.

The door to the boot room opened and the elderly lady from the day before entered.

'Mornin', my lovely. Where's that Anna to, then?'

'Hi, Mrs Lovelace.' Lauren gestured towards the hall. 'She's just talking to Oliver about something. Can I get you a coffee?'

'No, no, lovee. Can't stop today. Just on my way to see my friend, Cleggie. Been proper poorly, she has. Only I promised young Anna I'd drop off some running beans. Growed them m'self, you know.'

She placed a carrier bag on the table, then studied the sleeping Verity Blue. 'Little cherub. Grows proper fast, don't they? Be at school afore we know it.'

With that, she was gone, and Lauren walked over to study the sleeping child's face. She looked so benign, not capable of covering Oliver in whatever source came to hand.

Lauren swung around as the door to the hall opened. Anna looked anxious, but Oliver's expression was unreadable, a protective arm about his fiancée's shoulders.

'Is something wrong?' Lauren's brow furrowed as she looked between them.

Oliver, who had removed the soiled tie, spoke as they all took a seat at the scrubbed pine table again.

'I've been asked to stand in for a fellow historian, who's had to pull out of a lecture tour at short notice. It's for English students in Italy, two weeks, and I want Anna to come with me. She's been desperate to visit Rome and Florence.'

'Oh, you must go!' Lauren knew this had long been on Anna's wish list.

'But I can't.' Anna shook her head. 'It kicks off after the weekend, and I have guests booked in. Besides, you've only just arrived, and we wouldn't be back until Easter Monday. I can't desert you. You don't want to go back to Pateley Bridge early, and—'

Lauren took Anna's hand across the table, sending Oliver a reassuring look. Finally, she felt she had some purpose back, small though it was.

'I'm adaptable! I'll stay here, hold the fort.' A frisson of anticipation shot through Lauren, though she couldn't really account for it.

'Are you serious?' Anna looked astounded.

'Not much of a holiday for you,' Oliver added. 'And aren't you due back at your job?'

Feeling guilty for the continued pretence, Lauren tried not to think about what she didn't know about running a guesthouse.

'The joys of working from home these days. I can cook a decent breakfast, though I can't bake, so I'll have to buy bread.'

Oliver left them to it, but Anna looked torn between delight and concern. 'I can't leave you. You need—'

Lauren squeezed the hand she held and let it go. 'I'm at a loose end. Drifting. What I need is distraction and activity. You're doing me a favour, and I'll still be here when you get back if you'll have me a bit longer. Besides, I can work from here as well as anywhere.'

And so the deal was done. Anna and Oliver would leave for Italy in a few days' time, and Lauren – used to managing the global supply chain team in a large multi-national – would instead run the Westerleigh Cottage Bed & Breakfast in a little Cornish cove.

Chapter Four

Date Knight

Oliver shut himself away to prepare for the unexpected lecture tour and, after a quick lunch, Anna suggested showing Lauren where she shopped for her guests and, when they returned, running through the daily routine for the B&B.

As Anna began to prepare a pudding for that evening, she pointed to a peach in the fruit bowl. 'That's the size of your baby now.'

'You've lost me.' Lauren picked up the fruit, weighing it on her palm.

'I downloaded the Pregnancy+ app and put your date in.' Anna selected a couple of apples. 'They have a comparison thingy where there's a fruit, a dessert or an animal for the size of your baby each week. Fourteen weeks is a peach, although I think I might change over to the dessert. More my thing.'

'Are you serious?'

Lauren replaced the peach, eyeing Anna fondly as she headed back to the sink. It really should have been her friend who was pregnant. She'd have loved every minute.

–

Lauren had been shooed out of the kitchen as Anna cooked dinner, so she retreated to her room, sitting crossed-legged on the bed to work on a pitch on her laptop.

After a couple of hours, she stretched her arms above her head and put work aside. Checking her make up, Lauren eyed her softening haircut critically, then hurried from the room, enticed by the delicious aroma floating up the stairs. She'd cancelled her last appointment, which had been due the day she'd taken her third consecutive pregnancy test and finally accepted the result.

'Come and have a drink,' Oliver greeted Lauren as she entered the kitchen, and she joined him at the table, trying not to feel bad as he mixed what he assumed was a G&T for her.

'Ice?'

'Please.'

Oliver headed to the freezer as Anna came to join her, picking up a glass of wine and taking a long drink.

'How's the pitch coming along?'

'Slowly,' Lauren spoke quietly, aware Oliver was returning. 'Hoping I'll be more focused next week.'

Giving her a quick hug, Anna hurried back to the kitchen as Oliver handed the glass to Lauren.

'Anna tells me you're from a big family.'

'Three brothers, all older than me. It might sound like fun, but there are times when all you want is a bit of solitude, not your pigtails pulled and the smallest bedroom, full of clutter that isn't yours.'

Oliver's gaze drifted towards the kitchen and spoke quietly. 'I wish there was something I could do to fill that void for Anna.'

Lauren studied him thoughtfully. 'I don't want to be indelicate, but won't that be resolved one day – when you have a child?'

She almost held her breath as, worryingly, Oliver said nothing, his eyes fixed on his fiancée, humming to herself as she checked a pan in the oven.

Then, he turned his keen blue eyes on Lauren. 'If I can ever get her to commit to a date.'

'Oh.' Lauren frowned. Anna had never indicated any delay in getting married was down to her, she'd always assumed it was Oliver's reluctance.

Oliver shrugged. 'She doesn't want to rush me. But I didn't mean just having her own children. Anna feels not only her lack of parents, but also wider family like aunts, uncles, cousins – well, aside from the obvious…'

'Cousin Victoria? Yes, I know how awful she was to her. I mean, why even take a baby in if you're not going to cherish it?'

Lauren bit her lip, assailed by a sudden awful notion. What if she didn't love her child enough? Then, she brushed it aside. Of course she would. She had an abundance of affection to shower on someone, she just hadn't found the right person. The baby would surely fill that void.

–

As Saturday dawned, Lauren padded to the window to inspect the weather and was soon fastening her earphones and off for an early run. After a shower and donning her comfiest loungewear, she settled against her pillows, the laptop perched on a cushion, as she made some tweaks to a project brief for a company in Surrey.

Whenever Kit came to mind, Lauren forcefully shoved him aside. She couldn't forgive him, but she was beginning to understand his reaction more. Sadly, all that left her with was deep regret for their mutual weakness over giving in to their passion. What they had seemed so good and, between them, they had tossed it all away.

When Anna tapped on her door, Lauren emerged onto the landing thankful to be drawn from her incessant cycle of thoughts. The morning passed in a whirl, with Lauren shadowing Anna as she prepared and served breakfast, then was sat down to be taught the online booking system.

Oliver had been holed up in his office, working on lecture notes, which he promptly returned to after lunch. As it was such a mild April day, the women decided to take their drinks out onto the terrace and they sipped in silent appreciation of the view for a moment. Then, Anna squinted at Lauren, a hand held up to shield her eyes from the sun.

'Are you sure you'll be okay cooking mushrooms?'

Trying not to think about how nauseous a once-favourite food made her feel, Lauren sighed.

'I'm fine preparing them, it's just the taste.' Lauren eyed the rose lemonade with regret. 'Seriously hoping I don't have an aversion to wine at the end of all this.'

Anna laughed and turned back to the view. 'Me too. I miss my drinking bestie.'

'I'll be back.' Lauren stretched her legs out, enjoying the warmth of the spring sunshine in the sheltered spot. 'I've just been checking my diary, might need to move my next appointment on a bit.'

Anna turned in her seat. 'Oh, I never thought about that! I'm so sorry.'

'Don't be daft.' Lauren spoke reassuringly. 'It's routine, and it'll only be a week later. I'm in good health, past the all-important three-month mark. They listen for the heartbeat and start the bump measuring at this next one.' She eyed her midriff. 'Not much to measure yet. I wonder when it − sorry, the baby − will start to show?'

'You're so toned and it's a first pregnancy, so it'll be a while, I think.'

'*Think?*' Lauren tried not to laugh at Anna's culpable expression. 'You've been on those damn forums again.'

'It's fascinating.' Anna beamed. 'I can't wait until you find out the baby's sex.'

Lauren viewed Anna fondly. 'I promise you'll be the first to know. So, who is this lady Oliver is taking out to dinner tonight, and how come you're not madly jealous?'

Anna leaned forward to top up both their glasses. 'Cleggie. Mrs Clegg was his housekeeper over there.' She gestured towards Harbourwatch across the water. 'She's not been well lately, so wasn't able to mark her eighty-third birthday, and Oliver promised, once she was better, he'd take her out for dinner.'

'A riotous night ahead for Oliver, then.'

Anna laughed. 'She's expressed a desire to try a margarita, much to Oliver's surprise, so he's booked them into the bistro, as they have a good cocktail menu. I'm excused because I have a friend staying.' She winked at Lauren.

'Good to know I have my uses. What about us then, mate? Two young ladies, left to their own devices on a Saturday night. Polkerran Point at our disposal…'

'Leave it with me.' Anna drained her glass. 'Come on, let me show you where the linen is kept, and later I'll treat you to a night out in the cove as a thank you for standing in.'

Casting a speculative look towards the quaint village nestled around the harbour, Lauren shook her head as she followed Anna into the house.

Somehow, she didn't think it would be a late one.

–

Lauren reflected on the evening out as she dressed on Sunday morning. They'd had a lovely meal at the smart hotel at the top of the hill, then moved on to the Three Fishes pub on the harbour front before ending up in the wine bar attached to the bistro, although there was no sign of Oliver and his date by then.

They'd laughed so much, Lauren's cheeks ached, reminiscing about the days in the Harrogate house and their dating exploits.

She'd seen Daniel walking past the bistro with a couple of other young men. She hadn't mentioned it to Anna, who'd gone to the ladies', but he'd looked very cute and a lot smarter than she'd yet seen him. He was laughing and Lauren couldn't help but smile, hoping he wasn't dwelling too much on the absent Claudia. The wish they might bump into him on the walk home, she also kept to herself.

Once Sunday breakfast was over for the guests and they had checked out, Anna showed Lauren the rooms before running through what to do to turn them around. As it happened, no one was due in for a couple of days, which Anna said would give her friend the chance to find her feet and which Lauren secretly felt would give her time to spend on her laptop.

'We've kept the original flooring.' Anna indicated the oak floorboards of the landing, a stylish runner along its length. 'They're a bit creaky, but that's old houses for you.'

'Yes, there's a particularly squeaky one just where I get out of bed.'

They started down the stairs. 'Oliver had the ensuites installed, but we're not keen on making things too modern.'

'Did Daniel do them?'

'No. He's been too busy these last eight months.' Anna assumed a thoughtful expression as they reached the hall. 'I wish Daniel would cheer up. I worry about him.'

'I admit he's not quite what I expected from all you'd said of him.'

'He's become quite moody since he started dating Claudia.'

'That's not good.'

'I know. Opposites sometimes attract, but not in this case. Claudia can be quite demanding, and I think he's too distracted with the build to pay her enough attention. Trouble is, he'd crushed on her for so long, I don't think he knows how to stop, even though anyone can see it's not going well.'

'Poor man. Good job he's got the house to keep him occupied.'

Anna nodded. 'He has, up to a point, though he's not the actual builder. Daniel's been dabbling in DIY since he came back to the cove, but his real expertise is in finance.'

Lauren raised a brow. 'Quite the contrast.'

'I think when he escaped here from the City, the manual labour was the perfect antidote, so he's kept it up.'

Anna led the way back to the kitchen and reached for the kettle. 'Come on. Let's get the washing machine on, and we can have a cuppa before we clean.'

–

Anna and Oliver left for the airport at dawn on Monday, and Lauren saw to Heathcliff's needs and went for a run with Dougal, tuning into a new favourite podcast and watching the April sky turn from grey to pink as the sun rose over the hills surrounding the village.

'Let the new job begin,' Lauren murmured as she turned on the shower, relishing the feel of the water on her skin. 'But first, tea and toast and then a morning prepping another brief.'

Despite not having much time to herself over the first week Anna and Oliver were away, with guests in both rooms from mid-week, the visiting locals taking up several mornings, walking Dougal twice a day, coaxing a pining Heathcliff to eat, and Nicki's constant drop-ins to check she was coping okay, Lauren found she craved her former life. No amount of effort to relegate it to the past and shed its memories held sway against the sense of loss for all that was over.

Lauren hadn't only relished the challenges of her job, she'd thrived on the city lifestyle – the fabulous boutiques, coffee and patisseries in Harvey Nichols, after-work drinks with Kit before getting dressed up for dinner in the city or dancing the night away in her favourite club.

Waking each morning to the stillness of her room at Westerleigh, the expanse of an empty bed and no lingering scent of aftershave on the pillow beside her, Lauren's heart ached for the life she'd so recently had. The sounds were different too: no faint roar of traffic in the streets below, no aircraft droning overhead.

No, Polkerran first thing in the morning meant those damned ever-present gulls, wailing as they soared overhead, the dull chug of the fishing boats leaving for a day at sea and, if the tide was coming in, waves slamming against the rocks below the house.

'Never mind the old life, you have a new one to consider now, Kirkham,' Lauren intoned for what felt like the thousandth time on Monday morning, seven days after Anna and Oliver left, as she towelled down after a post-run shower. Wise words, and far easier to say than accept.

Lauren eyed her naked body in the mirror. It looked as it always did: petite, well-toned from keeping in good shape and no sign of life beneath the smooth skin of her taut belly. She tried to push her small, firm breasts closer together, to no avail.

'You never know, girls. You might even get to meet in a few months' time.'

Her phone vibrated, and Lauren snatched it up. A reminder to call one of her contacts at nine, and as it was a video call, she took care with her appearance, donning a smart shirt over her jeans.

Thankfully, there were no breakfasts to prepare, as the weekend guests had departed on Sunday. Their rooms, however, remained as they'd left them.

Lauren checked what she'd labelled Mission Improbable: her pregnancy timeline and appointment schedule, kept distinct from work projects, of course. After all, they were separate parts of her life, not to be mixed up – she'd colour-coded them to make sure.

Scrolling forward, she noted the appointments she'd rescheduled in Yorkshire with a sigh. Unlike Anna, Lauren wasn't in any rush to find out the baby's sex.

The video call went well, and Lauren made yet another cup of decaf tea, enviously eyeing the coffee maker, before settling back at the kitchen table. She skimmed through the podcasts on her phone, seeking one that would be motivational, but before Lauren could hit play, the boot room door opened and Daniel walked in.

Chapter Five

When in Roam

'Hey, long time no see.' Lauren closed the laptop and pinned on a smile, hoping Daniel wasn't the first of a crowd.

He hadn't called round all last week, and she'd assumed he was tied up with getting the house finished. Nicki had mentioned that Claudia was due back from her impromptu holiday over the weekend. Did that explain his current muted behaviour?

Daniel's frown took in the laptop, open notebook and the papers strewn across the table. 'Sorry.' He ran a hand through his thick, short hair, leaving it stuck up in a tuft. 'Forgot Anna was still away. I'll be off.'

His slightly bemused demeanour touched Lauren, and the smile became genuine as she made a mental note of what she needed to do later. 'Join me for a drink first? I was just about to take a break.' Liar, liar, pants on fire.

It's a thong, actually.

'I'd love one.'

Lauren blinked. 'Sorry? Oh yes, coffee?'

'Please. A strong one.'

'Go and sit on the terrace. Shame to waste such a lovely morning. I'll be out in a tic.'

Lauren eyed Daniel with interest through the window as she made him a coffee and poured herself a glass of water. He was in his overalls again today, but her heart went out to him as she took in the slumped shoulders.

Anna had always baked for the locals. Were there any goodies to hand? She opened the cupboard of the dresser and pulled out a tin labelled 'Naughties' in Anna's neat hand.

'Here you go.'

She placed the mug and the tin in front of Daniel, who'd taken a seat at the stone patio table.

'Perfect.' He leaned forward to breathe in the coffee, and Lauren took a seat opposite, feeling a tad guilty for having inhaled the aroma herself before handing it over.

'Sorry.' Daniel sent her a sheepish grin. 'Didn't sleep well. Claudia came back on Saturday.'

Lauren threw him an amused look. 'Are those two connected?'

Daniel's cheeks, above his neatly trimmed beard, filled with colour, and she waved a hand.

'Don't mind me. Have this awful tendency to say what I'm thinking. Must be great to have her back, though, catch up on each other's news.'

Silence followed, but then Daniel's warm, brown eyes fixed on Lauren.

'You're a girl, right?'

Was, last time I looked…

'Rumour has it.'

He smiled faintly. 'So, from your perspective, how do you know if it's been a good or a bad date-night? Or somewhere in between?'

'Hah! I always used to say to Anna, a good date was when he bothered to say goodbye the next morning.'

Daniel nodded slowly. 'Sounds promising. Claudia did at least kiss me before she left for the station this morning.'

'Anna says she works in Bristol?'

'Mainly, sometimes from London. She usually comes home on a Friday night so I stay at Pengillis over the weekend, then back to the cottage in the week. Am I being embarrassing? Anna's used to me waffling on, especially about Claudia.' Bashfulness overcame his face, and Lauren suppressed the urge to hug him. 'I had a mega crush on her for years.'

'I'm touched you feel you can talk to me. Somehow, I feel as though we go way back. Anna speaks of you often, and I know you were a good friend to her last year. I'd like to return the favour if I can.'

'I'd heard tons about you, too. It does feel like we know each other.' He indicated his mug. 'And you make great coffee.'

'That's my mate, Nespresso. We go even *further* back, although we're currently on a break.' Lauren tilted her head. 'Wanna talk it out more? Happy to be an ear. Fetch more cake. Dig out the tissues.'

Daniel picked up his mug, then drew in a short breath.

'Something's not right. Claud's acting oddly, but when I tell her I'm worried it's not going well, she insists we're fine, and it's my imagination.' Daniel huffed. 'Which is odd, because my English teacher said I never had one.'

Lauren's lips twitched. 'Hey, if she's reassuring you, that's got to be good, hasn't it?'

'I suppose so. And mostly, it's been so great I have to pinch myself. It's just lately, I dunno…' Daniel shrugged. 'Sorry, shouldn't have said anything. You're too good a listener.'

Part of Lauren was itching to get back to work, but Daniel intrigued her, so she offered a top-up, which gave her another chance to absorb the heady aroma of a hard coffee as she carried it out to him, the steam curling upwards towards her nostrils, and she sighed as she retook her seat and picked up the glass of water.

'So, how's it going running the B&B?'

Lauren pushed away the frisson of guilt over the current state of Anna's lovely guest rooms. 'Fine, I think.'

Daniel placed his mug on the table. 'And the locals?'

'I'll never remember who they all are, but I love the identifiers. Who wants to be just a name, anyway?'

'Indeed.' Daniel reached for a biscuit. 'And Mrs L? Come out with any classics lately?'

Lauren took a sip of water. 'Oh, yes. They were chatting last week about Mrs Clegg's belated birthday meal.'

'I did hear a rumour about Oliver taking her to the bistro for a cocktail, only to find out the margarita she wanted was a pizza?'

Chuckling, Lauren nodded. 'Mrs Lovelace isn't overly charmed by the bistro either, said she didn't like them,' she held up her hands to indicate quotes, '"putting scrotums on they'm salads".'

Daniel coughed. 'Sorry.' He wiped crumbs away with the back of his hand.

'She said they stuck in her teeth.'

Shoulders shaking, Daniel leaned back in his seat again. 'Love that woman! She told pretty much everyone in the village last year I'd done a proper job touching up the dildo rail in her back passage.'

'Oh no!' Lauren's cheeks dimpled. 'Poor Jean. She tries to check her, but it's like trying to stop a seagull stealing chips.'

Stretching his arms above his head, Daniel drained his mug. 'Right, I've taken up enough of your morning, so I think—'

Footsteps came towards them as he stood, and Nicki appeared round the corner, clutching a wriggling Heathcliff.

'Hi, guys. Found this scamp at the bottom on the lane. Doesn't normally venture so far from home.'

'I'd better be off.' Daniel sent Lauren a grateful look, tickled Heathcliff under the chin and left.

'Probably looking for Anna.' Lauren took the cat from Nicki, dropped a kiss on the fluffy head and carried her into the house. Spotting Dougal in his basket, Heathcliff trotted over to join him, turning round several times before settling down for a wash.

The morning was half gone, and Lauren sent her laptop a look of longing. Nicki, however, had already taken a seat at the table.

'Time for a cuppa?' Lauren gestured towards the kettle and Nicki beamed.

'Yes, please. Got a moment's peace. The boys are in school, and Hamish is out on the trawler.'

Lauren carried the drinks over to the table as the house phone rang. A booking for the next day, for two nights. Damn. She blocked the dates out on the website, releasing a huff of breath. She'd never get any work done at this rate!

'Problem?' Nicki's kind face was inviting.

'Guests, coming tomorrow, only I've not touched the rooms since the weekenders left.'

'Come on,' Nicki put down her mug. 'I'll give you a hand.'

Between them, they soon had the beds remade with fresh bedding from the linen press on the landing.

'How're you liking the cove?' Nicki tucked in a neat corner. 'Anna says you work in Leeds normally.'

Lauren plumped a pillow and put it in place. 'Polkerran is beautiful but I wonder how people fill their time. Anna loves it here, though.'

'Is she still having fun in Rome?'

'Doing lots of sightseeing when Oliver's lecturing. She was looking forward to using his Ancestry account this afternoon.'

Nicki frowned as she ran a cleaning wipe over the windowsill. 'Ancestry?'

'It's a website thing, where you can trace your ancestors. Apparently, Oliver set one up when he—' Lauren caught herself. It wasn't common knowledge that Meg was Oliver's grandmother. 'Anyway, he suggested she use it to try and find some distant relations.' Lauren shrugged at Nicki. 'They can't all be as bad as her cousin Victoria.'

Lauren's mobile rang: a hugely important potential new client. 'I just need to take this.'

Nicki waved a hand and headed for the bathroom as Lauren connected the call.

Five minutes later, after a swift negotiation, she joined Nicki, who was cleaning the sink.

'Is there a problem?' Nicki met Lauren's troubled gaze in the mirror, then swung around.

'A crucial meeting – for me, anyway. Should have been in Leeds on Friday but they can see me in London if I can do tomorrow.' Lauren bit her lip. 'I'm supposed to check this couple in.'

'I'm on an early, so I'll be back by lunchtime.' Nicki resumed her cleaning. 'Check with Anna, but assume I'll do it.'

They soon had the B&B restored to a satisfactory state of readiness, and as soon as Nicki left, Lauren whizzed a WhatsApp to Anna and grabbed her laptop to scan for trains from Par to London before turning her attention to prepping for the all-important meeting.

An hour later, she sat back and rubbed her eyes. She'd chosen what to wear – thank goodness she'd had the foresight to throw some business attire in to her suitcase in case of Zoom calls – and drafted a presentation. All she had left to do was source a diagram, and—

Her phone pinged with a notification: Anna.

> Of course it's fine! Nicki's done it before. Parking is dire at the station, so book a taxi.

> You're a darling. How's Rome?

> Sublime! We've been to the opera and Oliver took me to this gorgeous restaurant. Sorry, I'll gush when you're not busy. Get Nicki to do it. xx

Lauren stepped out into the chilly morning air on Tuesday, glancing at her phone. It would be five minutes before the taxi arrived and she leaned her laptop bag against the porch and walked round the terrace to where it faced the view.

Candy-floss clouds, dusted with pink and orange hues against the purple horizon, hung suspended above the rippling water. The 'chee-ow' call of a couple of choughs floated across the air as they circled above the small beach below Harbourwatch, and the faint throb of a fishing boat drifted upwards as it passed on its way out to sea.

Lauren leaned against the railing. Much as she appreciated the aesthetic beauty of the view, the expectation of being in London again excited her. City noises, city smells… they filled her with anticipation; the distant thrum of traffic through the corporate glazing, the chink and slosh of water being poured into glasses before a meeting and the copier, churning out page after page of handouts… how diverse were her comfort sounds to Anna's!

The purr of an engine drew Lauren's attention, and she returned to the driveway and scooped up her laptop bag. The train was only four minutes late, and as soon as she'd been served with tea from the cart, she opened her laptop and silently rehearsed her presentation. She knew it inside out, but her head didn't feel as on the ball as normal.

Nor could she quite explain why, as the train pulled into Paddington under leaden cloud, she had a sudden hankering for the wide open skies over Polkerran Point.

–

Lauren sailed down Millbank on a high after her meeting. This was the buzz she loved, and how she'd missed it these last few months! Looking across the Thames at the tall, glass buildings, dodging smartly dressed execs talking into their phones, absorbing brief soundbites of a myriad of accents, she soaked up the atmosphere. She'd be back, and perhaps London was the place to be? If she couldn't be abroad, Lauren would love to work in the capital, in plush offices like those of the multi-national Devere Corporation. Fingers crossed she had a foot in the door if she got this contract.

With time to spare, Lauren treated herself to an afternoon snack in Soho before heading to Regent Street to browse the shops until it was time to hail a cab to Paddington. Glued to her emails, Lauren was heedless of the traffic and the cursing of the driver, only tucking her phone away when he slid back the glass partition to tell her the fare.

Glancing at her watch, she studied the station departures board: her train was on time, and she scurried towards the platform, distracted by the ping of a text. It was from her mum.

'Oh, I'm sorry!' She looked up as she bumped into someone, only for her voice to fade in an instant.

Kit.

Chapter Six

Paddington Bare

Trying to ignore the swoop of her insides as she took in Kit's handsome features, Lauren side-stepped.

'Excuse me.'

'Wait, Lauren.' He stayed her with a hand on her arm, and she stared at it.

Those fingers had once entwined with hers when they lay beside each other in bed, had touched her with desire.

'Sorry.' He removed the hand, and Lauren was brought back to the present in an instant. 'I didn't expect to see you and had to—'

'You walked into me deliberately?'

'Well, no.' Kit smiled self-deprecatingly, and Lauren's heart twisted. She had loved the way his mouth curved. 'I walked towards you but you didn't stop.'

'I have a train to catch.'

'Me too. On my way back to King's Cross now.' Kit's smile widened. 'We can talk on the train.'

'Not to each other. Mine's heading west.' Hearing Kit's voice, seeing him, was doing Lauren no good. She'd made solid progress, or so she thought. Where was her anger now? She had to get away. 'Bye, Kit.'

Lauren glanced at her watch, then sped up. If she missed this train, she faced a much longer journey back.

Despite her best efforts, Lauren couldn't shed the sudden encounter with Kit until her train reached Taunton. Her emotions had come to the fore, and she'd felt naked and vulnerable, stripped of her former anger's protection. Now she was in the West Country, she began to relax, though why she had been so tense she had no idea. Kit and his north-bound train would be back in Leeds by now.

Frustrated with herself for letting Kit get to her, she tried calling the taxi firm to confirm her train but it was engaged, so she turned her attention to the laptop, which she'd stared at intermittently since opening it.

Come on, get on with it.

Lauren set to making some adjustments to the figures in a spreadsheet, then drafted several emails, tapping away on the keyboard and looking up with a start when she realised they were approaching Par. Damn, she'd forgotten to chase up the taxi company.

She stepped onto the platform, phone to her ear, but before it could connect, she was hailed from behind.

'Hey, Lauren!'

Spinning round, she smiled as Daniel reached her. 'Were you on this train?'

'Yes, I had to go up to Bristol to meet with Gerry. She's the producer on the TV show. Claudia joined us for dinner. Didn't expect to be this late back. Do you want a lift?'

He gestured towards the car park.

'You're an angel.' Lauren pocketed her phone and followed Daniel over to the familiar green Jeep.

'How come you didn't drive up there?'

'Wanted to get some work done.' Daniel patted the laptop bag slung across his body, and Lauren frowned. What sort of DIY required a computer?

They were soon in the car, and he expanded. 'I've taken on a consultant role, to keep the bank balance topped up.' He grimaced as he turned out of the station car park. 'The build has eaten money.'

Lauren almost mentioned her own fledgling consultancy, but then remembered no one knew she wasn't still working for her company back in Leeds.

'How about you? Didn't expect to see you on a train when you're running a village B&B.'

Lauren hugged the laptop bag to her chest. 'Had to meet a Supply Chain VP and his director who happened to be in London for meetings. Nicki kindly did a check-in for me.'

They were soon heading through Par, and exchanged news on their respective days, and within ten minutes, they'd reached the road to Polkerran. Lauren eyed the small rowing boat beneath the welcome sign, newly planted out with spring flowers. Recycling at its best.

'I wonder what happens to past-their-use execs,' she mused.

'Harsh,' Daniel chuckled. 'We repurpose ourselves. And *you*,' he added, as they skirted past the entrance to the cemetery and descended the hill, 'are amazing. Anna's told me all about your stellar career.'

Suppressing a shudder, Lauren resisted the unexpected urge to tell Daniel everything. He might well be into airing his feelings, and she did feel remarkably at ease with him, but she'd barely come to terms with the newness of her situation.

Dusk had long draped its veil over the sea, but Lauren could see the glisten of water in the harbour and lights in buildings on both sides of the cove. It was such a contrast to where she'd been.

'And the TV company were happy?'

'So they said.' Daniel waved an airy hand as they reached the harbour. 'I was upfront about likely completion on the interior, which is all they're waiting on. Gerry's a bit intense, but she was okay about it.'

'Nice.' She really shouldn't pry, but he had shared. 'And the Claudia thing?'

'Oh, fine.' Daniel threw her a quick smile. 'She's been lovely this evening and wants me to call her as soon as I'm home, because there are some things to talk about. Almost feel like a grown up.'

Unlike Lauren, who seemed incapable of acting like an adult around Kit. Then, she frowned. Daniel seemed to have taken Claudia's words positively, but they could have another purpose, and—

'What about you? Did the meeting go well?'

Lauren stroked the fine leather of the bag, reflecting on the intense two hours at the Devere Corporation. 'Promising.'

'Excellent.'

–

When Lauren's mobile pinged at two in the morning, she woke in an instant, conscious of the weight of Heathcliff's warm body against her leg.

She peered at her phone as the screen sprang into life. Then, muttering an expletive, she flopped back onto the pillow, giving Heathcliff a consoling stroke as she mewed in protest.

Kit.

> I need to see you.

Lauren huffed out a breath.

> I'll send you a photo.

> Come on, Lauren. We should talk.

> We really shouldn't.

> I miss you.

A fleeting moment of longing, but Lauren forced it aside, aware Kit was typing. What the hell was this all about? He must be drunk.

> Seeing you earlier made me realise there are things outstanding.

Yawning, Lauren's eyes closed, the hand holding the phone dropping heavily onto the coverlet. She really didn't need this, yet somehow it was a revelation. She didn't entirely *want* this either.

Lauren stroked Heathcliff with her free hand, smiling faintly at the responsive purring. Animals were so much less complicated than humans.

A notification pinged again, and she squinted at her phone.

> Come on. I know our future isn't together, but I need to know you're not alone.

Sitting up, Lauren tapped furiously into her phone, conscious of the cat's protesting mew.

> I'm not alone, in case you'd forgotten. There are two of us here.

> I'm sorry. I know you didn't want a kid either.

Not right now, she hadn't, but that was old history. It was a fait accompli – or rather, *fate* accompli. Lauren's lids were so heavy. She ought to just switch the phone off, but Kit was typing again. It was a long one.

> I got the director role in New Jersey. I start next month, but won't relocate until the autumn when the visa's sorted. I'll be over there a lot in the interim, but we need to talk before I start travelling. When are you home?

Home? She didn't exactly have one.

Before Kit could respond, Lauren switched off her phone, tucking it under her pillow.

'I'm going to lie awake now, thinking about him, aren't I?' she whispered to Heathcliff, who made no response, and Lauren flopped back against the pillows with a groan.

Men!

–

Later that morning, Lauren had barely closed the dishwasher on the breakfast crockery when the door opened and Nicki came in.

'Brought you some leftovers from last night.' She raised the covered pot she held and walked over to place it on the AGA.

'That's kind. Thanks so much again for yesterday.'

'Any time.'

Lauren poured a coffee and refreshed her own glass of water before sending Nicki an apologetic look.

'I really need to get this done. Do you mind if I work as we chat?'

'Of course not.' Nicki's expression was apologetic as she accepted the mug. 'Sorry, I forget you're not Anna.'

Lauren put the laptop aside. 'I'll take that as a compliment. I've got time for a drink.'

They exchanged some light conversation for half an hour, and once Nicki left, Lauren set to, polishing the amended proposal for the Devere Corporation, sending it off with a covering email and then stood up and stretched her back. Her body missed going to the gym more than ever.

Lauren checked her calendar. She couldn't believe she'd been in Cornwall two weeks and would have been, if all had gone to plan, headed back to North Yorkshire today. After Kit's intrusion, she was glad to be so far away. She'd do her B&B duties and go for a good long walk, clear her head of the tiresome man, and then—

Her phone pinged. Anna.

> I've just boarded a flight. I'll be in PP by evening.

Lauren stared at her screen, nonplussed.

> Has the tour ended early?

> No. I can't tell you in a message.

Lauren frowned at the exchange.

> You can't leave me hanging like that!

> Sorry. I'll explain when I get there.

And that was that.

Thoroughly confused, Lauren tidied the guest room in use before walking down into Polkerran to get something for supper. She tried to suppress her anxiety over what had happened to bring Anna home so precipitously, concern for her friend paramount in her mind. She emerged into the late morning sunshine with her purchases, shielding her eyes. She'd forgotten her sunglasses.

Easter would be upon them the following week, and Polkerran was noticeably busier. A few walkers lingered by the ferry, and a couple of people hovered outside the chip shop, waiting for it to open. A young woman walked past, leading half a dozen very young, chattering children, all holding hands and sporting hi-vis mini-vests, towards the little aquarium, another lady bringing up the rear.

Lauren smiled warmly, and the lady returned it.

'There's a new addition,' she gestured towards the small, square building housing Polkerran's attempt at Sea World. 'Bernard the Gurnard. We're all very excited.'

Lauren watched them snake their way along the narrow street, then continued along the harbour, her gaze drifting over the jumble of fishing boats and the few pleasure crafts brave enough to emerge from their winter storage.

In an attempt to put aside her worries about Anna, Lauren focused on work once she'd returned to the cottage, but her shoulders ached by the time she finished. Much as the view was fabulous, the kitchen table was not the ideal height for working – even if she perched on a couple of cushions.

Lauren prepared a salad, and made a quiche, ready to warm. She also put her friend's favourite wine to chill and added a couple of small bottles of the alcohol-free dry cider she'd taken to lately.

Checking her calendar, Lauren eyed with momentary regret the fun she would miss this coming weekend: a friend's thirtieth bash at a York hotel on Saturday night and an annual charity bed race on the Sunday – always a blast.

At least Anna was back that evening, but this reminder only served to bring Lauren's mood lower, concern for her friend foremost. What could possibly be serious enough to leave a dream trip and Oliver? Poor Anna!

'What is it, sweetie?' Dougal materialised by Lauren's chair, head to one side, tongue lolling, and he panted as though he'd been doing something other than snoozing in his basket for the last hour.

'Okay, I get it.'

Would fresh air help? She looked out the window: low tide. Closing the laptop and putting it on charge, Lauren grabbed her Barbour and shoved her feet into sturdy boots. The coat zipped up smoothly, and Lauren smiled as she fastened Dougal's lead. According to Anna the other day, the baby was almost the size of a doughnut.

They set off, the dog happily scampering ahead, his nose to the floor with Lauren pondering whether she was destined to end up having a Homer Simpson belly. Lord, she hoped not!

There was no sun now, and the frothy clouds picked up their skirts and scurried across the leaden skies as Lauren made her way up the lane to join the coastal path and, freeing Dougal from his lead, she turned her face into the stiff breeze, inhaling deeply. Funny how she'd grown to like the faint aroma of seaweed in the air, the ever-present wind on the clifftop tugging at her looser hairstyle.

The chimney of Daniel's house, The Lookout, loomed out of the trees to the left, but Lauren was determined not to dwell on his love life. It was none of her business, and she'd be gone from Polkerran in a week's time. Probably a good thing. Life in this small community wasn't exactly inspiring.

Soon, they'd reached Lauren's favourite place, the tidal beach tucked below the cliffs on which The Lookout perched, and she followed Dougal, who joyfully scampered down the steep steps, unheeding of Lauren's call of caution.

Making her way more carefully, she stepped onto firm sand, still damp from the receding tide, and began to walk towards the area of rock pools, but before long, she realised she wasn't alone.

Chapter Seven

Junk Male

'Hey.'

Daniel started, glancing over his shoulder as Lauren clambered onto the rock and settled beside him.

'What's happening?'

He held his hands up in a helpless gesture. 'Seeking direction.'

Daniel said nothing more, and Lauren called out to Dougal, who was playing cat and mouse with the shallow wavelets rolling onto the beach. He looked up, ran around in a circle, then gambolled towards them.

She really shouldn't pry, but he had shared. 'Is it Claudia?'

'It's not great.' Daniel threw her a quick smile. 'We talked last night, and it seems we're taking a break.'

'Oh.' Unsure what else to say, Lauren gazed out to sea, suppressing the urge to give Daniel a hug and uncertain why he seemed to draw a protective response from her.

Daniel held a flat piece of rock in his hand, his thumb repeatedly smoothing it, and Lauren suppressed the urge to reach out and still it. Then, he tossed the rock aside and it landed with a muffled splash in one of the pools.

'I suppose that doesn't end it yet, but how much more distance do you need when you spend most of the week 150 miles apart?'

There wasn't a lot Lauren could say to that, and they sat in contemplative silence for a moment.

'Ignore me.' Daniel straightened his shoulders, throwing Lauren a culpable look. 'I'm not surprised by her decision. It's just...' His voice tailed away.

Leaning forward a little, Lauren tried to catch his eye. 'So what else is on your mind?'

'The recording.' Daniel met her look, then shook his head. 'I never wanted to do the damned programme – the public sharing of my personal dream – only now it's intruding in ways I'd barely imagined.'

Lauren lifted her chin into the breeze. 'How come?'

'Claudia sort of set up the gig. She's got a friend who knows Gerry, the producer. There's this pattern to the series where they hone in on the motivation behind the build and the plans for the design in the first part of the episode. Then on the actual build in the second. Both of those are already recorded, but the final part of the episode is after it's finished, and they emphasise the human element, bring in those closest to the person whose dream build it is to get their take on the whole experience, and so on.'

The wind had ruffled Daniel's shortish hair into confused tufts, and Lauren tried not to find him attractive.

Epic fail.

Oblivious to his cuteness, Daniel continued. 'I had a call with Gerry this morning, and I mentioned Claud and I were on a break and didn't know for how long, but that I was happy to go it alone. Gerry isn't. She told me in no uncertain terms to get the relationship back on track.'

Wow. 'Tricky.'

'Indeed. Claud doesn't quite see it in the same light. I mean, she was looking forward to her bit of local fame, don't get me wrong, but as time's gone on and the build has become the wedge she sees as driving us apart…'

'She's not too amenable.' Lauren finished for him, eyeing Daniel with sympathy. 'Is the actual build complete?'

'It is structurally. There's a bit of finishing off to do, the landscaping, then it's onto decoration and furnishings.' His expression darkened. 'I tried to persuade Claud to help with that when we had dinner with Gerry, but I think it was the final straw. She's decided to work from London after Easter and says she won't have time to come down.'

Dougal, who waited patiently by Lauren's leg, nudged her pocket with his nose, and she fished inside for a biscuit, the offering soon vanishing. Patting the little dog absent-mindedly on the head, she turned back to Daniel. 'Furnishings will have quite a lead time, won't they?'

Daniel shifted his position a little. 'I've got some in storage, from the London flat, but not enough to fill the house. The ground floor is open plan, so it all has to flow.' He sent Lauren a rueful look. 'Never was into cushions and all that girlie stuff.'

Lauren swatted him gently on the arm. 'Hey, less of the stereotyping.'

Daniel got to his feet. 'Sorry.' Then, he held out his hand. 'Getting a bit numb, let's walk?'

As Daniel hauled her to her feet, Lauren really tried not to hold on too tightly, but he had lovely hands: warm, firm and with surprisingly smooth skin for someone who was so practical.

Daniel clearly wasn't aware of how pleasant he was to touch, releasing Lauren's hand and shoving his own into his jacket pockets as they began to walk back across the sands.

'I've had this huge crush on Claudia for years. Couldn't believe my luck when she agreed to go on a date. I feel like I've blown it now.'

They came to a halt as Lauren whistled to Dougal, who reluctantly abandoned whatever he'd found on the beach and trotted over to join them. 'Anna told me you had to cut your ponytail off.'

'It was a sad day.' Daniel pretended hurt, hand to his heart. 'Though I don't think I'd grow it back again. Much easier to get ready for the day when you don't have a mane to deal with.' He eyed Lauren's short cut, which was beginning to kink as it grew longer. 'Not something you worry about either.'

Lauren raised a hand to touch the hair against her cheekbone. 'I need a trim.' She'd book in with her usual salon in Leeds when she got back to the B&B.

'I like it. Softens your features.' Then, Daniel's skin went a dull red. 'Not that you need to... I mean, you look great anyway – er, no, that's – argh!'

Lauren's lips twitched as she fell into step beside him, Dougal at her heels now. 'I had my hair styled short and neat as soon as I started my first internship. With my small build, I felt I had to do everything to convince people I was a serious contender, a force to be reckoned with.'

Daniel threw her a keen look. 'And are you?'

Lauren shrugged, her gaze drifting across the sand towards the sea. 'I used to be. My career was going full tilt—' She stopped. 'Anyway, I hope you get the decor sorted. You must send some photos when I'm back home.'

For the first time, Lauren's heart didn't instinctively leap in anticipation at the idea of leaving Cornwall. She frowned as they reached the steps up to the cliff path. Was it the thought of being stuck at her parents' for months on end?

'There must be some vast empty walls, up there.' She gestured up to where The Lookout was located. 'How about some statement artwork? You could ask the gallery in the village for some.'

'It'd be a bit pricey. I'm not short of funds but can't justify those sums.'

'Not if they loan them.' Lauren called to Dougal, who scuttled up the steps ahead of them. 'Imagine the publicity of having their art on the walls for an episode of a TV show. They could get a piece in the local paper, and the village mag about it, so viewers knew where they'd come from.'

'Good idea,' Daniel mused as they scaled the steps. 'Shame you're not staying longer, I could have made use of you. Do you want to see it before you leave?'

Pushing aside a fleeting interest in extending her stay, Lauren grasped the wooden handrail as they neared the top of the steps. It was the first time the weariness had come back in a while, and the tops of her legs ached today, which was unlike her.

'I'd love to see it. Name the day, only make it soon.' She rested her hands on her hips as she reached the cliff path, then bent down to grasp her ankles, attempting to stretch away the ache.

Straightening, pink in the face, Lauren met Daniel's concerned expression.

'Are you okay?'

With a breathy laugh, Lauren nodded. 'Fine. Think it's just the baby-hormones making— ah.'

Daniel's confusion came to the fore again. 'Are you…' His glance dipped to her middle, then back to her face.

'I'm so sorry.' He ran a hand through his hair. 'I didn't mean to stare.'

'Hey.' Lauren laid a hand on his sleeve. Daniel's gaze had dropped to his feet, and she peeped up at him, striving to catch his eye. 'Not your fault. I've not told anyone — except Anna, of course — you weren't to know.'

Raising his gaze, Lauren was comforted by how warm his eyes were. 'Congratulations.' He essayed a smile. 'I hope?'

Lauren laughed, surprisingly relieved it was out there. Perhaps this time she would share. 'Let me fill you in on all my secrets.'

They began to walk again, picking their way along the cliff path, as Lauren spilled the beans.

—

Something felt good about telling Daniel the truth of her situation, not that Lauren could account for it, and she settled into work on her return with renewed vigour, buoyed by a text from Anna confirming she'd landed at Bristol and would be home in three hours.

So engrossed was Lauren in her work she looked up in surprise when she heard the front door close. Hurrying into the hallway, part anxious, part delighted, she found Anna kicking off her shoes.

'Well, this is a surprise.' Lauren stepped over a bag of duty free as her friend hung her jacket on the coat stand and turned to face her. 'What's up?'

Anna threw her arms around Lauren. 'I'm so glad you're here!' Her voice was strained and, when they entered the kitchen, she could see how pale Anna was.

'What's going on? Why are you alone?'

Anna summoned a smile. 'Oliver has to continue his lectures. He'll be back on Monday, as planned.'

Relieved, Lauren smiled.

'Tell me about it whilst we eat, you must be starved.' She walked over to pop the quiche into the AGA, grabbing cutlery and two plates along the way and headed towards the table. By the time she'd laid it, adding salt, pepper, the salad, dressing and a basket of bread, Anna had extracted her laptop from her bag and set it up at the far end of the table.

Lauren walked over. 'My curiosity is killing me.'

'Tell me about it.' Anna's voice was dry. 'Is there any wine?'

Lauren headed for the fridge. 'Always.'

She took a glass to her friend, pouring the cider for herself and taking a seat beside Anna in front of the now open laptop.

There was a chart on the screen, with names, dates and various symbols, and Lauren noted the Ancestry web address.

'This,' Anna spoke quietly, pointing to the line at the top, 'is my father, and this is my mother.' She indicated the entry beside it.

Anna scrolled down so that the screen moved upwards to reveal the line below, and Lauren gasped.

'Yes.' Anna swallowed visibly, her voice breaking. 'I'm not – or at least I wasn't – an only child. According to this, I have a brother.'

Chapter Eight

Three Go to Dorset

An astounded Lauren took in her friend's tortured expression, unsurprised when Anna's tears began to fall, and she leaned forward to hug her.

Letting her friend snuffle into her shoulder for a minute, Lauren waited until Anna raised her head and rubbed her eyes.

'Have some wine and tell me when you're ready.'

Doing as she was bid, Anna then pulled a handkerchief from her jeans pocket. 'Oliver's. He gave it to me when I left because I couldn't stop snivelling.' It was damp and crumpled, but Anna gave a watery giggle. 'He'd be appalled to see it in this state.'

Personally, Lauren suspected Oliver would be more disturbed by seeing his beloved Anna so upset.

Her expression sobering, Anna pocketed the handkerchief. 'I don't know where to begin.'

'Tell me how you found this.' Lauren gestured at the evidence on the screen.

'I was using Oliver's account, and I was quite excited about what I might find in terms of distant relations. Don't know why it never occurred to me before. I started in the obvious place, putting myself in, and then my parents. I knew their names and birth dates, thanks to cousin

Victoria…' Her expression became ominous. 'And that's when it came up. A suggestion of a connection, which I clicked on, and saw this.' Her voice hitched on the last word, and she took another sip of her drink.

'And what did Victoria have to say about it? You called her, yes?'

Anna drew in a short breath. 'I came right out with it: "do I have a brother?" And the line went dead.'

Wow!

'Guilty as charged, then.'

'Oliver was livid, and so protective of me. I've never seen him like that. If it wasn't for the tour, I think he'd have flown back on the next available flight and stormed over there to confront her.'

Lauren didn't know what to say. Anna's gaze was fixed on the screen as though hungry to absorb its content.

'Alistair Redding, born on the 28th January,' she whispered, as though for the first time.

Leaning forward, Lauren looked at the date. 'Two years older than you. And an Aquarius.'

Anna smiled faintly. She used to roll her eyes at her friend's enjoyment of reading newspaper horoscopes.

'I have to find out what happened, Lauren.'

'Of course you do. Victoria knows.'

'I must see her, face to face. Get her to talk.' Anna sent Lauren a tremulous look. 'Oliver wanted me to wait until he gets back, but I said I couldn't just stay in Italy, not knowing.' She put a hand to her chest. 'My heart aches, I told him I feel sick half the time, and I struggle to sleep.'

Sounds like my current life, mused Lauren silently, stretching her back, and Anna put a hand to her mouth.

'Oh my God! I'm so sorry. I didn't ask you how you are. Is everything okay with you, with the baby?'

'I'm— *we* are absolutely fine. Forget me, what can I do to help?'

Anna leaned forward earnestly. 'Will you come with me? To see Victoria? I don't think I can do this on my own.'

'Yes, of course.'

'Oh!' Anna looked askance. 'Do we have any guests?'

'Just one couple. No breakfast, as they're leaving early to get to Heathrow. No one due in tomorrow, but we're full from Friday for the Easter weekend.'

Anna drained her glass and pulled the laptop towards her. 'It'll have to be tomorrow, then. I'll change the online settings so we don't get any last-minute bookings, then pop upstairs to get into something comfy.'

While she waited for Anna to return, Lauren took some recycling out to the bins before walking round onto the main stretch of terrace facing the bay. It was dark and the stiff breeze from earlier continued to blow in from the sea. Her walk on the beach with Daniel seemed an age ago.

How could Anna make sense of this revelation?

Lauren wrapped her hands around her middle as she returned to the house. There *was* no sense to it, and no doubt Anna would lie awake all night, pondering what she was about to find out.

—

As Lauren suspected, Anna passed a restless night – she could hear her pacing upstairs in the early hours. Up early on Thursday to wave off the departing guests, she then popped by Anna's room with a mug of tea, only to find her friend in a deep sleep.

Leaving her to catch up on her rest, Lauren went for a run with Dougal – today's podcast was the latest from *Consultancy Insights* – and was back at Westerleigh by eight. After a quick shower, she threw on her dressing gown and – with no sign of Anna stirring – padded back downstairs to fire up the coffee machine.

Sod the advice. She needed a full-on caffeine fix!

Comfortably ensconced on the sofa, Heathcliff nestled by her side, Lauren tried to concentrate on a couple of emails that had come in overnight, but her thoughts were with her friend. Sounds of movement upstairs indicated Anna was up. She ought to move, cook bacon or something, but before she could get up, the boot room door opened.

'Morning, Daniel.'

He started as Lauren straightened carefully, trying not to disturb the cat.

'Oh God. Sorry, Lauren. Didn't see you over there.' He glanced at his watch. 'Damn, I didn't realise how early it was.'

Lauren re-fastened the belt on her dressing gown, stuffing her feet into her discarded slippers as she checked her phone. Still only nine. No danger of any other locals turning up yet.

'Hey, no problem. Want a coffee?'

'Only if you're sure?' Daniel hovered uneasily by the door. 'I'm an idiot. Just needed a bit of a yarn, as they say around here.'

Lauren hurried over to make the coffees and carried two mugs to the table, taking the seat beside Daniel.

'Talk it out.' She was used to listening to her brothers' tales of woe.

'You were such a good listener yesterday. I'm still trying to get my head around how I can use this break to make sure things are better afterwards. I think I need a female perspective. I'm not very good at this girlfriend stuff.'

Lauren opened the biscuit tin. He seemed convinced the break wasn't permanent, bless him. 'Go on. Try me.'

Daniel cast her a culpable glance as he took a biscuit.

'If Claud feels neglected, like the house means more to me than she does, what can I do? She's already said it's too early for us to live together, even when the house is finished.'

'Tricky. I mean, you can't help that it's a bit full-on trying to get it finished especially with the TV execs breathing down your neck, but she may have a point. Can you take a bit of time out, to make her feel loved? Do something special for her?'

'I've tried, but she's a bit high maintenance. Needs your full attention all the time or she gets distracted.'

'Sounds like Dougal.'

Daniel smiled faintly. 'Sadly, Claud's not that fond of going walkies.'

Having heard about her dress sense, I'm not surprised.

Lauren hesitated. Her instinct had been to lean forward and put an arm around Daniel's shoulder, but she was unsure whether he would appreciate the gesture. Besides, she was in nothing but her dressing gown, and it felt a tad inappropriate.

Daniel dunked his biscuit in his tea, but as the liquid was so hot, it broke off and fell in.

'Just about sums things up,' he said, then pulled a face. 'Claud says biscuit-dunking is uncouth.'

'There are worse habits.'

Daniel's gaze drifted out of the window. 'I just wonder if I'm a fool for clinging on to the hope that we'll ride this storm.' He stared across the water to Harbourwatch, much as Lauren knew her friend used to do.

This reminder of Anna and her imminent arrival in the kitchen roused Lauren, and she started to gather the things on the table.

'It's hard to let go, whether it's the real thing or just a crush, but—'

'Crushes have a way of coming back to bite you.' They both swung around as Anna came into the room. 'What did I miss?'

'Hey! When did you get back?' Daniel stood up in surprise, greeting Anna with a hug.

Anna threw Lauren an inquisitive look. 'You didn't tell him?'

'We had a lot to talk about.'

With a smirk, Anna headed for the coffee machine. 'Did you now?'

'Better make that three cups.' Lauren held up her hands. 'Mea culpa. I caved.' She patted her midriff. 'Sorry, Homer.'

A small gasp came from Anna, her gaze flying to Daniel. 'Did you—'

'I told Daniel about the job, Kit, the baby.'

'Did you now?' Anna repeated, the edges of her mouth twitching.

Lauren didn't mind the teasing. It was a relief to see her friend in better spirits. Besides, there was nothing between her and Daniel.

'But why are you here?' Daniel eyed Anna with confusion. 'And where's the big man?'

Placing the mugs on the table, Anna pulled out a chair as Lauren and Daniel resumed their seats. 'He'll be back next week, as planned. I've got something to tell you.'

Lauren gestured between them. 'Off you go. I've heard all this so I'll just indulge my fleeting and illicit reacquaintance with caffeine.'

An hour later, the three of them sat back in their seats, and Lauren looked from Anna to Daniel.

'I'm afraid we need to get going if we're to get to Dorset and back today.'

'Let me drive you.' Daniel turned to Anna. 'This is pretty huge, and it'll be easier for Lauren to support you if neither of you has to watch the road.'

Lauren let out a huff of laughter. 'What? In that Jeep?'

'Less of the mocking, please. I do have another car.'

'Are you sure?' Anna eyed Daniel warily. 'I mean, you've got a lot on your mind too. I'm sorry about the break with Claudia.'

Daniel shrugged. 'The news is already speeding round the village. It's exactly why I'd like the distraction *and* the chance to get away for a few hours.'

Lauren dimpled at Daniel's earnest expression, but Anna drew in a short breath.

'I'm dreading it, to be honest, but with Oliver away, having you two with me is the best possible thing.'

–

'Apparently, we've reached our destination.'

Daniel exited the satnav, and Lauren eyed the back of Anna's head as her friend stared to her left.

'That's it. Number Eleven.' Anna sniffed. 'It's... very *them.*'

The bungalow was pristine, with a well-maintained garden, borders of spring bulbs in serried ranks, every blade of grass in the neatly cut lawn standing to attention.

Daniel met Lauren's gaze through the rear-view mirror, but neither said anything.

It was three o'clock, but Anna didn't move.

'I haven't seen Victoria in person since leaving the house in Chiswick.' Anna made a small sound. 'I'd graduated university and couldn't wait to get my stuff and never go back.' She glanced over at Lauren with a faint smile. 'Thank God life took me to Harrogate all those years ago. I don't know what I'd do without you.'

Daniel stayed in the car, and they stood on the pavement, Lauren waiting for Anna's cue.

'I'm ready.' Anna straightened her shoulders, and Lauren took her hand, noticing her friend's feet, unseasonably shod in her sturdiest walk boots.

'You haven't said why you felt the need.' She pointed to the boots as they walked up the short drive, past a highly polished, immaculate hatchback.

'You'll see,' Anna warned as they waited for someone to answer the bell. No one came, so she tried again. 'What if she's out?' she whispered, but then there were sounds behind the door and it swung open.

As soon as Victoria saw who it was, she made to close the door, but Anna stuck her booted foot in the gap, and Lauren bit her lip as her friend winced when the door rammed against it.

'I'm not going away, Victoria. You have to let me in, or I'll stand in the street and shout loud enough for everyone to hear me.'

Cousin Victoria was a Dursley through and through. Making a scene in front of the neighbours would crucify her. The door opened slowly, and Victoria stood aside so they could enter. She was a sparse woman in her fifties, with drawn features and – at this moment – abject fear in her eyes.

'Who is it, Victoria?'

A man came into the hall, his eyes flying to meet his wife's frantic gaze as he spotted their visitor.

'Anna, dear. This is a surprise.'

'Is it?' Anna's voice was remarkably strong, considering how nervous Lauren knew her to be. 'Didn't your wife tell you what I found out?'

To Lauren's surprise, the man deflated. 'I told Victoria you would discover the truth one day. I said time and again she ought to tell you.'

'Shut up, Stephen.'

The mild-mannered man walked up to Victoria, who still held open the door as though hoping Anna would disappear through it. '*Enough*, my dear. Time to let it all out.'

He removed his wife's hand from the door and closed it. 'Come on. Let's have tea.'

Chapter Nine

Victoria Spongey

Exchanging a look, Lauren and Anna followed Stephen down the hall into a spacious kitchen, spotlessly clean and sporting every possible appliance known to man.

Lauren glanced over her shoulder. Victoria remained as though turned to stone by the front door.

Stephen rambled on about the weather as he attended to the kettle, asking Anna how she was and accepting the introduction to Lauren.

The tea was soon poured and they followed Stephen over to a circular table by some French doors overlooking a small terrace.

'I need to talk to Victoria, Stephen. Urgently.' Anna's voice was quiet but determined, and the man smiled vaguely.

'She'll be here. I rarely have the chance to express my opinion, and I doubt this will be one of those occasions.'

Suppressing a smile, Lauren sipped her tea. It was far too weak, but she needed the refreshment.

Stephen was right. The door was pushed aside, and Victoria came into the room. She looked a little more collected and sank into the vacant chair at the table. Anna's eyes were fixed upon her.

'Don't look at me like that.'

'How am I supposed to look at you?' Anna leaned forward, her voice hoarse with emotion. 'Why don't I know I have a brother? Where is he? What happened to him? Is he alive?'

'I don't know where he is. Why would I?' Victoria's tone was terse, but Lauren could sense her anxiety.

'Then at least tell me what you *do* know, because all I can see so far is that you've deceived me. You told me I was an only child, years ago. Did my brother die? Was he in the car accident too? I can't find a death certificate for him.'

Victoria shuddered, and Stephen pushed a cup towards her, then spooned sugar into it. 'Drink, my dear.'

With a shaking hand, Victoria raised the cup to her pinched lips for a moment before replacing it unsteadily on the saucer.

'Neither of you were in the car. You were with a babysitter at home. I told you that.'

'No. You told me *I* was at home with a babysitter.'

'Victoria,' Stephen, for all his mild air, spoke firmly. 'This must stop. It has haunted you for too many years. Anna deserves to hear the truth, and you need to be free of the secret.'

Getting to her feet, Victoria began to pace. 'I hadn't seen my cousin – your father – in years, you understand? There was quite an age gap between him and my father. I'd seen their boy once, when he was a baby, but that was the last time we'd had contact. When the accident happened…' She put a hand to her head and spun around to face them. 'My dad was the next of kin. Your parents had yet to make a will, so there was no indication of intended guardians. He dealt with the estate, but as a man in his late-fifties, living alone, he didn't feel equipped to raise two young children. He told me I'd have to do it.'

Lauren glanced at Anna to see how she was faring. Her complexion had paled, wide eyes fixed unwaveringly on her cousin.

Victoria seemed unable to continue, her face in her hands, and Stephen stood and put a hand on her arm. 'Sit down, dear. Come on.'

He led her to the table and she sank into her seat, her face mottled red and white and eyes strained. Taking a trembling sip of her tea, Victoria shuddered.

'Married just twelve months, in our early twenties, and we'd already said we didn't want a family. Neither of us were into children, it just wasn't... *us*.'

'That, at least, I can agree with.' Anna spoke quietly, and Victoria winced.

Lauren was conscious of a vague similarity to her own situation.

'I couldn't face taking on two young children. I agreed, reluctantly, to take the baby, and my father arranged for the boy to be privately adopted.'

A gasp came from Anna, and she clasped her hands on the table. 'Why didn't you tell me when I was old enough to understand?'

Victoria lowered her head but did not speak, and Stephen cleared his throat, as though waiting for his wife to tell him to shut up. When nothing happened, he looked over at Anna.

'Victoria feared you would want your brother to come and live with us. She was struggling to bring you up, found it a strain, that the life we had planned together had been stolen. The idea of taking on a growing boy, soon heading into teen years, was more than she could handle.'

'But if he was part of another family, that wouldn't have happened! At least I would have known him for most of my life instead of now being in my thirties and never having seen his face!' Emotion throbbed in Anna's voice, and Lauren placed a comforting hand on hers.

Victoria, however, raised her head. For once, the rigidness of her face had eased a little. 'I don't expect you to understand how I felt. It was a responsibility I never sought, never anticipated. The life I'd dreamed of was ruined, and yes, I resented you – and your parents for leaving you alone.'

It couldn't absolve the deceit Victoria had practised on Anna, or the years of silence, but Lauren found she empathised a little with her despair at unexpected parenthood.

'I want to find out what happened to him.'

There was silence for a moment, and then Victoria, not removing her gaze from Anna's determined face, spoke.

'Stephen, fetch the box.'

–

Lauren checked her phone, then tucked it in her pocket. Work emails could wait.

'How are you feeling? Stupid question, I suppose.' Anna had joined her in the rear seat as Daniel steered the BMW back towards the A303.

Raising her head from reading, yet again, the newspaper report of her parents' fatal accident, Lauren was unsurprised to see the mantle of sadness draped across her friend's shoulders and the dampness about her eyes.

'Not stupid.' Anna summoned a smile. 'Thank you so much for being with me.' Her voice wavered on the last word, and she swallowed visibly. 'I'm finding it hard to take in. There's a pressure inside me here.' She placed a hand to her breastbone as she laid the newspaper cutting on her lap.

'At least you have some photos now.'

Anna leaned back in her seat, her gaze drawn to the window. 'I can't believe they had them all this time and never gave them to me.' She glanced back over at Lauren. 'I mean, I had the few you've seen, none of which included a brother, but...' She shrugged.

There really wasn't much to say.

'Had she ever explained all that about your home before, how it was rented and how the estate was dealt with?'

'I did once ask, when I was about to leave for college, whether there had been any money from my parents. Victoria was her usual scathing self, saying they were too flighty to save for a house deposit, too busy travelling around to music festivals, trying to earn an income from performing.'

Lauren sighed. 'They do seem inordinately proud of their home.'

Anna rolled her eyes. 'Tell me about it. Show is everything to them. It's why they paid for my lessons – piano, riding, ballet.' She grinned. 'Victoria regretted that one when I became so tall.' Then, she sobered. 'All I wanted was love, not what their money could give me.'

There was a brief interruption as they reached the Devon border and Daniel reminded them they had a bag of sustenance between them, pleading for a wrap and a bottle of water. Once they were all supplied, they talked about what Anna could do next.

'Oliver might be able to help. He went through the process over how to contact a person connected to adoption when— once.'

They munched quietly on their sandwiches for a minute. Lauren didn't like to ask Anna if she'd considered her brother not wanting to know her. I mean, why would he not want to? It was just that she wasn't sure how many blows Anna could take. She had always been raw about her lack of family and her cold upbringing in a household where she was a burden rather than a delight.

Lauren's hand went to her middle. She may never have thought before now about life with a baby, as a mother, but every child deserved to be cherished by whoever raised it.

'I suppose we can assume your brother hasn't married or had children, as there was nothing on Ancestry? I mean, he probably has a copy of his own birth certificate, but he'd have been too young to have memories of your parents, and if he's never felt the need to research family history, he wouldn't have a clue about you.'

She reached over to retrieve the empty wrapper from Daniel. 'Want some chocolate?'

'Please.' Daniel met her gaze in the rear-view mirror but there was a strain about his eyes, and Lauren frowned. She sensed there was something on Daniel's mind that hadn't been there when they'd set off.

Silence fell for a while as the car ate up the miles, and when she next glanced at Anna, she'd fallen asleep, her head resting on her coat. Lauren carefully took the papers from her lap, leaving her grasping the photo of Anna's parents with their two small children.

'Thank you for driving.'

Daniel met Lauren's gaze in the mirror again. 'No problem.'

'Sorry we left you alone for so long.'

Daniel slowed the car as they reached a roundabout.

'I've been messaging Claud, but she's ghosting me. They're not even being read.' His eyes were solemn in the reflection, and Lauren instinctively laid her left hand on his shoulder, giving it a squeeze.

'Give her a bit of time and space. A break means a breather, a chance to think.'

To her surprise, Daniel's right hand landed on top of hers with a reciprocal tightening. 'Thank you, Lauren. I don't know what I would have done without you to talk to this last week.'

Their hands separated, and Lauren sat back in her seat. 'Any time.'

She meant it. Looking at her hand, she flexed the fingers. She could still feel the warmth of Daniel's skin upon hers, the firmness of his body beneath her touch on his shirt.

Rolling her eyes, she turned to stare out the window as Daniel turned up the radio and they sped along the A30.

It may have been your predilection in the past, Kirkham, but this is no time to be finding a man attractive.

Especially one who was clearly still hung up on someone else.

Chapter Ten

Fancy That

They'd made a late night of it after returning from Dorset. Daniel had been dispatched to Colin the Cod's to collect supper, and Lauren had helped Anna ready the guest rooms – one for a couple on a walking break, the other two for a young family making the most of the school holidays.

Anna hadn't stopped speculating about her brother, even though she had virtually no information, but as they sat around the coffee table, eating fish and chips off their laps, Daniel and Lauren listened patiently, and after they'd eaten, they all got on their various devices to search for advice on how to trace someone who'd been adopted.

The only helpful thing Victoria had offered was to contact her father to see if he could recall the name of the private adoption agency he'd used at the time. As the old man was in a home and suffering from the early stages of dementia, the odds weren't promising.

-

On Good Friday, Lauren settled at the table with her laptop and a cup of tea as Anna avidly studied the website of the adoption support agency Oliver had contacted when trying to find his grandmother, Meg.

'Any joy?' Lauren looked up as Anna closed her laptop.

'Sort of. I've made a few notes. I'll need to prove my relationship to Alistair, and they'll use what information I'm able to provide to try and locate him. If they do, they'll make an approach to see if he's willing to have his details shared with me. Oliver warned me these things move slowly.' Anna pulled a face. 'Not helpful when I want to know *now*.'

Lauren sent her a sympathetic look. 'Of course you do.'

'Good job we're full this weekend. It'll keep my mind busy.' Anna stood. 'Right, I need to stock up for the weekend. The farm shop's closed, so I'll pop to the supermarket in Port Wenneth. Can I get you anything?'

Lauren leaned back in her seat. 'Can you grab some more of that rose lemonade?'

Anna tapped into the Notes app on her phone. 'Can we tell Oliver when he's home? I hate that we're hiding something from him.'

'Yes, of course. I didn't mean to tell Daniel, it just slipped out.'

'I think Oliver has his suspicions.' Anna picked up some empties from the previous night and waved one of the rosé bottles Lauren was using. 'He asked me some odd questions the other day about alcohol and pregnancy. I reckon he spotted the alco-free bottles in the recycling.'

'I promise to fess up as soon as he's back.' Before long, everyone Lauren met would know about it.

Although it was a holiday, once Anna left, Lauren turned her attention to drafting a response to the rates negotiation email she'd received from HR at the Devere Corporation, then became engrossed with her inbox. It was an hour later that her mobile pinged, and she stretched her arms above her head before picking it up.

A WhatsApp from Daniel.

> Thanks for the ear. Are you free at the
> weekend to see the house?

> Anna's taken back the reins here, so I'm at
> a loose end after today.

> Let's do Saturday, 10 a.m.

Lauren put the phone on the table. She liked Daniel. He
was so easy to be around, and he deserved to be happy.
Her lips curved as she recalled their walk on the beach
the other day.

'Why are you looking like that?' Anna looked amused
as she came into the kitchen with the shopping.

'Daniel just messaged. Going to see the house in the
morning.'

Anna raised a brow as she placed her groceries on the
counter. 'You fancy him.'

Lauren gave a splutter of laughter as she walked over to
help. 'Don't be daft. Of course I don't.'

'Fibber.'

'Be quiet.'

Anna smirked. 'I know that smile, Lauren Kirkham,
once champion serial dater of Harrogate.' She sobered.
'It's not a crime to like someone, you know.'

'I'm pregnant, in case you haven't noticed.'

'So?' Anna laughed. 'Has it shut your eyesight off?'

'I—' Being lost for words was an unfamiliar sensation
to Lauren.

'Is that why you're watching back-to-back *Poldark* on Netflix?' Anna's lips twitched as she headed for the utility with some of her purchases. 'Well, Daniel did grow up in Cornwall and he's very... muscley.'

Lauren burst out laughing. 'Stop it!' She was secretly relieved Anna had cheered up and she was prepared to humour her to keep it going, so the teasing continued as they made lunch.

After they cleared the table and Anna popped upstairs with fresh milk for the hospitality trays, Lauren opened her laptop again, then paused to think. She'd always had an eye for a good-looking man, and her casual dating had been notorious, though it had only rarely led beyond dessert. She'd never been just friends with a man, but with Daniel it felt so natural. Did she like him beyond it, though?

Lauren pushed the notion aside, but struggled to settle back into her work, her gaze constantly drifting outside. It was a grey day, though relatively mild. Rain threatened on the horizon, but even so, the view remained as charming as ever.

She really needed to think about heading back up north. She'd only moved her next midwife appointment on a week, and it would be stupid to miss it. Besides, her mother was pressing for her to go home.

Park it, Kirkham. Get on with some work.

Lauren eyed the open PowerPoint slides with distaste. It was a long weekend, and she really wasn't in the mood. What with Anna's predicament, Daniel's stress levels, and her own uncertain future, there was enough to think about without scanning through the terms and conditions of a new contract.

The boot room door opened, and for the first time since she'd arrived, Lauren was grateful for the interruption as Nicki, Mrs Lovelace and another elderly lady trooped in.

Then, she frowned, looking at the time.

'Afternoon, ladies. This is a surprise.'

'I saw Anna going past earlier,' Nicki smiled. 'Word soon gets about.'

Mrs Lovelace beamed at Lauren, then looked around. 'Where's our Anna to, then?'

'Upstairs. She won't be a minute.'

'Don't mind us, my lovely. This here's Cleggie.' Mrs Lovelace took the seat opposite, indicating the other lady, who smiled kindly at Lauren as she settled beside her friend. 'Used to housekeep for young Mr Seymour.'

'Lovely to meet you, Mrs Clegg. I'm Anna's friend, Lauren.'

'We saw you, my lovely. Didn't we, 'Melza?' She nodded at Mrs Lovelace. 'When you'm first came to the cove, 'aving a moment with young Daniel. We came soon as we 'eard young Anna was back. Where be that Master Seymour, then?'

'Anna needed to pop home early. Oliver will be back Monday.'

'Have we interrupted you?' Nicki nodded at Lauren's laptop. 'Hoped you might be having a day off.'

Lauren sent her a warm smile. 'I was just contemplating doing so.'

'Shall I make the drinks?' Nicki wandered over to the sink, and Lauren willingly closed her laptop only to meet Mrs Lovelace's enquiring look.

'When you'm heading back up country? Anna's goin' to miss you.'

Lauren laughed. 'I doubt it, not once she's got her man back. I came down for two weeks initially, but I'm staying into next week to make up for not seeing much of them.'

She got up to fetch the cake tin, still battling a strange sense of disquiet over returning to Yorkshire, then went to call up the stairs to say there were visitors, before resuming her seat.

'Hello, everyone!' Anna's gaze roamed over the assembled ladies as she came into the room. 'To what do we owe this afternoon honour?'

'Bank Holiday weather,' Nicki said sagely from by the kettle, waving a hand at the darkening skies. 'The boys' kayak lesson ended early, so Hamish has taken them to see his parents.'

Anna sent Mrs Clegg a kind look. 'Are you feeling better?'

Mrs Lovelace sniffed. 'They'm saying she's got to see one of them gynaeropodists.'

'Gynaecologists,' Nicki interjected from over by the sink.

'That's what I says.' Mrs Lovelace turned back to Anna. 'Cleggie's havin' a few...' She lowered her voice. '*Problems*.'

'I'm sorry you're not well, Mrs Clegg.' Lauren frowned. 'It's nothing serious, I hope?'

To her surprise, the old lady beamed. 'Don't mind me, my lovely. Looking forward to it, as it happens. Been a long time since anyone's had a fumble with me bits.'

Under cover of the general amusement, Lauren sat back in her chair, nursing her mug. It would drive her mad if this was her permanent life, but there was no denying she'd miss these moments around Anna's kitchen table, taking in the scenery and listening to the barmy locals.

Who would have thought she'd find some contentment is such a sedentary way of life?

You'd have enjoyed it more if Daniel had turned up...

Shut up.

–

Lauren arrived at The Lookout on Saturday morning, excited to see the house she'd heard so much about. Thankfully, the overnight rain had moved on and although it wasn't sunny, the air was mild and small white clouds scurried across the pale grey backdrop as though chased by a shepherding dog.

As Lauren got out of her Mini, she looked around. The grounds were pretty much still a building site. Daniel's Jeep was parked over by a cabin, where he was in conversation with a woman dressed in mud-spattered overalls – someone to do with landscaping, if the van's logo was any guide.

Lauren's gaze drifted towards the house. She liked the look of it immediately. Though a new build, there was plenty of character in the thick wooden beams below the Cornish slate roof and she loved the almost gothic-style front door.

She leaned against the bonnet of the car, waiting for Daniel to finish his conversation. He looked far more animated this morning, and she smiled faintly. They had fallen into such an easy friendship.

'Sorry about that.' Lauren straightened as Daniel came towards her, waving off the lady in her van before gesturing towards the house. 'Shall we?'

'Anna's very jealous.'

Daniel laughed. 'She keeps ribbing me, saying I should charge for entry as the house is going to be famous.'

They were soon inside, and the pride in Daniel's voice was evident as he showed Lauren around.

'Wow!' They had come into what Daniel said would be the main living area: large, open plan, with flagstones and floor-to-ceiling, timber-framed windows looking straight out to sea. Even with bare plaster and the odd wire poking out of the walls, it was breathtaking. 'This is amazing.'

'I've got contractors finishing off once the long weekend's over. The plaster's dry enough to put a sealing coat on and then it's down to choosing the colour palette.'

Lauren turned around on her heel. The rest of the space contained a large wood burner under a huge beam, a sweeping bay window and, at the far end of the room, looking over fields towards the sea further down the coast, a stylish kitchen.

The ceiling was vaulted, with exposed timbers, and Lauren took it all in before looking over to the silent man by the wall. His gaze wasn't on the interior but on Lauren, and her brow furrowed as she took in his unreadable expression.

'Are you okay?'

Daniel straightened. 'I'm just watching your reaction. You like it?'

'I *love* it! It's stunning, and the *views*!'

'Come and inspect the kitchen.'

It was a fabulous room, with every modern appliance anyone could possibly need. 'Are you into cooking?'

Daniel shook his head. 'Not as a habit, but Anna inspires me. I decided I'd get the best equipped kitchen I could and then start learning.' He turned around. 'With that view to keep me company, I think I'll do okay.'

Lauren's brow furrowed at his darkening expression. As Daniel had said, it was a big house to rattle round in on his own.

'And here?' She walked over to the large curved window. 'This is the perfect spot for a table.' Her gaze roamed over the clifftop field, scattered with sheep grazing, and then beyond to the sea. 'What a heavenly spot. I could happily work from home with that on the office doorstep.'

'That's the plan, though there is a study. To be honest, it was designed so there aren't any bad views, thanks to the clifftop promontory.'

He showed her the cosy snug, with a smaller log burner.

'I'm going to have a massive screen here.' Daniel placed his hands on the longest wall. 'Got to have somewhere to play *Red Dead Redemption*.'

Lauren laughed. 'I'm well jealous. Been playing Play-Station games with my brothers for years. I became quite the demon at uni. We'll have to play whenever I next come back to see Anna.'

They viewed the aforementioned study – small, but well-equipped with power and charging points and a floor-length window facing the stunning scenery. There was also a spacious utility and a wet room.

'Wondered if I should get a rescue dog.' Daniel tapped his foot on the tiled floor. 'This would work well as somewhere to wash muddy paws.'

They were about to climb the striking curved oak staircase to the upper floor when Daniel's mobile rang, and he glanced at it.

'Gerry. I'd better take it. You go on up and explore.'

Lauren found three fairly equally sized rooms, all a blank canvas but with more gorgeous views. There was a sophisticated bathroom with a huge bathtub placed before a large, circular window so you could soak and enjoy the outside vista at the same time.

The master bedroom elicited another whispered 'wow', with another vaulted ceiling and stylish en suite as well as a vast alcove with sliding doors to what Lauren suspected would be a dressing room.

Lauren came out onto the landing, filled with light from the skylights, and went down the stairs, her hand running over the smooth wood of the bannister.

Daniel was still on the phone, and she could see a couple of men out in the yard, measuring and making notes, so Lauren wandered around the room, admiring the finishing touches, her mind happily engaged in how she'd furnish it, given the chance. Then, her eyes lighted on a framed photo on the hearth, and she leaned down to study it: a stunning photo of a beautiful woman, sporting long jet black hair, a gorgeous smile and a designer jacket. Surely, this had to be—

'Claudia.'

Daniel had ended the call and came to stand beside Lauren. He bent down and picked up the frame. 'She gave it to me about a month ago, said it would remind me what she looked like, as I was never around.'

Ouch.

He let out a huff of breath. 'Gerry's not cutting me any slack. She says,' he assumed an accent. '"Get the girl back, Danny-boy, or get a new'un."'

Lauren clamped down on the offer that almost sprang to her lips.

'You're serious?'

'She says it's all in the contract: a family member or equivalent to participate in the final recording. They like to add that personal touch.' Daniel shrugged. 'At this rate, I'll be having to ask Mrs L to do me the favour or drag my aunt down from Tremayne Manor.'

'You got a minute, mate?'

They both looked around as one of the men appeared in the doorway, and Daniel's mouth curved. 'I'll go and chat with these chaps and then I'll make us a cuppa in the cabin and share my thoughts for the gardens with you.'

Chapter Eleven

My Little Phoney

The conversation at The Lookout had gone down an unexpected route, and a preoccupied Lauren arrived back at Westerleigh Cottage to find Anna busy laying the table for lunch.

'How did it go?'

Dropping her bag onto the sofa, Lauren followed Anna back over to the kitchen.

'Good, I think.' Her mind wasn't really on the house. 'I saw a photo of Claudia, in Chanel, no less. She makes me feel like I forgot to check the mirror before going out.'

Anna laughed as she rinsed a bowl under the tap. 'I know what you mean. She's stunning.'

Lauren leaned back against the kitchen island. 'They seem incredibly mismatched, but then, they say opposites attract.' Then, she frowned. 'Daniel's getting some flack from the TV producer. Seems dead set on him having either a girlfriend or close relative in tow for this last bit of filming.'

'They do like to play that card, I've seen earlier series. Lord, I hope he doesn't bring Alex down from London!'

'You're surely well over him?'

'Entirely.' Anna checked the pan on the AGA, and started to plate up. 'I just hate the condescending way he looks at Oliver.'

They enjoyed a leisurely lunch, and in an attempt to distract her friend from going round in circles about the elusive brother, Lauren enthusiastically described the layout of The Lookout, all the time ordering her mind for what she wanted to run past Anna.

'Daniel needs help with the interiors.' Lauren shrugged. 'I'd love to do it – such a dream house to furnish. I said it was a shame I'm going home in a matter of days, and he asked me why I didn't stay.'

Anna's lips lifted as she exclaimed, 'Oh my God! Why don't you?'

'I can't stay this far from everything.' For some reason, Lauren's mood had sunk again. Was it her mum's last WhatsApp message about setting up a nursery for the baby?

Anna filled their glasses with homemade lemonade. 'What's "everything"? We have electricity and running water, you know.'

'Pillock.' Lauren picked up a glass, then lowered it. 'Work, especially my northern aspirations. Ditto to family support. Access to big cities, my medical people.'

Anna shrugged. 'So? You have your clients and me. I'm only sorry you can't stay here, but your room is booked most of the summer.' Her face brightened as she took a seat. 'You could always take on a holiday let.'

Lauren's spirits fizzled even lower. 'Suppose.' She'd gone from the bustle of the family home to various uni digs and then the house share in Harrogate. Living alone wasn't her thing. 'Mum is pushing for me to be at home, and I don't really see I've any choice in the short term, although transport links in Pateley Bridge aren't exactly first class.'

She helped herself to an apple from the bowl on the table.

'Then stay here for the summer and just go home for the birth, so your mum feels involved.'

Lauren stared at Anna, the apple half raised to her mouth as wheels began to turn in her head. She lowered her hand as her eyes drifted to the scene outside. 'I miss Leeds. The lifestyle you know?' The wheels accelerated. 'But that won't be my life for a while. It might be feasible, and going home for the birth might appease Mum.'

'You said yourself, you can work from anywhere these days. There are several direct trains to London a day if you need to be there. It's not much longer a journey than from the Dales, and we're only forty minutes from Newquay airport if you need to go further.'

'But what about my appointments?'

With a laugh, Anna selected a handful of grapes from the bowl. 'We do have midwives here too.'

Lauren took a bite of the apple and chewed thoughtfully. 'I'm not too keen on the idea of a holiday let, but it would work as they're furnished.' She glanced at Anna. 'Provided there's a proper desk. Much as I love being here, this table's not good for my back.'

'You've got plenty of project work on to tide you over and the big companies will be snapping your hand off once you're back on the job market. Oh, Lauren,' Anna grasped her friend's hand. 'It would be so great to have you stay longer. I think I'm going to go mad in the wait for news on Alistair otherwise.'

It was a timely reminder. Oliver, she knew, had a busy summer ahead. Anna would need a friend more than ever.

Lauren squeezed Anna's hand before relinquishing it. 'Being here for you is the best incentive. I'm sure I can make it work. Besides,' she smirked at Anna. 'It will give me plenty of time to help Daniel if I stay.'

A frisson of delight sped through Lauren, and Anna raised an amused brow.

'Daniel? Is that your reason, then?'

'Of course not.' Lauren pushed the notion away. 'Men aren't even "Any Other Business" on my agenda. Besides, no one's going to be interested in me in my condition. Good way of keeping them at bay, though.'

Glancing at the clock as she popped the last grape into her mouth, Anna got to her feet. 'I need to call Oliver and update him on Alistair. I'm not sure if I'm excited or terrified about what I'm going to find out.'

Lauren glanced at the clock. 'I'll leave you to it, I'm going for a run. See you later.'

The run and a shower failed to cease Lauren's speculations, but deep down, she knew exactly what she was going to do. For herself, she had a myriad of doubts, but when it came to her friend, there were none.

Anna might well think Lauren needed a friend around her for the next few months, but Lauren believed – even though she had Oliver – Anna also needed a mate onside as she faced the dilemma of her lost sibling.

–

On Easter Monday, the B&B guests departed, and Anna went to make up the beds ready for the next arrivals, leaving Lauren to work, but so far, the bulk of her productivity amounted to making several cups of tea and staring at the view from the window.

A small trawler bobbed and weaved like an aquatic boxer as it crested the waves outside the harbour entrance, seagulls winging overhead in hopes of stealing some of the catch. There was a light breeze, the sky was blue and there was a hint of the approaching warmer months in the air, but despite the serenity of nature, Lauren's mind was on the call she needed to make.

Mrs Kirkham wasn't at all impressed with her daughter's thinking and continued to press her to go home as soon as possible. Lauren felt blessed to have such a caring mother, but it was obvious she still believed she knew best for all her children, despite the eldest being nearly forty.

Lauren started as Anna came hurrying into the room clutching her mobile, her face alight with joy.

'Oliver's nearly home. Managed to change to an earlier flight. Oh!' Her face fell as she looked over to the kitchen. 'I need to go shopping. I'm out of bacon and still need to get something in for supper.'

'Can't you go out, enjoy an evening together?'

Anna shook her head. 'Oliver said how much he was looking forward to being at home. He's not that fond of eating out.'

'Morning, ladies. Has the Home for Loose Ends got room for a stray?'

Perking up, Lauren smiled warmly at Daniel, keen to tell him her news.

'Rude!'

Anna, however, laughed. 'There's always room at my table. I have to dash, or I'll not be here when Oliver arrives. Lauren can look after you.'

She turned her attention to tapping a shopping list into her phone, checking the fridge and cupboards as Lauren made coffee for Daniel and yet another mug of tea for herself.

Lauren eyed Daniel covertly as she joined him at the table with the drinks. No overalls today, just jeans and a polo shirt sporting a logo. He looked a little tired around the eyes. Not moping for Claudia, she hoped. 'You're our only caller today.'

Daniel took an appreciative sip of his coffee. 'Nothing happening at the build either, it'll all kick off again tomorrow.'

Anna came in from the utility to say she wouldn't be long, and Daniel turned to Lauren as the door closed.

'How's she doing? Has there been any more news about this brother?'

'It's just a waiting game, I think. Oliver's been keeping her going over video and voice calls, reassuring her.'

'That's the big man for you, always a steadying hand.'

With a smile, Lauren picked up her mug. 'Hey, I'm going with your suggestion and staying for a while, just going home for the birth – my mum's taking some convincing, but luckily she's far enough away for me to stand my ground.'

'That's brilliant news!'

Lauren tried – *really* tried – to suppress the quick skip of her heart as his face infused with obvious pleasure. Was he *that* pleased? And why did that excite her?

'You can help with the interiors after all.'

Ah… okay.

Soon, they'd drained their mugs, and Daniel gestured towards Lauren's open laptop. 'What are you working on?'

'Invoicing.' She faked a yawn. 'Boring but necessary.'

'What are you using?'

Lauren turned the laptop so Daniel could see.

'There's a much better one. May I?'

'Feel free.'

Daniel sourced the app and downloaded it, running through the basics. They were so engrossed, they both jumped when Anna came back through the door laden with shopping.

Lifting the heavy basket onto the counter, Daniel then left with a cheery wave.

'Someone seems happier,' Anna said dryly as she stocked the fridge but Lauren shook her head.

'He's pleased there'll be someone to help with the furnishings.'

Wanting to leave Anna alone for when Oliver arrived, Lauren attached the lead and took Dougal off on a walk along the cliff path. The chimney of The Lookout could be seen poking up through the trees. It would be so much fun helping Daniel to furnish such a stunning property, but probably a good job he was off limits. She was hardly in a position to try dating again and Daniel certainly didn't need someone like Lauren, with her track record.

Lauren walked on for half an hour before whistling to Dougal and retracing their steps, returning to delicious smells emanating from the kitchen.

Anna was nowhere to be seen, although there was evidence of her recent activity, with the table laid, a basket of bread on the island and a pot bubbling away on the AGA.

Opening the fridge, Lauren eyed with resignation the rose lemonade, hiding away in its wine bottle cloak. She longed for a nicely chilled glass of wine. With a sigh, she poured the lemonade into a wine glass and headed out to the terrace.

Sitting by the patio table, Lauren took a sip, trying really hard to pretend it tasted like wine. Not remotely close. She shivered as a breeze swept across the terrace, and sitting up she pulled the two sides of her light-weight jacket together, then sighed.

'Here we go.'

She could have done the buttons up if she'd wanted to, but it wouldn't have been as comfortable as it used to be.

'There you are!'

Lauren's head spun to the left as Anna hurried across the terrace.

'Hey. Where's Oliver? Have you worn him out?'

'Cheeky! He's fine, went up to his office to put the trip paperwork to bed.' She waved a hand towards the back of the clifftop garden. 'Except...' A frown creased Anna's brow as she took the seat opposite.

Lauren leaned forward. 'Except?'

'It's odd. He seems wary about my pursuing the search for Alistair.'

That was a surprise. 'Did he say why? I thought he'd been supportive?'

'He has.' Anna nodded firmly. 'He kept saying these things take time, I wasn't to get too stressed.'

Lauren sent her a sympathetic smile. Anna's aunt Meg had suffered a disappointment when searching for her adopted child, Oliver's mother, who hadn't wanted to know her.

'He's only looking out for you.'

'I know.' Anna smiled warmly. 'And I love him for it. He's been incredibly protective of me since the news came out.' She glanced at her watch and let out a small yelp. 'I'd best put the finishing touches to our supper. Can you go and give Oliver a nudge? The office is round the corner, up the stone steps at the back of the garden. Let him know it'll be on the table in about fifteen?'

Keen to see Oliver's bolthole, Lauren drained her glass as they stood. 'Gladly.'

'Oh, and Lauren?' Anna held out her hand for the empty glass. 'Now you're staying, please tell him about the baby.'

'Of course.'

Lauren followed the side terrace round to a flight of steps at the back of the garden, which led to a stone building sporting a solid-looking door. It looked hewn from the rocks behind it.

She started as the door opened. Oliver's expression was grim, and she rushed into speech.

'You've been summoned. Dinner on the table in fifteen.'

Oliver held up a small alarm clock. 'I've learned. Come on in. I just need to tidy a few things away.'

Curious, Lauren stepped inside.

'Gosh!'

Oliver walked over to the solid desk beneath a large window fronting out to sea. 'This outbuilding belonged to the property next up the cliff from us.' He glanced over his shoulder, his glasses perched on the end of his nose. 'Used to be a disused barn. Became a joint project for Daniel and I last autumn, when he was awaiting planning approval.'

Lauren walked slowly around the vast room, wondering how to open the conversation and fess up. Oliver's closed expression didn't excite confidence.

'It's stunning.'

It had a high roof with exposed beams, but the walls were all painted white, and it was incredibly light, mainly due to the large skylights fitted into the roof. The room ran for some feet away from the main door, fitted on both sides with cabinets and shelving, holding an array of treasures – antiques, she suspected, knowing from Anna his passion for them – and row upon row of books.

Oliver glanced over at Lauren as she hovered near one of the cabinets, uncertain how to begin. 'Needed somewhere to store my things.'

Come on, Kirkham. Carpe Diem and all that.

Walking over to Oliver's desk, Lauren was about to launch into speech when she noticed one of the empty alcohol-free gin bottles by the bin.

Did this make things easier or not? Lauren wasn't sure, but – despite her inability to decide on where to live – she wasn't into procrastination either.

'There's something I need to tell you. About *that*.' Lauren pointed to the empty bottle.

Placing his glasses on the desk, Oliver turned to face her, his countenance unreadable and his piercing blue gaze holding hers.

Lord, it was like standing in front of her old headmistress when she'd been caught throwing crab apples from the grounds at the boys from the school across the road.

Oliver raised his chin. 'I've known for a couple of weeks. Couldn't work out why Anna hadn't spoken. I didn't want to confront her, so I've just been keeping an eye, hoping she'd tell me when she felt ready. This discovery of a brother isn't helping, she's so stressed by it, and I know she's anxious about... my past determination to avoid family ties of any sort. Since we got together, I've done my best to convince her I'm fine with us having a child. Children, even.' The edges of his mouth turned up. 'Though I think we might have to compromise on how many.'

Oh. My. God!

Chapter Twelve

Pregnant Pause

'Oliver! Anna's not pregnant! *I* am.'

Oliver almost swayed as his skin paled, and Lauren instinctively put out a hand – not that she was going to be able to support this giant of a man – as he sat heavily in his chair, his head dropping into his hands.

'Are you okay? I'm so sorry for not being open about it. It's not Anna's fault. I begged her to keep my secret, thinking I'd be gone within a fortnight.'

Slowly, Oliver raised his head. Colour had returned to his skin, and the blue eyes were as searching as ever.

'Forgive me. It's a bit of a shock.'

'It was for me, too,' Lauren intoned dryly, and a hint of a smile touched his mouth.

'Anna's got an app on her phone, I saw it, and—'

'Jumped to inclusions, as Mrs L would say?'

He blew out a breath. 'God, I've been wondering why she was drinking, then came across that.' He pointed to the infamous bottle. 'I went back to the hotel once, to collect a memory stick, and she was in the bathroom. Her laptop was open on a website about exercise during pregnancy. It all made sense at the time.'

Lauren sank onto a nearby chair, her gaze resting on Oliver.

'Anna's feeling bad about it – all my fault for putting this on her.'

A flash of emotion washed over Oliver's face, gone in an instant. 'I assumed she wasn't ready to tell me. I've been married to my job for so long, we needed time to adjust to being together.' He sent Lauren a self-deprecating look. 'Anna believed *I* needed time.'

'Again, I'm so sorry to have put you both through this when you've been so good to me.' Lauren felt truly dreadful. 'And are you okay now the truth is out there?'

To her surprise, Oliver laughed, then leaned forward in his seat with an earnest look. 'The truth isn't fully out there. I need to talk to Anna. No doubt she'll fill you in on the shock factor later. Come on, let's go before we're in trouble.'

They headed for the door, but as they stepped out onto the small lawn outside the barn, Oliver squinted over at Lauren.

'Are *you* okay? I hope delaying your return home hasn't upset your boss. You've been so kind to accommodate us.'

'Let's just say, my truth isn't fully out there yet either. Anna and I can fill you in over supper.'

They headed down the steps and along the side terrace, but before they entered the house, Oliver stopped and turned to face her.

'I thought I knew everything I wanted, Lauren. Be wary of getting a fixation in your head of how your life is going to pan out. Sometimes a curve ball is entirely what you need. When Anna came into my life, it didn't take me long to realise I hadn't got a clue what I really longed for. She changed me – for the better, I might add – and helped me to see what life *could* be.'

Lauren stared at him as his words washed over her.

'What is it?' Oliver's brow furrowed.

'Nothing.' Rousing herself, Lauren summoned a smile. 'I'm just beginning to understand myself a little more, that's all.'

Once in the kitchen, Oliver swept Anna from the room, a gentle hand about her shoulders as she protested the meal would spoil.

'I'm on it!' Lauren called reassuringly after their departing backs, then hurried to grab a pan from the AGA, pouring the contents into the drainer and looking round for the dish to put them in. Opening the oven, she found it warming, and she added it to the rest of the meal, turning the temperature low.

Relieved she had come clean, at least about the baby, Lauren carried the basket of bread rolls over to the table. Wouldn't it be better to leave them in peace this evening? She didn't relish being alone, but Oliver had only just returned and who knew how their conversation was going?

It was only as Lauren reached out to straighten a napkin, she noticed the four place settings, and before she could speculate, the boot room door opened, and Daniel walked in. Her spirits rising, Lauren beamed at him.

'Hey, wasn't expecting you.'

'Got a message from Anna, inviting me to join you all. Said she didn't want you to feel like a spare part at supper.'

Lauren smirked. 'That girl knows me too well. I was contemplating taking a tray up to my room.'

Daniel placed a bottle of wine on the island and Lauren tried not to covet it.

'Where are love's young dream, then? Not still in hiding since Oliver's return?' Daniel waggled his brows, and Lauren laughed.

'They had something to talk about, and—' They looked over at the sound of approaching footsteps. 'Here they are.'

Anna had been crying, but there was a glow about her, and she sent Lauren the widest smile as Oliver crossed the room to greet Daniel, and under cover of the distraction, Lauren joined her friend.

'Okay?'

A tremulous smile. 'More than. I'll tell you all about it tomorrow.' Anna hugged Lauren, then headed for the kitchen. 'Right, let's get this show on the road.'

Lauren passed a reflective night. The previous evening had been fun and informative. She'd finally shared *all* her news with her host, Anna and Oliver had recounted tales from their travels and Lauren had confirmed two things she already knew: Anna was tying herself up in knots over the mystery of her long-lost brother, and Daniel was not only an exceptionally good listener, but she was finding him way too attractive.

With Oliver engrossed in his work in the barn the next morning, and the B&B sorted, Lauren put aside her laptop as she and Anna had a chance to catch up.

It turned out Oliver's shock – much to his own surprise – had been how devastated he was to learn Anna *wasn't* expecting. He'd been a combination of frustrated by his level of anxiety for her and disbelieving of his own happiness at what he'd suspected.

Anna had finally accepted Oliver meant every word of his commitment to her. Once the outcome of the search for the missing brother was known, they would set a date to marry, her dream being – because, as Lauren pointed out, Anna always had a dream – that said brother would be there to give her away.

Lauren was thankful she'd be there for Anna and whatever she might face in the coming months. What was more, Oliver's words of wisdom had given her pause for thought. The decision to remain in Polkerran until a few weeks before the baby was due now seemed like a perfect piece of serendipity.

–

With the commitment made to staying in Cornwall, Lauren's impetus and former vigour returned with ferocity. The next ten days sped by as – urged by Anna, who was desperate to know the baby's sex – she moved her gender scan appointment to the nearest private hospital and registered with a local midwife, duly attending for her overdue tests.

Lauren also started the search for somewhere to live, making enquiries at all the holiday letting companies serving Polkerran Point. She spent every spare minute she wasn't working at The Lookout, talking choices with Daniel as the finishing touches were done: chrome plates on the switches and sockets, removing all the inner packaging from the many appliances and taking delivery of the furniture he'd had in storage since he sold his flat in London.

Helping Daniel with his interiors, however, although a nice balance from the intensity of her work, gave Lauren pause for thought. Spending time with him was fun, but was it becoming too much so? She definitely found him a bit of a dish, especially after turning up at the site to find him stripped to the waist and wielding an axe with impressive strength as he chopped some logs. Was it really a good idea to be around him so much?

Furthermore, the cove's rumour mill had clicked into action, as the locals eagerly consumed every possible sighting of Daniel and Lauren, be it heads together as they poured over plant catalogues outside The Lookout, argued over paint colour cards when grabbing a quick lunch in town or were caught sharing a laugh inside one of Polkerran's smart interiors shops.

Lauren chose to ignore it, completing another project she'd taken on well ahead of the deadline, and delighted with the promise of more work in future. Having won the tender for the Devere Corporation, she also accompanied the Procurement Director to a lead supplier, which involved an overnight stay in Kent and continued to work on existing projects from dawn until dusk, pausing only to go for a run with Dougal or eat a hurried meal.

Kit sent her a couple of messages, but she ignored them. It was funny how fast his influence upon her heart faded. Had it truly been nothing more than a foolish, blinkered crush? She and Anna had always laughed about that being her friend's territory. What an idiot Lauren felt she'd been...

Nicki came round and trimmed her hair, commenting on how thick it was, and Lauren eyed the chic chin-length tousled bob with surprise at how much she liked it. She'd also felt a strange fluttering in her middle, which Anna had excitedly proclaimed to be the baby. Lauren was pretty certain it was just wind.

There was no denying her waistline had thickened slightly, though, and she could detect a slight mound when naked – under which, allegedly, something the size of a slice of cake was growing. Lauren hoped it was one for someone with a small appetite.

The day before the scan was taking place, Lauren headed downstairs in time to help Anna clear up after the guests' breakfasts. Oliver had decamped to his barn office and, despite an early morning run, Lauren felt unusually tired.

'I need a caffeine fix today.' She stopped, a hand shooting instinctively to her middle. There was that butterfly sensation again. Could it really be the baby, when it was still so small?

'Oliver says you're doing too much,' Anna cautioned as she picked up her cleaning trug. 'And he's right.'

'So does Daniel.' Lauren sipped her coffee. 'I had a lecture yesterday when we were ordering a dining table.'

'You're like Bilbo Baggins,' Anna added as she paused by the table.

'Rude!' Lauren laughed. 'I can't help being vertically challenged.'

Anna, however, wasn't amused. 'I meant that quote from *The Fellowship of the Ring*, when Bilbo says something about feeling stretched, like butter scraped over too much bread.'

Opening her laptop, Lauren squinted at the screen. Her eyes were certainly scratchy. 'I have to do some research this morning, so that's a nice change.'

'And I need to clean some rooms before people turn up.'

Lauren glanced over as Anna headed for the door. 'Expecting the usual crowd later?'

'I've learned never to expect, but they are more likely to turn up than not.'

An hour later, Lauren welcomed the interruption of Nicki coming in through the boot room door, even though she'd not got very far with her work. Her shoulders were seriously starting to protest over the unsuitable chair height.

'Just dropping some of these off.' Nicki tapped the leaflets she'd pulled from her bag. 'Anna puts them out for guests.'

Intrigued now, Lauren leaned over to read the heading on the top page.

'There's an art and music festival in Polkerran?' Judging by Nicki's expression, she'd failed to keep the incredulity out of her voice.

'Don't be so sceptical. It's non-stop here, there's always something going on.' Nicki handed the flyer to Lauren. 'There's a well-established and very popular one in Fowey every year, draws some big names down from up country. The cove decided to set up a fringe fest to showcase local talent. This is the second year.'

'Oliver says there isn't a sane month in Polkerran,' Anna added as she came into the room bearing a tray of used cups and empty biscuit jars.

Nicki laughed. 'He hides away in that man cave of his and only emerges when he thinks it's safe to do so.'

'So, what's on?' Anna picked up the top sheet and perused it just as the door opened and Mrs Lovelace came in, followed by her daughter, Jean.

Lauren joined Anna in making the coffee and tea and putting out a plate of cakes and biscuits.

'How's Mrs Clegg?' Anna handed out paper napkins. 'Did her appointment go okay?'

'Fair to middling, my lovely.' Mrs Lovelace gestured at her daughter. 'Jeannie here's tekkin' her back to the hospital next week.'

'A few more tests. She feels okay in herself. Thanks, Lauren.'

Stretching over the table to hand Jean a plate, Lauren's shirt – which she'd taken to wearing loose over her unbuttoned skinny jeans – rose up, and when she reclaimed her seat, Mrs Lovelace's beady eye was on her.

'You'm been eating one too many pasties, young'un.' Mrs Lovelace indicated Lauren's middle.

'*Mum!*' Jean protested.

She exchanged a look with Anna. 'Don't worry, it's time to fess up.' She smiled kindly at the elderly lady. 'I'm having a baby, Mrs Lovelace.'

'Gisson!' The lady's eyes widened, but Jean's smile was warm.

'Congratulations! When's it due?'

'End of September.'

'Lauren is eighteen weeks pregnant and the baby is currently the size of a pomegranate, a slice of cake or a baby hedgehog,' recited Anna.

'Nearly halfway there,' Nicki said, patting Lauren's arm. 'Congrats!'

Mrs Lovelace looked puzzled. 'But we saw you meet young Daniel. Me and Cleggie, in the cafe. Nay so many months back.'

'It's not Daniel's baby.' Lauren spoke gently.

Mrs Lovelace folded her arms under her ample bosom, but Jean frowned. 'But you're together now?'

'Course they are, Jeanie.' Mrs Lovelace sniffed. 'Old Patrick told us, he did. Said you was both cuddled up close on that sofa in the window at Karma. Seen you when waterin' the flower trough on the front there, he did.'

Lauren choked on a laugh, ignoring Anna's amused look. 'We're not a couple! We'd been to measure up shutters for the house and had lunch while we went through the brochures.'

'Of course you did,' Nicki said soothingly, but with a glint in her eye.

'Lauren was in a relationship in Leeds before she came here,' Anna interjected.

Mrs Lovelace reached for a shortbread. 'Well, young'un, where's that father to?' She waved it, and a few crumbs flew off. 'You'm been here awhile. He must be missin' you.'

Allegedly.

'He's busy preparing to live abroad.' Lauren hesitated, then decided, as she was staying in Polkerran for now, she may as well be honest. 'We're no longer together, I'm afraid.'

Expressions of regret were followed by a ream of questions, which Anna did her best to help Lauren field, culminating in:

'Do you know the sex?'

Eager eyes fixed on Lauren, and she smiled.

'Tomorrow.'

'Well now, young'un.' Mrs Lovelace rummaged in the bag at her side. 'You take it easy. None of that hunching over your machine-thing or you'll squash the little one.' She pointed to Lauren's neglected laptop, then smiled warmly, waving her retrieved knitting needles. 'I'll knit something for the baby.'

'Thank you.'

I think.

Chapter Thirteen

Life's a Beach

On Friday morning, the overdue gender scan took place, a fairly straightforward ultrasound, after which Lauren headed back to Polkerran, barely noticing the journey.

Parking the car in the driveway to Westerleigh Cottage, unaware how she'd got there, her head awash and her heart full of emotion, Lauren sat for a minute, then dug in her bag for the envelope Pauline, the midwife, had bestowed on her.

I'm having a baby!

Suddenly, this had become Mission Improbababy – a real tiny person, at the mercy of Lauren's every action and decision.

Releasing her seatbelt, she pulled the scan from the envelope.

'Hello, little one,' she whispered. 'I'm your mummy. I'm going to love you *so* much.' Lauren's voice hitched. 'I already do, I just didn't realise it. How stupid am I?'

She hiccupped a laugh, then realised Anna was hurrying towards the car.

'Hey, how'd it go? What are you having?' Her friend's anticipation was palpable, and Lauren handed her the scan then got out of the car.

'A chalk monster, apparently. And all is fine.' Lauren peered at the scan in Anna's hand. 'It's not obvious, but apparently it's a girl.'

Anna's eyes filled with tears as she examined the grainy image. 'Oh, Lauren! It makes you realise it's happening, doesn't it?'

'Just a bit.' Lauren took the image back and tucked it into the envelope. 'I feel like I've been hit with a soft hammer.'

'You do seem a bit dazed.' Anna laughed. 'I wondered when it would sink in.'

Lauren shook her head. 'I'm such an idiot.'

'No, you're not,' Anna spoke affectionately. 'You're just adjusting, one step at a time.'

By mid-afternoon, Lauren had told her mum, who'd been ecstatic at the news, drafted several emails that needed a damn good proof-read and attempted to listen in to a meeting on her laptop, but her mind was elsewhere.

A baby girl. A day ago, Lauren had been driven to succeed because she didn't know any other way to be. Now, she had a new mission, and a fierce instinct to do everything in her power to give her daughter the best possible life.

'Hello, my little one,' Lauren whispered to her belly.

Suddenly, this had become incredibly real.

The early May Bank Holiday weekend passed in enjoyable fashion, with Lauren exploring Truro, as Anna had bookings for her room. She added some key items to her maternity wardrobe, to supplement her online purchases, and then spent an enjoyable few hours pricing up cots and buggies. The evenings were passed in the hotel bar, drinking her usual and ignoring yet another message from Kit, catching up on emails but now and again – or, in fact, most of the time – googling for 'latest fashion trends for baby girls' and fielding her mum's suggestions for baby names, all of which were popular thirty years ago.

–

Lauren was at The Lookout a week later, her laptop open on a lighting website, brochures spread across the kitchen island, when her mum messaged asking for a video chat.

She busied herself making a cup of tea as her mum ran through an update on each of her children before fixing her well-meaning eye on her youngest.

'Now, what's happening with you, love? And how's my granddaughter?' Voice softening, Lauren's mum leaned closer to the screen. 'I'm glad you're coming home at the end of the summer. You're going to be lonely in a holiday cottage, you're not used to living alone. Kit said the same when—'

'Whoa!' Lauren's eyes widened as she too leaned forward to stare at her mother. '*Kit?* When have you been talking to him?'

Looking a little discomfited, Mrs Kirkham bit her lip. 'Sorry, love. He just turned up here. Your dad was at work and the poor lad looked like he needed to talk, so—'

'You offered him tea, followed by lunch and then dinner?'

A sheepish smile. 'Something like that. He's very charming.'

Isn't he just.

Lauren was so busy grilling her mum, she didn't hear the front door close or realise Daniel had returned until…

'Oh! Who's that young man?'

Daniel, phone to his ear, had wandered into view, oblivious to Lauren at the kitchen island.

'That's Daniel.' Lauren turned back to the screen. 'This is his house. I told you, he's a friend of Anna's.'

'You never said it was a *man* friend,' Mrs Kirkham all but hissed at her daughter.

Lauren rolled her eyes.

'Don't you pull that face at me, Lauren Primrose Kirkham,' the lady admonished. 'You deliberately withheld that piece of pertinent information.'

'*Mum.*' Lauren spoke quietly. 'There's nothing to say. We're friends, nothing more. I'm helping Daniel choose the interiors for his new house.' She waved an arm around, but it connected with something solid.

'Argh!'

Lauren half laughed as Daniel pretended injury. 'Sorry. Didn't see you there.'

'I thought I heard my name mentioned.'

Lauren sighed at her mother's expectant expression.

'Mum, this is my *friend*, Daniel. Daniel, this is my mum.'

Daniel pocketed his phone and waved a hand. 'Pleased to meet you, Mrs Kirkham.'

'Oh, call me Linda. Please.'

Lauren shook her head at her mum, who smiled widely at Daniel.

'So, Daniel, how did you and Lauren meet?'

'Er,' he threw Lauren a startled glance. 'In a coffee shop?'

Daniel's voice ended in a sort of squeak, and Lauren sucked on her cheeks. If he only knew, he was feeding her mother's dreams.

'How lovely!' Linda clapped her hands together. 'So much nicer than when you say a nightclub, Lauren.'

'Well, we have to go, don't we, Daniel?' Lauren gave him what she hoped was a discreet nudge in the ribs.

'Yes! Yes, we do.' Daniel folded his arms, nudging Lauren's with his knuckles. 'Lovely to meet you, Mrs... Linda.'

'I'll call you in a few days, Mum.' Lauren exchanged blown kisses with the screen and ended the call, swinging round on her stool to face Daniel.

He eyed her with amusement. 'Primrose?'

'Shut up.'

'No, seriously. *Primrose?*'

Lauren made a small sound. Very few people knew about her middle name! 'She'd had three boys already. Had a stack of girls' names she hadn't been able to use including that of her favourite doll from childhood. I'm just thankful Dad insisted on it being my second name.'

–

The conversation reminded Lauren of her friend's latest pursuit: researching baby names and mainly coming up with ones associated with her favourite books.

Lauren had left Anna to it. She'd already made a decision, just not decided to share. Anna was having far too much fun for her to end it so precipitously.

Cousin Victoria had surprisingly messaged with the name of the private adoption agency involved in placing the missing brother and, after a conversation with them, Anna was flitting between hope and despair over what might happen next. Any distraction was good for her, as Oliver attested.

One morning, with Anna busy doing admin for the B&B and free of any calls for a few hours, Lauren shrugged into her jacket, which no longer met up, and tugged on her walking boots. It was a mild day, and she had no desire to walk into the town.

Turning towards the coastal path, Lauren soon reached the steps down to the beach below The Lookout. A solitary gull winged overhead, silent for once, and she lifted her face to the warm breeze scooting inland across the rippling sea. The sun peeped out intermittently from the bulbous scattered cloud and the water sported white caps today as the waves performed their incessant dance.

Leaning on the railing at the top of the steep steps, Lauren's gaze roamed the horizon. The sea and sky merged into one in a haze more reminiscent of a summer's day, and for a moment, she simply let the view wash over her.

There's a sense of peace here, little one. It's taken me a while to feel it, but now I do, I can see why people come back time and again…

Something caught Lauren's eye, and glancing down onto the beach, she smiled. A lone figure – a man – skimmed a stone across the shoreline, his fist pumping the air as the pebble bounced four times before disappearing.

Making her way down the steps, Lauren called out to Daniel. His head whipped around, and he tossed a handful of stones into the waves sliding along the sand.

'Is this a favourite haunt, then?' Lauren gestured with her arm as she approached him. 'Or just coincidence? Hope I'm not intruding.'

Daniel covered the remaining few paces between them. Today, he sported a greyish-green, oversized cable-knit sweater and faded jeans tucked into muddy Hunters.

'One of my happy places.' The sentiment seemed contradictory to the delivery, and Lauren peered at him.

'Shall I leave you alone? Happiness I do not detect.'

'Sorry.' Daniel shoved his hands into his pockets. 'How's it going? I saw Anna earlier, said you'd been to the surgery.'

'Routine check with the midwife. All fine until the next one.'

A fishing boat came into sight, far out to sea, the usual flock of seagulls hovering in its wake. 'And?' She squinted at Daniel, but his head didn't turn. 'Haven't seen you since Friday. How's it going with you?'

'Oh, you know. Seeing the midwife next week.'

'Twit!' Lauren pretend-swatted his arm, and he winked at her.

'I'm fine.' Daniel stretched his arms above his head. 'Needed to get away from the house for a bit. You're right,' he waved a hand, 'I come here a lot. There's something about the fact you're down here, away from everything.' He tugged his phone out of his pocket. 'Not much signal, either.'

Daniel shoved his hands into his pockets again. The breeze stirred the hair on his forehead as he scanned the open sea, Lauren touched his arm, and he looked at her.

'Want to talk? I can do a nice line in silence too if you prefer.'

'Claudia finally got in touch.'

'That's great.' But not really.

'She's going on a date.'

Ah.

Daniel let out a huff of breath. 'She said she was fed up waiting for me to get over a house that I've more hots for than her. She's all I ever wanted but I couldn't hold onto her.'

Lauren reflected briefly on all she'd ever wanted: the career, the stylish city flat, the executive boyfriend with the same ambitions…

'Sometimes,' she said softly, recalling Oliver's words, 'life doesn't turn out how you expected, and that's often not a bad thing.'

'Such wisdom in one so young.' Daniel's voice was slightly mocking, and Lauren frowned at him.

'Hey, squirt. I'm only a year younger than you.' Then, she smirked. 'Anna told me.'

A rueful smile formed. 'Come on, the tide's on the turn.'

Lauren followed him across the firmer sand to the bottom of the steps, negotiating the small rock pools at their base. They clambered in silence, but when they reached the top, Daniel stopped and leaned, much as Lauren had done earlier, on the railing, and she joined him to catch her breath.

'Look, Daniel, a date's just that.' She smiled. 'I should know. It doesn't mean a thing, really, other than you're not exclusive right now. It might make her realise what a good thing she had in you.'

'And if it doesn't?'

Lauren shrugged. 'Then you don't have much choice. Perhaps that's a good thing too.'

'I'm angry with myself.'

'Don't be. I've been down that road. It's a dead end.'

They began to pick their way along the cliff path, soon reaching a stile, where Daniel stopped.

'I'm going this way,' he pointed towards the cliff path as it ran away from Polkerran. 'Need to stretch my legs.'

'I'll see you tomorrow, then.'

Lauren followed the path she'd taken earlier, but her mind remained with Daniel. He needed something – or someone – to lift him out of the mire.

'*Idiot*,' she muttered as she walked towards the gate to the cottage. 'Starting to care about what Daniel wants is the last thing you need right now. Let it go…'

For once, the mantra didn't work, and Lauren entered the house in even deeper thought than she'd left it some hours ago.

Chapter Fourteen

Karma Chameleons

The following week sped past in a flurry of work for Lauren, interspersed with phone calls to chase deliveries for The Lookout, WhatsApp messages with Daniel to agree the budget for soft furnishings – he'd gone up to London at short notice on a project for his old firm – and continuing to try and find a local let with availability across the whole summer, which was proving tricky.

Unable to sleep, her head full of decisions on work projects, fabric samples and whether a quaint former fisherman's cottage with steep stone stairs was really the answer for a pregnant woman living alone, Lauren rose early on the Friday and went for a long run. She was twenty weeks along now, and her stretchy running zipper hugged her slowly increasing midriff.

Lauren was on her way back through the village just after eight, jogging along the harbour front and looking over at Hamish's boat as he unloaded the night-time catch when she bumped elbows with someone coming in the opposite direction.

'Oh, I'm sorry!' Lauren tried to catch her breath, only to have it swept from her body when she saw who it was.

Daniel shoved his hands in his coat pockets. 'Hi. How's things? Only got back late last night. Couldn't sleep.'

Conscious of her lack of make up and wind-tousled hair, Lauren stirred under his brown gaze. Why did she feel so… vulnerable, uncertain?

'Hey, Lauren?' A smile tugged at Daniel's mouth as he waved a hand at her face.

Pulling herself together, Lauren fell into step beside him. 'Me neither. Needed to do a bit of thinking.'

'Shall I leave you alone? I'm only on my way to the Spar. Run out of milk.' Daniel gestured along the road.

'No, please don't. I'm not very happy with my own company right now.'

'Hmph. I know that feeling. I don't suppose you've got time for a coffee? They've just opened up.'

Lauren smiled. 'Coffee, no, but an alternative, always.'

They shed their coats and settled into the sofa by the window in Karma, and Lauren cast a quick glance outside to see if Old Patrick was lurking with his watering can. No sign so far.

'Have you had time to check this week's deliveries?' Lauren wished her heart would settle down. Was the extended run causing it to pound like this? 'I took the packaging away, but I'll need a hand to move some things around.'

Daniel didn't answer for a moment, placing his mug on the table and leaning back in his seat. Lauren hid her smile. He looked about as unkempt as she felt, his hair sticking up in its usual tuft and his T-shirt having seen no sign of an iron lately.

'I hate the bloody house.'

A jolt shot through Lauren. 'Oh! I'm so sorry.' She felt awful, but more than that, she was hurt. Hadn't they made most of those choices together?

'God, no. It's me who's sorry.' Daniel reached over and took her hand, and Lauren cursed her heart from upping its tempo. 'That's not what I meant. It's the damn recording. I hate the pressure they're putting on me. I wish Claudia had never put the idea forward, made the introductions.'

He gave her hand a quick squeeze and released it, and Lauren slumped back against the cushions.

'But building the house is your dream.'

'It was.'

Lauren held his gaze firmly. 'So take it back. Forget the recording.' She waved a hand as he went to speak. 'I know, you have to go ahead, there's a signed contract, and you need someone close to you who can talk about what life was like living through the build. I get it. But…' This time she grabbed *his* hand. 'That's going to be a few hours out of the life of The Lookout, of *your* life. Put it from your mind until the date it happens. There'll be so many more days to enjoy.'

To Lauren's surprise, Daniel placed his mug on the table, his second hand coming down on top of hers.

'You're good at this problem-solving thing.'

Lauren shook her head. 'Not where my own life's concerned.' Her gaze dropped to their clasped hands just as he released her. Why did she feel like a teenager all of a sudden?

'Tell me, then. What's bothering you?'

Stirring under Daniel's keen look, Lauren picked up her mug and drank some tea. It had cooled a bit too much for her taste.

'Summer's coming, and I'm struggling to find a let that's available for several months on end. There's this one tiny cottage with a tiny desk and Wi-Fi, but… I don't know.' She sighed. 'Is it the idea of living somewhere so opposite to my taste? It's quite dark, with its low ceilings and rustic charm. Or is it my mum, who keeps reminding me how much I'll hate living on my own? I'm meant to be a grown up, in my thirties, having a baby.' She rested a hand on her small bump. 'But Mum still knows me better than I know myself. She just won't let it drop, and I know it's because she cares, but—'

'You could move into The Lookout.'

Lauren blinked. 'What about you?'

'I meant with me. Well, not literally.'

Sadly.

'No, of course.' Lauren's brow furrowed. 'Are you serious?'

He drained his mug. 'Living alone doesn't bother me, but I'm more than happy to have a lodger for a few months if it will help you out. You know it's got the best Wi-Fi set up in the cove, and there are two workstations, with the desk in the study and the one in the snug.'

They both got to their feet. Ridiculous as it sounded at first, the more Lauren liked the idea.

'Be warned. My mum will assume the worst.'

Daniel frowned. 'What's that?'

'That we're a couple.'

'I think I should be offended.' He pouted as he held the door open for her. 'The worst?'

'For you, yes!'

Trust me.

Lauren laughed at his expression as they emerged into the street, delighted their friendship had resulted in such an offer.

Friendship? Who are you kidding, Kirkham? There's no anything-ship here, just you, clinging to a buoy.

132

Daniel glanced at his watch.

'I'd better get this milk and head back. Gerry's coming to check on the house and set the filming dates. You're right. The sooner it's over the better. Perhaps then I'll stand a chance of winning Claudia back.'

'I'll be over this afternoon to unpack the lamps. Maybe I'll choose a room, too.'

'Happy to be my lodger?'

'Definitely.'

I think…

'Then it's a deal.' Daniel held out his hand, and Lauren grasped it, but to her surprise, he pulled her close as his arms came around her back and dropped a kiss on her head, with a whispered 'thank you for giving me some direction' in her ear.

Lauren closed her eyes. Daniel smelled rather nice, and had such a solid body.

When they parted, however, Lauren noticed a car pulled over on double yellow lines, and a tall woman bearing down on them.

'Danny-boy!'

'Oh God.' Daniel released Lauren. 'Sorry about this. It's Gerry.'

The introductions were made, and Lauren blinked at the almost wolf-like grin spreading across the lady's face and within minutes it was clear why. Gerry had assumed Lauren was Daniel's 'new'un'.

'Lauren's my lodger,' Daniel repeated for the third time.

'Living in the house with you, then?' Gerry nodded, and Lauren could swear she could hear the woman's brain ticking.

'Yes, but only for a few months.'

Gerry swung to face Lauren. 'Planning to be here early September?'

'Just about. I'm heading north on the—'

'Great.' She swung back to Daniel. 'We plan to film commencing on the fourth – two days, weather dependent. Will firm it up when we get to the house.'

Lauren shook her head. 'I haven't moved—'

'Now, Laura, was it? Danny-boy mentioned you choosing the furnishings. We'll do a piece on camera about that too.'

'It's Lauren,' Daniel said through gritted teeth, and Lauren laid a consoling hand on his arm.

'And you know all about the build, Laura?'

'Well, some of it.' Lauren glanced at Daniel.

'I've discussesd some of it with *Lauren*, but not the early stuff.'

Flicking her hand dismissively as her phone started ringing, Gerry tugged it out and took the call. 'You can soon catch her up.'

'Why don't people listen,' Lauren hissed at Daniel as Gerry gushed into her phone, and he shrugged.

'I don't think it was ever on Gerry's school syllabus.'

'Fab. See you there.' Gerry ended her call and fastened her bright gaze on them. 'Right, Danny-boy. See you at the house in ten.'

She was already in her car even as Daniel made to speak, and Lauren tugged at his sleeve.

'You okay, Daniel? Sorry if that—'

'No, it's fine. I'll put her straight when we talk.' He gave a sheepish grin, making him, if he only knew it, even more adorable. 'Gerry's great really… if you like steamrollers fuelled by Irn-Bru.'

Lauren laughed, then glanced at her phone. 'Oh Lord. I'm supposed to be on a conference call in about an hour. I need to get back and shower.'

'Thought I could smell something.' Daniel smirked at her pretend outrage.

'It's a good job that's a technology they've yet to land on us. Aromazoom.'

To her surprise, Daniel dropped another kiss on her cheek. 'Let's chat later about a move-in date.'

Lauren headed for the passenger ferry, intent upon getting back and making herself presentable for the meeting, but as she waited for the little boat to dock, her gaze remained fixed on the figure of a man walking along the harbour front to his dirty green Jeep.

They were both oblivious to the interested stares of two elderly knitting ladies as they waited in the bus shelter opposite Karma for the small minibus to take them to Port Wenneth to buy more wool.

–

'You're doing what?'

Lauren's meeting had concluded, and she and Anna were busy pulling sheets out of the tumble drier.

'I'm moving into The Lookout.'

Anna sent Lauren a knowing look as she delved inside the drier for a missing pillowcase. 'I knew you fancied Daniel.'

'Anna!' A strange flutter passed through Lauren, and she couldn't help but laugh at her friend's smirk. 'Daniel's a very nice man, but he's—'

'Also single. And I agree, he's a *very* nice man.'

'He's on a break. That doesn't mean it's over. And Daniel's still completely besotted.' Lauren placed the last sheet on top of the ironing basket. 'I'm doing him a favour with the interiors, and he's doing me one in return. There is a slight complication, though.'

Anna closed the door of the drier. 'Go on, spill the beans.'

'I seem to be Gerry's answer to "get another one".'

Anna's brow furrowed. 'I don't understand.'

'This producer woman has latched onto me to provide the heart to Daniel's episode.'

'And you agreed.' A smile formed. 'Of course you did, Little Miss Spontaneous.'

Lauren shook her head. 'I didn't need to. She jumped to the conclusion we're a couple.'

'Seems to be an occupational hazard where you're both concerned. What happened this time?'

'She came across us in the street having a hug.' The words came out in a rush, and Lauren peeped at Anna as they made for the door.

Her friend looked nonplussed, as well she might.

'It was a friend thing. You know, seal the deal and all that.'

This banter was all very well, but there really wasn't anything between her and Daniel, and nor was there likely to be. Ignoring the flicker of dissatisfaction this truth brought, Lauren followed Anna into the kitchen and went over to the put the kettle on. 'Cuppa?'

'Please.'

Anna dug out the usual crockery and placed it on the table by the window. 'Warm the coffee pot too. It's nearly eleven and someone will be here before we know it.'

Lauren did as she was bid, but then her friend joined her, placing an arm about her shoulders.

'I think moving in at The Lookout is a great idea. You'll have the space you need and a proper desk to work at…'

'But?' Lauren had a feeling she knew what was coming.

'I know I'm teasing you, but take care of your heart, Lauren. Daniel's in a very complicated place and it's hard not to—'

'It's okay.' Lauren eyed Anna with deep affection. 'I'm not in any danger. Gerry can think what she likes. I'll do what's asked of me for the recording, but it doesn't change how things are behind closed doors. Daniel's off limits, his heart is rigidly attached to Claudia, and if I needed any other barrier, there couldn't be a better one than this.' She rested a hand on her bump.

'Good.' Anna's relief was clear as she hurried back to the cupboard to search for cakes but, returning her attention to the coffee, Lauren couldn't help but wonder if she'd dropped herself into yet another challenging situation.

Then, she shrugged. What could possibly go wrong?

Chapter Fifteen

Barrow Boy

Life fell into a pattern over the next couple of weeks, with Lauren working hard for her clients, but taking time to go through interior design choices, placing orders and compromising on choices where the lead times were too long.

Daniel seemed happier, for some reason, and Lauren attended her appointments, listening intently to the baby's heartbeat and smiling wryly as the midwife confirmed the latest bump measurement. She didn't need Pauline to tell her she was increasing in size.

Still enjoying her morning runs, listening to various podcasts – though there was a mix now of business and baby topics – Lauren stopped to gather her breath one morning, only to clutch her middle. She waited. It happened again and, her heart pulsating with emotion, she kept her hand on the bump. It was more substantial than the flutterings of recent weeks. Was this the first kick Anna had been eagerly anticipating? No further sensation followed, and Lauren adjusted her headphones and resumed her run, only at a gentler pace.

'Sorry, Kitten,' she huffed. 'Don't mean to jostle you.' She'd reached the lane where it ran past The Lookout, and took another breather. 'Think you were meant to be a small melon or dessert something, but my mate changed the app to animals last week.'

'Hey, Lauren!'

Looking over, Lauren waved at Daniel as he appeared from beside the cabin, clamping down on the frisson of pleasure that accompanied every sight of him lately. Hell, he'd got his bloody shirt off again!

Conscious of her sweaty running gear, hair scraped back in a band, Lauren walked to meet him in the driveway.

'Should you still be running?' Daniel frowned. 'Is it… you know, safe?'

Lauren trained her eyes on his face. 'Perfectly, as an experienced runner. Wouldn't be quite so wise to take it up as a new sport in this condition.'

His expression darkened. 'Promise me you don't go down onto the beach? Those steps are pretty treacherous as it is.'

'I haven't.' Lauren assumed interest. 'But now you mention it, I—'

'Please don't!'

With a laugh, she put a hand on his arm, dropping it instantly.

'I promise I won't run on the beach. Or up and down the steps.'

'Good. Have you finished, got time for a cuppa?'

'Always.'

Daniel soon had the kettle boiling on the little stove in the cabin, and Lauren did a few warm-down stretches, tucking her earphones into her pocket.

The sun had not long risen, and the glassy sea reflected the paleness of the skies above it. A wood pigeon chorus trilled from the treetops and the faint chug-chug of fishing boats leaving the harbour drifted upwards on the still air.

Lauren rested a hand on her growing bump, hoping for another kick. Kitten did not indulge her, and she shrugged. Cats were known for being disobliging.

'Here you go.' Daniel handed over a mug, placing his own on the ground. 'Do you mind if I finish off?'

'Carry on. What time did you say the landscaper's due?'

'About now. I was just moving some sand when I heard someone on the lane and thought it might be you.'

She looked around for somewhere to sit, and Daniel paused his shovelling.

'If you wait a minute, you can sit in this.'

He indicated the over-sized wheelbarrow, and Lauren eyed him in disbelief.

'Thanks, but no thanks. I'm happy on a crate.' She perched on a nearby one. 'What's in here?'

Daniel paused again, leaning on his shovel, and Lauren eyed him covertly. He seemed to be getting more attractive to her every day. What would those hands feel like on her...

'It's the slate for the hearth in the snug. It's being fitted later. Oh, and good news,' he picked up the shovel again. 'The entertainment unit arrives tomorrow, and the sofas and dining furniture the following week.'

Daniel and Lauren had agreed she'd join him when the last of the furniture arrived.

'Great,' Lauren sipped her tea, savouring its heat as it trickled down her throat. 'I can't wait to move in.' Before she did, she really needed to get a grip. Perhaps she ought to distract herself with the finer things, like cushions and ornaments.

A notification pinged on her phone, and Lauren pulled it out. Kit, damn him. She skimmed the message, a longer one this time, then sighed. He was as persistent as a gnat. She'd need a giant bottle of spray to get rid of him. Or just a massive swatter.

'So.' Daniel had discarded the giant barrow by the cabin, tugged a T-shirt over his head, much to Lauren's relief, and retrieved his mug. 'How's it going?'

'Fine, other than this.' She waved the phone. 'My ex is constantly messaging.'

Daniel's eyes narrowed. 'The baby's father?'

'Yes. He's got this fixation – fuelled no doubt by my mum – about my being alone.'

'But he chose not to be part of this, didn't he?'

'There's no logic to it. I'm a grown-up, reasonably intelligent woman, but they just don't seem to think I'm capable of coping without help.'

Lauren checked the time. 'Best go shower. Due on a call at nine-thirty. Thanks for the tea.'

She crossed the driveway, already marked out by the landscape team, and cast a look back before heading down the lane into the village.

Daniel had disappeared inside the cabin, and she chewed on her lip as she walked. These stupid feelings were persistent little buggers and, like the bump on her front, seemed to be making their presence felt more by the day. Was it wise to move in with Daniel?

Then Lauren shook the concern aside. It was an arrangement, nothing more, and would serve them both equally. Besides, she really liked Daniel. They got on well. It would be like staying with one of her brothers.

Liar, liar, pants on—

Don't start!

The next ten days flew by for Lauren, with little time for her to dwell on either the cuteness of Daniel Tremayne and her wisdom in moving into his home, or the impending change to her life.

Aside from her daily work, she had to visit a supplier in Hertfordshire, onto which she was able to tag a meeting at the Devere Corporation in London. Deciding to make the journey worthwhile, she stayed over in her favourite hotel, the Montague near Russell Square, so she could shop and do a show, before calling at another supplier in Southampton the following day.

It had been a successful trip, both from a business and shopping perspective, but for the first time, Lauren had found the crowds around Oxford Circus a little too much. She wasn't too keen on being bumped into from every side on the Tube, either, and had forgotten how pungent some of the less pleasant odours could be in the passageways.

Once back in Polkerran, Lauren started to pack up her things, hardly able to believe she'd been staying at Westerleigh Cottage for two and a half months. She would miss the lovely room, with its gorgeous view, old beams and even the creaky floorboard by the bed. Lauren smiled to herself as she made her way down the stairs. She'd miss her friend's constant companionship too, but she was looking forward to having a bit more space and a proper desk to work at.

On her last evening, as they finished their main course, Lauren leaned back in her chair, thankful for her new looser clothing. 'I can't thank you both enough for putting up with me all this time.'

'I've loved it!' Anna beamed at her. 'It's been almost like the old days.'

'Thanks,' Oliver said dryly as he picked up his wine glass.

Anna reached up and kissed his cheek. 'And I wouldn't change things for the world.'

'I think the old days were a little wilder.' Lauren smirked at Anna, then added to Oliver. 'Well, for me, anyway. And I have news. Thanks to the Peanut app, I've chosen the baby's name.'

Anna clapped her hands together. 'Please tell me you went with Darcey.'

'Sorry, love, no. I've decided on Amelia Grace.'

Already on her phone, Anna looked up. 'Amelia means hard-working and industrious. Sounds more like her mother.'

'And Grace is one of the meanings of Anna,' Lauren said, feeling quite emotional as realisation dawned on her friend, who all but chucked her phone at Oliver as she leapt to her feet to come and hug her.

'I don't care about Darcey. It's a beautiful name,' Anna sniffed through her tears, and Oliver made an exaggerated sigh as he extracted another of his neatly pressed handkerchiefs and handed it over.

Once this little bit of excitement was over, they all cleared the table, but then Anna – as was her tendency – shooed them away so she could finish off the dessert, and as they resumed their seats, Lauren smiled at Oliver.

'Anna is a gem. Is there no end to her talents?'

Oliver cradled his glass in both hands. 'Don't tell her I said so, but no, I don't think there is. She'll be an amazing mother when the time comes.'

Lauren laughed. 'She's far more ready for this than I am, a fount of information, forever sending me links to articles or podcasts she's come across. None of them to do with baking, I might add.'

'No.' Oliver met Lauren's amused gaze with a serious one of his own. 'Don't take this as a dig at your situation, but Anna is ever the traditionalist. I'd like to get a wedding ring on her finger before we head down the parenting route.'

'And are you truly ready for it?'

Oliver remained silent for a moment, his startlingly blue gaze on Lauren.

'Anna has such faith, for one who never knew what it was to grow up in a loving family.'

'From what she's told me, you didn't have a great experience either.'

'It was different. I had the family, it just wasn't a happy one. Talking of which, my father has been in touch. He's not got long, apparently.'

'I'm so sorry.'

Oliver shrugged. 'The circle of life. We've never been close, but I'm the only child. He's been in Dubai for years, but he's had to drop everything. He came home a month ago and went into a hospice near London. He's asked for me.'

'And your mother died some time ago?'

'About four years now. She had little time for me, but what her passing gave me was my grandmother, without whom I'd never have met Anna.' He met Lauren's interested gaze openly. 'I'd had a failed marriage, was convinced history would repeat itself, that it was best avoided. Until Anna came along.'

His gaze rested on her friend, his normally inscrutable expression absent, and Lauren could see exactly why her friend had fallen for him. He was adorable.

'I'll be glad when this damn search is over. I'd like to set a date.' He sent Lauren a sheepish smile. 'I'm not getting any younger.'

Lauren emitted a ladylike snort. 'You're what… mid-forties? And in your prime.' She smirked. 'So Anna tells me.'

Oliver almost choked on his drink.

'Sorry. Couldn't resist. We don't talk intimacies, but I've known her long enough to realise how happy she is.'

They sipped their drinks in unison for a minute, but then Oliver said, 'You don't seem overly fazed by what's coming. Aren't you anxious?'

'Deep down. It's a huge responsibility.' Lauren gave a small laugh. 'And it's assuming much larger proportions than managing a team.'

'You'll be fine. Ah, here she is.'

It was as Anna placed a slice of homemade tiramisu on Lauren's plate that she noticed the striking engagement ring again.

'Do you know its history?' She pointed to it before picking up her spoon.

'Not really. Aunt Meg kept it in an old tea caddy, which she said contained the things that mattered most to her. It was in a leather box and, curious in the way all kids are, I opened it once. She took it from me, then snapped the lid shut, burying it beneath some papers.'

'Did she say anything?'

Anna shook her head. 'I said how pretty it was, but she said something like, "it's just a ring".'

Oliver sipped his coffee. 'We realise it had to be more than that to be in the caddy.'

Lauren eyed it keenly. 'It's definitely a one-off.'

'I agree.' Oliver took Anna's hand and placed a kiss on it. 'As is Anna.'

With a smile, Lauren tucked into her dessert. 'This is so delicious.' She let the creamy dessert dissipate in her mouth before loading another spoonful. 'How is it you're not the size of a house, Oliver?'

'Because every now and again, she lets me do the cooking, and that is guaranteed to reduce your appetite.'

Anna laughed as they polished off the remains of the dessert. 'Oliver is selling himself short. He's a great cook.'

Lauren looked from one to the other, but she didn't envy them because it warmed her trampled heart. Their happiness gave her hope for the future.

Amelia gave Lauren a resounding kick or two, and she rested a hand on her bump. The immediate future, however, looked like it could be fun – despite her misgivings over how attractive she found Daniel – and Lauren's spirits lifted in anticipation of her move into The Lookout the following day.

Chapter Sixteen

Mat-er-knitty

Lauren awoke to mixed emotions the next day. Her life may have been turned on its head but living at Westerleigh Cottage had brought its own routine: the view from the window each morning, changing only with the weather and the seasons, the smell of breakfast being prepared for the guests, the constant interruption of her work by the locals calling for sustenance and a chat.

What would life at The Lookout bring?

'Only one way to find out,' Lauren announced to the room as she donned her recently acquired supportive running gear. She would hit the twenty-four-week mark within days. The celebration was another check up with Pauline – more bump measuring and listening to Amelia's heartbeat, which had become Lauren's absolute favourite thing.

Going running remained invigorating, but Lauren had started to take a less strenuous route through the village and back, rather than along the cliff path, with its challenging terrain.

What the run didn't succeed in dispelling that morning, however, was the rather erotic dream she'd had in the night, triggered, no doubt, by the memory of a shirtless Daniel chopping wood, his torso tanned and lean, the taut muscles in his arms rippling as he wielded the axe.

As Lauren showered, towelled dry and rubbed cream onto her distended belly, she fought the wisps of the dream. Then, catching sight of her flushed face in the mirror, she shook her head in admonishing fashion at her reflection.

'Grow up, Lauren Kirkham. You're just missing not having had sex for months.' With a small smile, she rested her hands on her bump. 'Sorry, sweetie. You shouldn't have to listen to this. Mummy's just being silly.'

That's all it was. The inability to satisfy her natural desires. Lust, basically.

Lauren dressed and headed down the stairs, but despite the attempt at justification for her attraction to Daniel, some misgivings persisted as she ate breakfast with her friend, and as they enjoyed a last cup of tea, she aired them.

'I'm wavering between being excited for the move and questioning the wisdom of it.'

'Because you fancy Daniel?'

'A bit.'

Anna reached for her cup. 'It's not like you to have second thoughts. You're the decisive one, the grab the opportunity girl. You don't get lost in dreams like I do.'

Lauren's dreams were best kept to herself. 'It seemed the perfect solution at the time – a win-win on all sides.'

Anna sipped her tea. 'You're right, it serves more than one purpose. You need somewhere to stay where you're not living alone, and I need your room for bookings. And you're helping Daniel by taking that producer woman's pressure off over having someone else in that last section.'

'All true.' Why did she have such misgivings? 'It's just me being me, isn't it? You know what I'm like, I have to fancy someone, and Daniel's hard not to crush on. I think I feel a bit underhand, finding him attractive.'

'Don't,' Anna admonished. 'He's a grown man, going into this of his own free will. Besides, he's still besotted with Claudia.'

Lauren pushed away a spasm of hurt. Ridiculous.

'Who wouldn't be?' She summoned a rueful smile. 'Hell, I could fall for her myself!'

Anna's lips twitched but she said nothing, merely eyeing her friend in a knowing way over the rim of her cup.

'Stop it, Anna!' Lauren's gaze dropped to the more prominent mound. Her child. Her daughter. Every decision now needed to be with Amelia's happiness, safety and future in mind.

'You are still allowed a life, you know?' Anna spoke softly, and Lauren raised her eyes to meet her friend's kind face.

'Not yet.'

Anna went to speak, but the boot room door opened and Mrs Lovelace came in with Jean and Mrs Clegg.

After the latter's health had been enquired after, Mrs Lovelace settled opposite Lauren. 'Wasson, young'un?'

She sent Lauren a sly look, and Jean shook her head. '*Mum.*' Her tone was cautionary, and one Lauren had heard before. Mrs Lovelace never took any notice of it, and she was fairly certain she knew the gossip that was coming. It was only fair to let the lady have her moment.

'There's talk you'm movin' out.' Mrs Lovelace rummaged in the bag on her lap, and Jean sent Lauren a sympathetic look.

'I'm sure it's just tittle-tattle. You know how it is in the cove.'

Lauren and Anna exchanged a look. There was no point in being coy.

'It's true,' Lauren said brightly, as Mrs Lovelace placed an oddly shaped package on the table. 'I'm moving into Daniel's new house; going this evening, actually, after work.'

'So, it's true, then.' Jean looked taken aback.

'I'm not sure what's been said, but yes. I'm moving up the hill.' Lauren looked from Jean to her mother and back. 'We're just friends, Daniel and I, and he's got spare rooms and Anna hasn't.'

'That's... lovely,' said Jean, throwing her mother a cautioning look.

'Men and women friends didn't hug in public in my day.' Mrs Lovelace eyed Lauren keenly, and she squirmed under the scrutiny. 'You'm spending a fair bit of time with each other.'

Not as much as we're about to...

'And we see'd the way you look at each other, didn't we, 'Melza?' Mrs Clegg's dark and beady eyes were on Lauren, and Mrs Lovelace nodded with enthusiasm.

'Leave it be, Mum,' Jean warned, but before anything more could be said, the door opened and Nicki breezed in.

'Morning!' She took the seat beside Jean. 'What's the latest?'

'This maid,' Mrs Lovelace waved a hand at Lauren, then delved back into her bag to withdraw her knitting. 'Is a movin' in with our young Daniel.'

'So I've heard.' Nicki sent Lauren an impish look. 'And it's a nice big house, according to rumour.'

'Stunning,' said Lauren. 'And it's perfect timing. I can't keep taking up a letting room here with summer approaching, and Daniel would rattle around in The Lookout on his own.'

'Aye, and the babe will need space.' Mrs Lovelace nodded towards Lauren's bump. 'What semester are you now?'

'Second trimester, but won't be long before I'm in the last one.' No need to tell the locals Lauren would be back in Yorkshire before the birth.

'And time she started to slow down a bit.' Anna mock glared at Lauren before going to fetch another mug. 'You take on too much.'

'I'm fine. And the commute's a doddle.'

'What's that, Mrs L?' Nicki pointed to the package on the table, tied with a jaunty ribbon.

'This is for you, dearie.' Mrs Lovelace offered it to Lauren. 'A gift for the wee one.'

Touched, Lauren took it. 'That's so kind, thank you.'

Mrs Lovelace beamed. 'First go at mekkin' something with no pattern. Can get back now to twiddlin' my muffs.'

Nicki spluttered into her coffee, but Lauren hid her smile. 'Oh, what's that?'

'Twiddle muffs, for the nursing home,' Jean explained, reaching for a biscuit. 'The Knit and Natter Group make these squares from left over wool.'

'They form them into hand muffs,' added Anna as she joined them with a plate of scones, some jam and clotted cream. 'And sew things onto them—'

'Buttons and the like,' chimed in Mrs Clegg.

'For the ones with old-timers' disease.'

'Alzheimer's, Mum,' Jean intoned.

Mrs Lovelace sent her an irritated look. 'Zackly.'

'You made one for Meg, didn't you, Mrs L?' Anna offered her the plate.

'Ah, Meg.' Mrs Lovelace took a scone and sighed. 'Still miss her, I does.'

Lauren smiled kindly at the old lady. 'I'm sure she knew how much you loved her.'

There was a change of conversation as the scones were slathered with jam and cream, and Lauren sipped her tea, trying not to think about the work she hadn't done this morning.

'We should 'ave one of them parties. You know, 'Melza.' Mrs Clegg nudged her friend, whose tea slopped over the edge of her cup. 'Young Phee 'ad one afore Verity Blue were born.'

Mrs Lovelace nodded enthusiastically, patting the spilt tea with her hankie. 'A baby bath.'

'It was a shower, Mrs L.' Nicki chuckled. 'A baby shower.'

Mrs Lovelace sent her an aggrieved look. 'Babies don't need no shower, they'm in need of a bath.'

'That's very kind of you,' Lauren looked around the table at the expectant faces. 'Really sweet, but the baby doesn't need anything. Honestly.' She held her hands up, palm upwards. 'My mum's pretty much bought out the local baby store, and I've ordered enough to last her until she's eighteen.'

Anna nodded solemnly. 'She's not joking.'

No more mention was made of Lauren's impending move, or of her and Daniel being a couple, but as she let the conversation wash over her, her gaze drifted, as it so often did, to the bay window.

Were the old ladies merely indulging in wishful thinking, or was Lauren's attraction to Daniel detectable by others?

Anna noticed some time ago…

As the words whispered through Lauren's mind, she clamped down on it. She'd have to be super careful, that's all.

–

It was early evening by the time Lauren left Westerleigh Cottage in the Mini, mainly because she'd had to work late, and partly because Anna hadn't wanted her to go.

Bearing in mind she would be just up the lane, Lauren was a mixture of touched and amused by her friend's sadness on her departure. Oliver assured her he would soon take Anna's mind off things and, laughing at her friend's expression, Lauren drove out of the gates, took a right up the hill and within minutes arrived at The Lookout. She pulled into the tarmacked parking space, between Daniel's Jeep and the BMW, and unfastened her seatbelt.

'Here we go, Mia. Next stage in our adventures.'

There was no reply when she knocked, but the door was ajar, so Lauren walked into the hall, excitement and trepidation wrestling for attention in her head. She could hear Daniel on the phone, but when she put her head around the door, he waved a hand towards the kitchen island, which housed a coffee pot and mugs, and Lauren busied herself pouring one for him and finding a glass for water, then eased herself up onto one of the stools.

Once the call was over, he joined her, smiling.

'Welcome to The Lookout. I'll get your bags in when we've had this.' He settled on the stool opposite and picked up his mug.

'I'm quite capable of carrying my own bags.'

'Did I say you weren't?'

Lauren sighed. 'Sorry. I have this giant chip on my small shoulders. People always assume because I'm petite I'm physically unable to do normal things like carry a bag up a flight of stairs.'

'Well, there is the added factor of your condition, you know.'

She raised her chin. 'Let's compromise.'

'Deal.'

Daniel fetched her suitcase and the holdall, and Lauren slung her laptop bag over her shoulder and carried a bag for life crammed with things she'd acquired during the first few months of her stay.

'What on earth is *that*?'

Lauren followed Daniel's pointing finger, then laughed and pulled the soft toy from the carrier.

'This is Twiddler. Isn't he cute?'

'No!' Daniel took the knitted creature from her. 'The baby will be traumatised! Tell me someone gave this to you, and you couldn't refuse?'

Tempted to pretend otherwise, Lauren hesitated, then confessed. 'Mrs Lovelace made it. Not sure it will be safe for a newborn.' Taking the strange-shaped animal back from Daniel, Lauren dropped a kiss on its mis-formed head.

'I can't even work out what it is.' Daniel remained nonplussed, and Lauren placed Twiddler back in the carrier. Then, he frowned. 'Why's it called Twiddler?'

Lauren laughed. 'You don't want to know. And it doesn't matter what *he* is, does it? Twiddler needs a home, and I've given it to him.'

She bit her lip. Technically, Daniel had given her a home.

'Precisely.' He smirked. 'I'm not sure about this sub-tenancy to a misfit.'

Lauren tapped him playfully on the arm as they reached the stairs. 'Don't be rude. He has feelings.'

'He may do, but just make sure he never creeps up on me unawares!'

Chapter Seventeen

Check Mate

Lauren was delighted with her room. Despite having chosen the furniture, bedding, blinds and decorative pieces, it was fantastic to see how well it had all come together, and the view from the window was stunning. Below the house was a meadow, then the cliff path and beyond was nothing but an expanse of blue.

It didn't take her long to unpack, and she joined Daniel in the kitchen, perched on a stool at the island as he rustled up what he called his best curry for dinner.

They talked about many things as they ate: the small tweaks he wanted to make to the property and grounds, the recording later in the summer and then, Lauren's work. Daniel – a former stockbroker – outlined some of the consultancy work he'd been doing, and recommended Lauren set up a private company, citing the tax benefits. Lauren agreed to research it.

When they'd eaten, Daniel insisted on clearing up his mess, and Lauren wandered into the open-plan sitting room, admiring the furnishings and the vast artwork on loan from the gallery, which adorned the expanse of wall opposite the floor-to-ceiling windows. Her hand ran over the ornaments, lamps and tables as she toured the room, satisfied that it had all come together well, both the new furniture and Daniel's existing pieces from the London flat. She sent a fond look at the vast armchair in the window bay, facing out towards the spectacular view. He'd insisted on keeping it, despite it not fitting in with anything else. It had been his gran's chair, and his only concession was for Lauren to drape a plain, soft throw over it to hide the chintzy upholstery.

'Here we go.'

She turned around as Daniel approached, taking the offered glass from him and sniffing it. 'Where's this one from?'

He'd sourced another alcohol-free cider, said she ought to try it. 'A farm in Somerset. They've had a cider mill there for centuries. Friend of mine now runs it.'

Lauren tried it, letting the ice-cold liquid slide down her throat. 'Oooh, that's *good*! I don't know how they got it so dry, but I could almost think it was the real thing.'

'Great, because I bought a crate!'

With a laugh, Lauren sank onto the new sofa, and Daniel sat beside her, but at the other end, for which she was thankful. There was a strange intimacy about them being here in the house alone, now it was a home.

For a few minutes, they sat in silence. Then, Daniel stirred in his seat.

'Does this feel a bit weird to you?'

Lauren dimpled. 'Regretting asking me?'

He shook his head, grabbing his beer from the table. 'I didn't mean it like that. I'm used to being on tenterhooks, wary of putting a foot – or a word – wrong around Claud.'

'That's so sad, Daniel!' Lauren drank a little more of the cider. 'Surely there were good times, too?'

He said nothing for a moment, his gaze fixed on the vast hearth. Then, he sighed. 'The sex was always good.'

Unable to help herself, Lauren laughed, though a frisson of something stirred in her breast. She wasn't a prude; talking about sex didn't bother her. Was she actually jealous?

Discomfited, she took another sip of her drink, wishing it had that alcoholic kick that eased all cares away.

'We laughed…' He paused, a frown on his brow. 'Though now I come to think of it, I'm not sure it was at the same things. Claud's very kind-hearted, though.' He smiled at Lauren's sceptical look. 'Seriously. Beneath the glamour and the glossy exterior, I've seen her be generous with her time and caring towards others.'

'But not you?'

'Doesn't feel like it now. How stupid am I?'

Lauren leaned over, placing a hand on Daniel's arm and giving it a gentle squeeze. 'Sometimes, we only see what we want to. At least you don't have the repercussions I do.' She smoothed a hand over her growing belly, filled with a new contentment. 'Not that I regret this one.'

'Good to know. Right.' Daniel drained his bottle. 'Fancy a game of *Final Fantasy*?'

Placing her now empty glass on the table, Lauren stood up. 'Always. Hope you're not a bad loser.'

Daniel headed to the kitchen with the empties and retrieved two fresh bottles from the Smeg refrigerator. 'Time will tell.'

'Is this the time I fess up to being a closet Zelda fan? Never quite grew out of it.'

Daniel laughed as they made their way into the snug and he powered up the games console and massive screen hanging on the natural stone wall.

'I'll save my guilty secrets for another day.' He handed a controller to Lauren, who settled into one of two leather recliners.

'Normally, I'd be sat cross-legged on the sofa, but I'm not sure my body can manage that anymore.' She released the catch so the footrest came out, resting her legs with a contented sigh. 'Bliss. Do you think I'll ever be able to touch my toes again?'

Daniel's gaze followed her pointing hand, then turned a frowning visage in Lauren's direction. 'Your ankles are a bit puffy. You're doing too much. On your feet too long as well, with all that running and going for long walks.'

Touched by his concern, Lauren sent him a reassuring smile. 'I'll ease off the running soon, I promise. Thanks for being a friend, Daniel. I love that you care.'

He looked a little uncomfortable, so Lauren turned to the screen. 'Come on, let's play. And be warned, I take no prisoners.'

'Love the challenge of a competitive woman,' Daniel retorted as he set the game in motion, sinking into the other leather chair. 'Be prepared to lose, mate.'

Smiling to herself, Lauren adjusted her position, the controller gripped in two hands. Did he but know it, Daniel had just fed her the word she needed to get through this. *Mate.* Friends. Pals.

That's what they were, and that's how it was going to stay.

–

After breakfast the following morning – Daniel had insisted on making scrambled eggs for her – Lauren settled at the island as he went outside to take some photos to send on to Gerry, to give her an idea of how the landscaping was coming on.

She'd barely completed a purchase for a gorgeous maternity dress she'd found on Vinted when her mum video-called her.

'Mum, we're just friends. I'm a lodger. Daniel offered me a room in his house. It's big.'

Lauren was becoming tempted to get a badge made, so often did she seem to say the words.

'I said to your dad, when you emailed that change of address through, you'd found a new man. I guessed you must be living with him.'

'I *am*, but—'

'It's okay, love. I don't mind. You need someone by your side at a time like this, and if it can't be Kit, then Daniel will do.'

'*Mum!*'

'Can I talk to him again?'

'No.'

'Why?'

'He's not here.'

'Er, I am, actually?'

Lauren looked over her shoulder to where Daniel stood. 'I didn't hear you come in.'

'I'm not surprised,' Daniel began to walk over, but Lauren frantically waved him back.

He took no notice, taking a seat beside Lauren, who resignedly adjusted the laptop so they were both visible.

'Morning, Linda. How are you?'

'Oh, Daniel,' Lauren's mother gushed. 'I'm so pleased Lauren's moved in with you. I worry about her so much. She's just not good on her own.'

Lauren could see Daniel's smile from the corner of her eye, but was too busy glaring at her mum to stall the conversation.

'Lauren's fine, Linda. She's got lots of space here, and a proper office desk to work from.'

'I really think she should have come home, so I could be on hand, Daniel. Lauren needs people around her. Did you know she used to take a blanket into one of her brothers' rooms when she was little, curl up on the floor in there, because she didn't want to be in a room on her own?'

'That's very... sweet.'

'And she had all these dolls. Used to line them,' Linda gestured with an arm, 'across her pillow, so she could talk to them as she fell asleep.'

'Hey, I'm still here!'

Lauren sent Daniel an indignant look, but he merely smirked, and said quietly, 'Should I be worried? I might have to lock my door.'

Lauren nudged him hard in the ribs, but Mrs Kirkham was continuing.

'I do feel comforted, knowing she's got you.'

'I do *not* have Daniel,' Lauren said through gritted teeth, wishing she did. She wouldn't mind lining him up on her pillow, that's for sure.

Mrs Kirkham sent her daughter a knowing look. 'Always in denial, this girl, Daniel. Never wanting to commit. She was moving in with Kit before she said anything about them being serious. And then she was moving out again.' She brightened. 'Still, every cloud, as they say. You take good care of our girl, now, Daniel.'

'That I do promise to do, and the house is all finished, so there's lots of space for her to spread out.'

Linda waxed lyrical for a moment about how lovely it all looked from what she could see – which was nothing but a run of kitchen cabinets – and Daniel said out the side of his mouth, 'Plenty of room for your dolls, too, if you want to move them in. Ouch.'

Daniel rubbed his arm, and Lauren whispered 'sorry'. She had rapped it a bit harder than she'd intended.

'It does sounds super, Daniel. I'd so love to see it.'

'If you're ever down this way, you're most welcome—'

Daniel's mobile saved them both, and while he took the call, Lauren ended hers with her mother, promising to speak soon.

'What was that all about, saying she was welcome?' She demanded when he pocketed his phone.

'I was just reassuring her. She's worried about you.'

'I wish she'd just leave me alone. I can't bear all the fussing. Or the implication I can't function on my own!'

Ping. A text from her mum.

> Daniel's SO charming! I'm very happy for you, love. I can't wait to tell your dad.

'Bloody hell!'

'What's the matter?'

'See?' Lauren showed him the message, expecting him to be horrified, but Daniel shrugged.

'She's jumped to her own conclusions. If it makes her happy…'

'Fine. Thank goodness she's a long way away.'

'Look, if it will get her off your back for now, leave her to it. Your parents live hundreds of miles away. If it puts their minds at rest, who can it hurt?'

'But Gerry thinks we're an item, and so do the locals. Why does no one *listen*?'

Daniel laughed. 'Stop fretting. We know the truth, and it will all be fine.'

Chapter Eighteen

Who's that Man?

Daniel worked on the garden for the rest of the weekend, and on the Monday morning, Lauren took herself off for an early walk around the harbour, stopping to call in on Anna on the way back up the lane.

It was a grey day, with a typically Cornish mizzle in the air, and Lauren scurried past a vintage dark green Jag in the driveway and made her way round to the kitchen. Anna was busy dishing food onto plates, and Lauren was surprised to see an elderly man standing by the table, looking across at Harbourwatch.

'Is that a guest?' She spoke quietly, taking plates from Anna and placing them on a tray.

Anna shook her head as they carried the trays to the dining room and served the guests, indulging in a little small talk, pausing before re-entering the kitchen.

'He turned up on the doorstep just now. Asked if he could walk round to the terrace and look at the view from this side of the bay.'

Lauren shrugged. 'So why is he in your kitchen?'

'It's wet and miserable, so I invited him in. He was wistful, seemed quite sad.'

They returned to the kitchen, where the gentleman stood as they'd left him, one hand resting on a chair, his back to the room, but he must have heard them for he swung around and dashed a hand across his eyes.

'Forgive the intrusion.' His shoulders, which had seemed slumped at first, straightened, and he walked with a surprisingly light step towards them. 'I am indebted to you, my dear.' His smile was warm, and he included Lauren in it. 'It is many a year since I've seen that particular view.'

'Did you live here, then?' Lauren returned his smile. He was still a handsome man.

The gentleman didn't answer for a moment, his gaze returning to the view, but then he faced them both again. 'After a fashion.' There was a hesitation, as his gaze fell to Anna's hand. 'Forgive my curiosity. I noticed the lovely ring. May I?'

'Of course.' Anna raised her hand and he laid a gentle finger on the central stone. 'It belonged to my Aunt Meg, but we don't know its origin.'

He whispered something, and Lauren and Anna exchanged an amused look as the man straightened.

'I'll leave you in peace, ladies. Thank you again, my dear.'

'Can you spare time for a cuppa?' Lauren looked over at the pile of dirty dishes on the island. 'I know you're full at the moment.'

'I've always got time for you, mate.'

Five minutes later, they settled in their usual seats at the scrubbed pine table. Despite the dullness of the day, it was mild, and the doors to the terrace were open. Heathcliff could be seen lurking in the flowerbeds, and the call of gulls drifted in on the morning air.

'When does Oliver leave?'

Anna sighed. 'Tomorrow. He and his dad have always had a cantankerous relationship. The prospect is making him a bit of a grump. Not with me,' she added hastily. Leaning forward, Anna grasped Lauren's hand. 'I'm so glad you decided to stay in Cornwall. There's a lady from the adoption agency calling next week. She sounds lovely on the phone, but I'm so nervous.'

Squeezing Anna's hand, Lauren released it and leaned back in her seat, eyeing her bump, which felt like it became more pronounced by the day. 'It's another step forward, so see it that way. Oh!' she exclaimed, and Anna's eyes brightened.

'She kicked again, didn't she?'

Lauren nodded, taking Anna's hand and placing it on the solid mound of her middle. 'You slightly freaked me out, telling me she was currently the size of a Maltese pup. Had to google it to ensure she hadn't ballooned overnight.'

'Shhh,' Anna cautioned, her hand spread out on Lauren's bump.

Lauren eyed her friend with affection. 'You're feeling for a kick, not listening for it, bean brain!' She spoke softly, amused by the concentration on Anna's face.

'*There!*'

'Happy now?' Lauren smiled as Anna sat back in her seat, her features infused with contentment.

'Aunty Anna is more than happy, thank you.'

'Good.' Lauren checked her phone as Anna headed to the sink with the mugs. A WhatsApp from Daniel. A large Amazon delivery had arrived, when would she be back?

Suppressing the urge to drop everything, Lauren schooled her mind as she tapped a reply: will be about an hour.

'Daniel's off limits, remember,' she intoned silently. 'And you are – apparently – growing a puppy. Get back in your basket.'

As June continued, Lauren lost herself in work once more. The Lookout was all but finished, and Daniel wasn't around much. All she discerned from him, over the occasional rushed meal, was that he had a lot of work on and that the recording would go ahead as planned, the first week of September. Realising it was for the best they didn't have too much down time together, Lauren channelled her energies into her consultancy and plans for the future.

Anna's meeting with the adoption people had gone smoothly, and she now understood the process and possible timescale. It was all a question of waiting, but thankfully, Anna was also extremely busy, managing a very full B&B with constant turnover.

Several packages arrived, containing stylish maternity clothes, along with cute outfits for the baby which Lauren took to show Anna, who went all mushy, and Oliver – back from seeing his father – rolled his eyes, before agreeing they were the best thing he'd seen since they'd raised the *Mary Rose*.

Lauren was now six months pregnant, all of which she appeared to be carrying on her front. She still managed to run, though not at her usual speed, but the exercise gave her distance from her work – something she never used to hanker for – and she spent it listening to podcasts about the ups and downs of single parenting, how to avoid stretch marks and speculating on how soon she would get back into her jeans.

On a Friday in mid-June, Lauren was disturbed in the early hours by yet another notification from Kit, this time a voice note.

She'd tried to ignore it, but unable to get back to sleep, Lauren gave in and listened. He was nothing if not persistent.

'Wish I knew what to do,' she muttered to the baby, who responded with a few kicks. A smile tugged at Lauren's lips as she sank back against the pillows, the phone still clutched in her hand. 'Sorry, sweetie. Did I wake you up?'

Sleep was intermittent after that, and although she didn't feel up to a run when she woke, Lauren tugged on some soft trousers, a loose top and a light coat she'd found in the boutique in Polkerran in a few sizes up from her usual. A walk would have to suffice today.

She headed down into Polkerran, not in the mood for walking along the cliffs, deep in thought and struggling to suppress her frustration with Kit's persistence.

'Damn it,' she muttered as she stepped up to the wall bounding the harbour, her eyes taking in the scene before her. The fishing boats were all out, the sea glistening in the distance like glittering shards of glass. The aroma of fresh coffee wafted across the road from Karma, and Lauren inhaled deeply. The number of pleasure crafts moored in Polkerran was increasing almost by the day, and the rattle of sail lines against the masts mingled with the ever-present hammering from the boatyard.

It was too early for most tourists to be about. A small group of school kids wended their way along the street before disappearing up the road to the top of the hill where the village school was located, their chirping voices drifting towards Lauren on the cool morning air.

She closed her eyes, breathing deeply.

'Let it go.' Her habitual mantra began its repeat, and she raised her lids, letting the beauty of the location in. 'This would be a wonderful place for you to grow up, little one. It's a shame there's nothing for your mummy here.'

Lauren turned her head to survey Westerleigh, perched on its rocky outcrop. It had felt such a sanctuary when she'd first arrived, somewhere to escape to for a few weeks, giving her time to regroup, sort out a new plan for her altered life. All her thoughts had been about obliterating Kit from her life, getting through the next months and then starting her career afresh, but listening to his voice note this morning had brought a moment of reflection.

With a sigh, Lauren turned her back on the view and leaned against the wall. Was she being selfish, or sensible? Kit *was* the biological father, after all. Was she right to continue her resistance to his demand that he had a right to be heard?

It wasn't that he wanted to reverse things, he merely wanted to talk with Lauren. Even Kit seemed uncertain about what, and letting out a huff of breath, Lauren pushed away from the wall and set off at a rapid pace along the waterfront.

That was enough time given over to a man whom she'd once imagined herself in love with – not that they'd ever said those words. Mutual passion and the common ground of being rising execs in the corporate world had blinded her to the truth, and though Lauren would never have wanted things to end like they did, it was better for them both it was over.

–

Lauren returned to The Lookout, pleased to see both the Jeep and BMW in their parking slots. Daniel had returned late the previous night from several days in London, and they'd stayed up for hours, catching up on each other's news. Hopefully, he'd be around a bit more now he'd completed his project.

As she crossed the drive, Lauren looked around, trying to see the exterior as Gerry would. Although Daniel had sent photos, the producer hadn't been back since the landscapers moved in, and they'd done a brilliant job, laying lawns, and a gravel driveway which formed a circular sweep outside the vast stone steps up to the front door. Daniel had plans to convert a couple of sheds into garages at a later date, but for now they'd placed some bushy shrubs in huge pots around the buildings to screen them.

'Daniel? Are you home?'

Lauren dropped her bag on the kitchen island and looked around the ground floor. He wasn't in the snug or the study, and although the glass doors to the terrace were open, he wasn't out there either.

Shedding her lightweight jacket, Lauren made her way upstairs. Daniel's door was closed, so she assumed he was in there. She'd grab her book and sit outside, wait for him to come downstairs.

It wasn't on the bedside table, and then she remembered: she'd had a long soak in the candle-lit bathroom last night as she immersed herself in the book. It did have a prevalence of sex over plot, and Lauren was enjoying it immensely, the experience enhanced by the silkiness of the bubbles and warm water caressing her skin as she read.

With a soft smile, she crossed the landing and walked into the room, only to emit a small squeak as she almost walked into Daniel's back.

Chapter Nineteen

Porn Salad

'Hellocks!' Daniel spun around, clutching the towel around his waist.

'Oh my God!' Lauren put a hand to her mouth. 'I'm sorry! I had no idea—'

'Not your fault. Damn, is the lock faulty too?'

Daniel's brow furrowed as he stepped past Lauren to check it, and she tried not to admire his lean torso as he passed.

'Nope. Just operator error. Sorry.' He straightened and turned around.

Lauren feigned nonchalance. 'Er, why are you in here?'

'I had a problem with my shower just now. Decided to use this one, then check it later.'

Lauren swallowed quickly, struggling to drag her gaze from a rivulet of water slowly sliding over the rise of Daniel's chest before rolling quickly down his abs to meet the embrace of the towel.

'I— er...' She dragged her gaze to meet Daniel's. Was he laughing at her? 'I left my book.' She snatched it up from the stand resting across the bath and fled from the room.

Lord, this really wasn't helping her pathetic attempts to regulate Daniel to the back of her mind!

That night, Lauren struggled with the next chapter of her book, staring so hard at the words her head began to ache in an attempt not to think about Daniel in nothing but a towel.

'Damn it,' she muttered, throwing the book down and swinging her legs out of bed. She padded over to the window and peered into the blackness, a hand caressing her bump. Rain lashed against the panes, trickles of water cascading down the glass, and Lauren watched them for a moment, then straightened her shoulders and raised her chin.

'Come on, girl. You're a career-focused, successful businesswoman, experienced in compartmentalising problems, shutting them away to concentrate on priorities. Daniel Tremayne is not – *cannot* – be part of any to-do list, so relegate him. With immediate effect!'

There. Job done. Clambering back into bed, Lauren lay on her side and closed her eyes. She'd think about something mundane... like knitting or baking. She fell into a deep sleep, and if her slumbering mind did venture anywhere near rainwater droplets on glass becoming hot water streaming down the insides of a showerscreen, she refused to acknowledge it the next day.

'He's your landlord,' she chanted to herself as she dressed. 'He's also mad for someone else,' she added as she left her room. 'For goodness sake, control your mind!'

Best-laid plans are, of course, destined to go awry. Over breakfast, Daniel decided they should go out for dinner and, moreover, make it a weekly thing.

'Why? I mean, I love going out, but won't we just stoke the rumours the locals are perpetuating?'

'Does it bother you?'

'No.'

'Me neither. It's not like we're going to hold hands across the table.'

Pity.

Stop it.

'Besides,' Daniel continued as he scraped butter across his toast. 'You keep saying you're finding it hard to think of things to say to your mum that don't bend the truth but keep her happy. If we make it a habit of going out to dinner now and again, you can tell her we did that. She'll misconstrue that it's a date.' He shrugged. 'Win-win?'

Lauren watched as he unscrewed the top on the marmalade, then licked a finger at its stickiness. She cleared her throat. 'Agreed.'

Daniel booked an early table at the bistro, saying he knew eating late aggravated Lauren's heartburn, and they walked down into the village ahead of time to stroll along the harbour for a while, talking nonsense, and Lauren tried not to feel a thrill of pleasure every time she managed to elicit a laugh from him.

They sat on a bench, waiting until their booking time. It was a calm evening after the recent rain storm, and they exchanged greetings with the occasional passer-by. Daniel began demonstrating to Lauren what had been wrong with the shower, and although it wasn't the most riveting subject, she couldn't take her eyes off his gesturing hands.

It didn't help, once in the bistro, that Daniel opted for the prawn dish either. Lauren couldn't stop staring as his firm fingers freed them of their shells before popping the plump fleshy bodies into his mouth.

A choked sound escaped Lauren, and Daniel's hands paused in stripping another pale specimen as he raised an expectant brow.

'What's up? Have I got food on my chin or something?'

'No.' She tried to be serious. It was, after all, very immature. Still, weren't prawns considered an aphrodisiac? Lauren was certain she'd read somewhere that shellfish encouraged sexual vitality.

A langoustine with a stopwatch and a training manual popped straight into her mind.

'I'm... so... sorry.' Lauren's voice broke on the last word, and she grabbed her glass, taking a slug of water.

Daniel leaned back in his seat, his prawns abandoned as he eyed her with confusion.

'Did you want some?'

Yes, please!

The bubble rose in Lauren's throat again.

'No, I'm good with the salad, thanks.'

When they'd finished their meal and the table had been cleared, Daniel fixed Lauren with a look.

'Much as it's great to see you having fun at my expense, is there something I should know?'

You definitely shouldn't know this.

'No.' Lauren schooled her misbehaving thoughts into order. 'Sorry. Must be the heady delight of being out. Feels a bit like a date.' She caught herself, expecting Daniel to draw the evening to a quick end, but he stilled, then the edges of his mouth twitched.

'You miss it. The dating.'

Lauren smiled warmly at Daniel, conscious they were attracting interest from a nearby table hosting two couples she recognised from the village.

'Well, in case rumours travel up north...' He reached across the table for her hand, and she happily placed it in his and immediately wished she hadn't when he began stroking his thumb across her palm.

Dear Lord, she'd always loved a good old-fashioned crush, but this was definitely testing her playing-hard-to-get skills!

'Would you like dessert?'

'Ice cream,' Lauren blurted out, without even a glance at the menu. Perhaps it would help her cool off.

Once she'd reclaimed her hand and drained her glass of water, Lauren pulled herself together. She couldn't account for why she found this man so attractive. He was easy on the eye, without question, but so far from her usual type.

All the same, later that night, Lauren buried her latest read inside her suitcase and put the bag at the back of her wardrobe.

Instead, she started on the first in a popular cosy mystery series she'd added to her e-reader some time ago, and although it was a page-turner, she found a chapter was all she needed for her lids to droop and rest to claim her.

—

Lauren woke the following morning from a dreamless sleep and, taking it as a sign, downloaded the rest of the books in the series, firmly quashing any thoughts of Daniel that went beyond them being house-sharers and platonic friends. It worked to a point, and life at The Lookout settled into a more realistic pattern.

With Lauren working feverishly to complete her assignment for the Devere Corporation and a smaller project for a Hampshire-based company, the weeks flew by. Offers of consultancy work were beginning to come in regularly, and she hated having to turn some away. A couple didn't start until the autumn, but she didn't want to tie herself into anything long term. By then, she planned to be on her way to finding a new permanent role.

Besides, kick counting had become far more enjoyable than stakeholder updates.

The baby was now the size of a bunny, so Anna said. Judging by how she felt, Lauren assumed it was the Easter variety. She couldn't say she was enjoying her increasing size, even though it was indicative of the most wonderful thing happening inside.

She had heartburn most nights – seriously, shares in Gaviscon had become a distinct possibility – Amelia was kicking for England, and Lauren's ankles came and went like they were performing in a peep show. The running had all but stopped, although she still went out early for a brisk walk along the cliff path, if the ground conditions allowed. She enjoyed soaking up the sounds and smells of the sea, audible even as she listened to her latest podcast, as she'd taken to just using one earpiece.

Lauren had been amused to come across Daniel shoving a magazine under a cushion when she'd walked in from the study one evening, after she'd finished a late video call with a US supplier. Sneaking a peek when he went to make her a hot water bottle and a much-needed cup of tea, she'd expected a sports mag – Daniel loved football. When it turned out to be a copy of a parenting magazine, she'd stowed it back in place and said nothing.

Anna had come up for dinner a few times, as Oliver was back in London. His father had passed away after his short illness, and there'd been the funeral to arrange and a complicated inheritance to go through with the legal firm who'd represented Mr Seymour Senior's affairs.

Her friend had been agitated and excited, having heard the same day that it was believed her brother had been located. Now came the delicate stage for the intermediary to establish contact, after which Anna would find out if this really was the right person, and whether he wanted to be in touch with a sister he probably never knew he had.

'I'll come over.' When Anna hesitated, Lauren's brow creased. 'Sorry, bad timing?'

'No, no.' There was a rustling sound. 'How about in a half hour? Just finishing something off.'

'Perfect. See you shortly.'

Anna being who she was, spent most of the evening wavering from hope to despair, convinced it would be a red herring and, if it was Alistair, he'd want nothing to do with her. After all, wouldn't he have been told he was an only child too? And if he *had* known he had a sister, why hadn't he sought *her* out?

Round and round went the questions, and Lauren was grateful to be in Polkerran with her at such a difficult time, especially with Oliver away. Anna had not forgotten how Meg's own adopted child – Oliver's mother – had refused to acknowledge her, choosing not to know or meet her.

How would Anna cope if she suffered the same fate?

–

Daniel had been waiting up for her when she arrived back at The Lookout, and they shared a nightcap, sitting in the bay window, Daniel in his new chair and Lauren curled up in the embrace of the old one, which she'd rather taken to.

They talked about their respective days, with Lauren sneaking surreptitious looks at the man to her right – he was too cute, not even her normal type, yet something about him appealed inexplicably to her inner core.

Oblivious, Daniel's gaze rested, for the most part, on the windows. It was a week since the longest day, and it had been warm, sunny and cloudless. Facing west, there was still light on the horizon and the skies were yet to assume their full, inky-black cloak of night.

Leaning back in her seat, a glass of water cradled in her lap below her bump, Lauren wriggled around, trying to get comfortable.

After an hour of desultory conversation, they agreed to call it a day, and Daniel hauled Lauren out of the seat, which was awkward enough when you had a waistline and could bend, only she stumbled as she put her feet down, and he grasped hold of her.

For a moment, they both stared at each other in the dim light of a nearby lamp. Daniel had a firm hold of one arm, but the other had come around her shoulder, and Lauren had no incentive to move.

Daniel's gaze flicked to her mouth and then his warm, brown eyes met hers again.

'Sorry.' He let her go, swallowing visibly. 'I worried you were going to topple over.'

Pulling herself together, Lauren shook her head. 'Not with your lightning reflexes. Thanks, Daniel.' She hesitated, touched his arm gently, then turned away. 'Night.'

'Goodnight, Lauren.'

–

Lauren's phone woke her at just gone eight the next morning.

'Hey, what's up?' Lauren yawned widely. 'Sorry. Bad night.'

'I hate to call so early, but it's a bit urgent.' Anna spoke quietly, and Lauren's mind snapped into gear. Could an email have come through about the missing brother?

'Tell me.'

There was a pause, then: 'Kit's here.'

Chapter Twenty

Conversion Kit

Lauren blinked owlishly. 'What? *How?*'

'No idea.'

'Did you send him packing?' Lauren knew the answer. Anna didn't have it in her to send someone away.

'He just turned up, saying he'd arrived late the day before and stayed at the hotel overnight. He explained that he knew you weren't staying here, but expected I'd know where you were.'

Staring blankly at the clock on the bedside table, Lauren tried to think straight.

'He asked me to contact you, said you weren't taking his messages. He seems *really* keen to talk to you. Serious. Earnest.'

Lauren flopped back against the pillows, a hand cupping her bump; her baby; *their* baby. Time to be a grown up. 'I have to come and see him, don't I?'

'I suppose so. He's hardly likely to tell me what he wants. We'd never met before.'

'Fine. I need to shower. Give me a half hour.'

'I'll cook him a very slow full English.' There was a pause, then, 'And Lauren?'

'What?'

'Don't hate me, but he seems quite nice.'

He was. No denying it. She'd not have taken her first step towards commitment if he hadn't been.

Daniel was in the kitchen when Lauren came down-stairs.

'Hey.' He looked a little self-conscious, so Lauren smiled warmly at him.

'Morning.'

'Tea?' He raised the pot, but regretfully, she shook her head, conscious of tendrils of hair brushing her cheeks.

'Sorry, got to dash over to Anna's. Be back soon. Got a ton of work to get through.' The urge to kiss his cheek before she left was strong, so Lauren grabbed her bag from the counter before she could do anything quite so stupid and fled the house.

Anna was waiting on the doorstep, and they hurried down the hallway to the kitchen and took a seat opposite each other at the table.

'He's just finished eating.'

'Does he know I'm coming?'

Anna shook her head. 'I said I'd let you know he was in town, nothing else. How are you feeling about seeing him? I mean…' Anna looked uncomfortable. 'You haven't mentioned him in ages.'

Lauren shrugged, and Anna patted her friend's arm. 'I'll go and let him know you're here.'

Getting to her feet, Lauren stood before the window and looked out across the cove. Life in North Yorkshire was becoming a distant memory, almost as though it belonged to someone else entirely.

Am I that changed?

Yes. Everything was different now, including Lauren. She'd come to Cornwall in April for a reprieve, a few weeks' escape, a chance to rethink her future. Months later, and the baby's needs had become paramount. The burning ambition had coalesced into something else: a drive and determination to make the best possible life for her child.

Lost in thought, she started when Anna touched her gently on the shoulder. Kit stood behind her friend.

—

Anna left the room, and Lauren drew in a shallow breath. 'Hey, there.'

'Lauren.'

Kit was tall, though not in the same realm as Oliver, with finely drawn, handsome features. The anger she'd still borne towards him when they'd bumped into each other at Paddington had eased away, but Lauren was relieved the smile that had once charmed her drew no reaction.

'This is unexpected, Kit.'

'Sorry if it seems dramatic, but you wouldn't take my calls or respond to messages.'

Lauren dimpled. 'You were becoming a bit of a nuisance. Why are you here? More to the point, *how* are you here?'

'Your mum told me you'd moved in with someone down here.' Kit looked a little awkward.

'And the why?'

'Two reasons, I suppose.' Kit's gaze flicked over Lauren's bump and away. 'Shall we sit? Will your friend mind?'

'I doubt it.' She led him over to the seating area in front of the log burner, taking Oliver's usual chair as it was sturdier and had a higher back than the sofa, and Kit dropped into an armchair opposite.

'How're you doing?' He ventured a smile. 'You appear well. Blooming, in fact.'

That old adage! Nonetheless, Lauren returned the smile.

'I'm fine. No major issues, other than I can't see my feet unless I'm sitting down and put them up.' No need to bore him with what was bordering on an addiction to Gaviscon.

'And,' he hesitated. 'The... er...'

Lauren raised a brow. 'Do you mean, how is the baby? Is he or she well, developing normally?'

Kit sat forward, resting his elbows on his knees. 'Don't get defensive on me, Lauren. You know I never wanted kids.'

'Yes, I know. I get it. Your ultimatum may have been harsh, but I'm not a fool.'

'That's the first reason I came, why I've wanted a moment to talk.' Kit reached out a hand, palm up and Lauren eyed it, glanced at his face, then took it.

Her body recognised his touch, but her heart remained firm. Kit no longer had emotional power over her reactions.

'I'm sorry, Lauren. It was such a shock.'

With a wry smile, Lauren reclaimed her hand. 'For me too.'

'I didn't mean it to come out so bluntly.'

Lauren leaned back in her seat, wishing she had a hot water bottle. 'Wouldn't have made much difference. There's no easy way to say, "it's the baby or me". Besides,' she sent Kit a reassuring look, 'you're right. We'd barely known each other long enough to explore our thoughts on family.'

Kit remained hunched over, his elbows on his knees. 'It doesn't alter the fact this is life-changing for you.'

'I've adjusted. It now feels like the finest kismet ever.'

'Really?'

Lauren placed both hands on Amelia, caressing the firm mound, smiling softly. 'It took a while to sink in, but I can't wait to meet my daughter.' She raised her eyes to Kit's. 'I get why you wanted to apologise. It wasn't your finest moment, but it's in the past now. What's the second reason?'

Kit huffed out a breath, then got to his feet, and Lauren made to move but he waved a hand. 'No, don't get up. I just need to pace. Is that okay?'

Lauren settled back into Oliver's chair. Kit had liked to pace when working out a problem in his head. 'Feel free.'

Walking over to the kitchen island, Kit turned on his heel and marched back. He was about to set off again, when he stopped and faced Lauren.

'I wish this hadn't happened to us, and I—' He broke off, flexing his shoulders. Lauren's heart went out to him. He looked like a little schoolboy who needed to fess up to something. She waited, and then he resumed pacing, before stopping again on the other side of the room.

'I think there's a part of me that will always have feelings for you, Lauren. You're the first person I've met who I felt might be that elusive "one", and I think you felt the same.'

With a sigh – and a bit of a wriggle – Lauren got up. 'I did, for a while.' She walked over to where Kit stood and peered up at him. 'What are you trying to say?'

An hour later, Lauren walked with Kit out to his car.

'Are you sure this chap you're living with is on the level?' Kit flinched as a seabird swooped low across the driveway to deposit a poop on the bonnet of the Audi before settling on its roof and letting out a loud 'caw, caw, caw'. 'It's so far from civilisation. Shoo! Bugger *off*! You stupid seagull.'

'Chough.'

'What?'

'It's a chough, not a seagull.'

Kit glared at the bird. 'Whatever.' He waved his hands ineffectually but the bird merely flicked feathers and flew off with few regrets.

Lauren touched his arm to get Kit's attention.

'Daniel's a good man. There's nothing to worry about.' She wasn't prepared to elaborate on that, and she was fed up with trying to explain the real situation. Her mum, it seemed, had done a good enough job of not only convincing herself Lauren and Daniel were a couple, but she'd also swayed Kit into believing it too. Honestly, Linda Kirkham really should have been in sales, not nursing!

'It's all a bit sudden.'

Lauren huffed on a short laugh. 'So were we, Kit, especially when it came to ending it.'

Kit's mobile rang, and Lauren waited, mulling over whether she was doing the right thing in letting him believe she was with someone. What would Daniel suggest she do?

Five minutes later, after finishing his call, Lauren waved Kit off, returning to the house engrossed with all he'd said.

'Hey, got time for a cold drink?' Anna waved a jug of homemade lemonade. 'You don't have to tell me anything, but the company will help me. I can't stop refreshing my email in hopes of news about Alistair.'

Lauren glanced at her watch. 'The boss says yes.'

She'd work late to make up the time. Besides, she needed to talk this out, and who better to listen than her best mate?

Lauren helped Anna carry the glasses and jug out onto the terrace to enjoy the fine weather.

The clunk-thud-splash of the gig rowers' oars could be heard from the water below, accompanied by the calls of the cox, and Lauren sank carefully onto a chair, never tiring of the panoramic views the terrace commanded.

'Do you feel better for seeing him?'

Lauren watched Anna pour the drinks. 'Definitely. Despite everything, I like Kit, but I wouldn't go back to him, even if he had a highly unlikely personality change and decided he wanted to raise the baby as a hands-on father.'

'Good. Because you deserve better than that.'

Placing her glass on the table, Lauren squinted over at Anna, wishing she'd brought her sunglasses with her. 'But we have a connection neither of us sought, and Kit wanted to talk that through, because he's lost. He doesn't know how to deal with it in a caring way, but not be involved.'

'He's still taking the job in the States?'

'Yes, his career trajectory is steadily upward.' She shook her head as Anna went to speak. 'It's fine. I no longer need to wail about how mine isn't. Something has changed inside me.' Lauren laughed as her friend's gaze went instinctively to her bump. 'Not the physical change. More here and here.' She pressed her heart, then touched her head. 'God, this is like being in therapy.'

It was Anna's turn to laugh. 'It's the magic of escaping to Polkerran Point.'

Lauren mulled on this, then smiled. 'I think you're right. Part of it's being here, so far out of my normal

187

way of life, and the other is realising that I have the skills and experience to provide for my child regardless of any company and their whims, and I'm young enough to still reach those goals, but now I have a greater motive to succeed than purely for myself.'

'Did Kit come to any conclusion on a way forward?'

'He's still working on it, and I want to leave him to do that. The only givens so far are that we will always look out for each other.'

—

Kit's visit had been cathartic, and he'd already done a great deal for Lauren without even realising it. It felt liberating to let go of the remnants of her regrets, and also her resentment towards him. Towards *them*, for their foolishness.

Lauren stayed in the driving seat after pulling into a space outside The Lookout. She loved the house, but finding her housemate so attractive wasn't conducive to a relaxing time. She couldn't shake the memory of being held in Daniel's arms last night, albeit in an accidental embrace. Was this because she fancied him, or was it the damn hormones affecting her judgement?

It was a timely reminder. The pregnancy certainly helped provide a barrier, as did Daniel's being besotted by Claudia, but the former was a temporary condition, and what if he and Claudia remained apart?

The image of an almost naked Daniel in nothing but a towel kindly presented itself, and feeling heat course through her skin, Lauren hurriedly grabbed her bag and got out of the car.

Walking into the hall, Lauren peeked at her reflection in the ornate mirror. She'd become accustomed to the softer chin-length hairstyle – a flirty, according to Nicki, layered bob which highlighted her cheekbones – but her flushed face was testament to the recent direction of her thoughts. Perhaps Daniel would be in his office and she'd be able to cool down and think pious thoughts before they met?

'What happened?' Daniel leapt up from his stool at the kitchen island as she entered the room. 'You've been gone ages.'

Lauren dumped her bag on the counter and removed her driving glasses, willing her colour to return to normal.

'Kit – my ex – turned up at Anna's and wanted to see me.'

Daniel's expression darkened.

'He has no right to do that.'

Lauren smiled faintly. 'Do what, exactly?'

Gesturing with a hand, Daniel huffed a breath. 'Turn up out of the blue. Upset you.'

Touched by his displeasure, Lauren walked over to join him, leaning on the island.

'I'm not upset.'

Daniel snorted. 'Right. Course you're not. You're pink in the face and trembling. Must be the effect *I* have on you.'

If you only knew.

'I'm only flushed from the walk.'

'From the car?'

'And I'm not trembling. Maybe I shivered.'

'It's a hot day.'

Lauren couldn't help but laugh at his disgruntled demeanour.

'Daniel,' she placed a hand on his shoulder, enjoying the warmth through the fabric of his shirt, 'I'm fine. Kit had things he wanted to say, and I'd been being a brat and ghosting him.' She lowered her hand, feeling as though she were consoling a new graduate who'd been told off for something.

Releasing a breath, Daniel's uncharacteristically stern features softened. 'Sorry. This must be what it's like having a sister. Brought out some sort of protective instinct.'

Lauren walked over to put the kettle on. Was that how Daniel saw her?

Footsteps indicated his approach, and she pinned a smile on her face. She was in no condition to consider anything else.

'Sister?' She cast him a sideways glance as she gathered mugs and the tea caddy. 'I don't see you as a brother.'

Daniel seemed surprised. 'What do you see me as then?'

Probably best not to say.

Lauren summoned a smile. 'The best landlord anyone ever had.'

She found his expression hard to read as she followed him over to the table. Best to put aside these silly thoughts, stay calm for Amelia's sake. With a rueful smile, she patted her bump.

Dreadful timing, Kirkham. Time to get a handle on this stupid infatuation and concentrate on what really matters.

Chapter Twenty-One

Mulled Whine

Lauren had wondered when Claudia might be in touch with Daniel regarding her on-hold relationship with him, or whether indeed she already had been. Daniel had said nothing, and his mood had been upbeat, but a week later, she got an answer of sorts. The lady in question was clearly on a video call with him when Lauren arrived in the kitchen.

If she hadn't needed to prepare for an important call herself in half an hour, Lauren would have returned upstairs, but she crossed the room to the study, closing the door firmly on the pair. Perhaps they would finally sort themselves out.

Putting on an playlist, Lauren opened the laptop, losing herself in work until the call was due, updating the client on a project and then fielding some phone calls as she amended her calendar. When she ventured to peek out of the door a couple of hours later, all was quiet.

Daniel had his head down at his laptop on the kitchen island but looked up with a smile as Lauren approached.

'Too early for lunch?'

Lauren smiled, patting her bump. 'This is one hungry baby today. Am I interrupting?'

'Nope.' He leaned back in his stool and stretched his arms above his head. 'I'd forgotten how all-consuming the financial sector can be. Definitely time for a break.'

They lunched quickly, agreeing it was a beautiful day for a walk on the beach, coming to a mutual decision to down tools around five and go out.

It was closer to six by the time Lauren had been up to change and Daniel had ended his last call, and they walked in silence for a while, and Lauren tried to curb her desire to ask about how things had gone with Claudia. Daniel seemed engrossed in the horizon, once they'd descended the steps to the beach – the first time after warning Lauren not to attempt them on her own – so she held her tongue, attempting instead to embrace the beautiful evening.

The sky remained clear of clouds, a deep blue reflected in the water and a light, mild wind ruffled her already tousled hair. Lauren wrinkled her nose as they crunched their way over a run of dried-out seaweed, soon reaching flat sand again, but Daniel's strides were too long for her now, and she fell behind.

Fondly, she watched him walk on, oblivious to being alone, the breeze tugging at his hair. His hands were shoved deep into his pockets, and he kicked at a stone, then stopped suddenly and turned around.

Lauren waved as she attempted to catch up, but he wasn't smiling when she joined him.

'Sorry.'

'Can I help? Be an ear?'

Daniel shook his head. 'This dating of Claudia's seems to have become a habit. She's been on three, now.'

'Oh. Well, she's probably just getting something out of her system.'

'Me, I suspect. All three were with the same chap.'

Lauren tilted her head as she observed the troubled man beside her. His eyes were dull – much as hers had been when she'd looked in the mirror the day after Kit told her it was over.

'Still, she barely knows them.'

'God.' Daniel sighed heavily. 'I'd talked myself into thinking we'd be okay, that Claud's break would skim us past the rest of the build. What a bloody fool I am.'

'Look, there's no reason to judge Claudia, is there? It's a few dates, that's all. Lord, I've been on enough of them myself and they rarely last beyond dinner.'

'I think I need to give up on women. Not you.' Daniel cast a glance at Lauren. 'Mates like you and Anna are great. I've had two doomed relationships that left me rock bottom. I either choose badly or mess it up. Either way, I'm avoiding it going forward.'

'And if Claudia decides she wants to try again?'

He raised his hands, then dropped them. 'I've crushed on her for as long as I can remember. Not sure I know how to stop.'

'Falling in love with someone who's good for you might help.'

'Easier said than done.'

'It worked for Anna.'

Daniel shook his head. 'She saw through Alex just by being with him. Why can't I get over Claud in the same way?'

'Maybe you're just not ready. Besides, Alex was a cheat. Would you…' Lauren hesitated, not sure she wanted to know the answer. 'Do you *want* it to work, to try again with Claudia?'

'Probably.' He sighed. 'Am I weak to say that?'

Smiling faintly as they began to walk again, Lauren nudged his arm. 'No, of course not. We're all different. Look,' she pointed ahead, 'there's our rock. Shall we sit and mull for a while?'

'I like mulling with you.' Daniel offered his arm and Lauren slipped her hand through it.

If she wasn't carrying a baby, she'd be doing more than mulling to help him over Claudia!

Lauren said nothing more as they walked to the rock they'd shared before.

'How's your mum?'

'Remarkably quiet now she thinks I have someone. I've spent my adult life trying to convince my parents I'm no longer a child. I may be the youngest, but no matter what I say or do, they just expect me to only be whole if I'm part of a couple.'

—

Later that evening, after enjoying their supper, they settled in their usual seats, and Lauren eyed Daniel covertly over the top of her magazine. It wasn't just that she found him attractive; he was kind, thoughtful and she more than liked him.

With a suppressed sigh, she lowered her gaze to stare at the glossy images of the capsule wardrobe for autumn. She was seven months in, for heaven's sake, and whilst she wasn't oblivious to the glow of her skin and the brightness of her eyes, a woman with a large bump on her front couldn't possibly be attractive... could she?

Daniel confused her. They got on so well, and there were times when she caught him looking at her in a way she was sure was complimentary, yet he seemed doggedly attached to Claudia.

Lauren stirred in her seat. Her back was aching, but she was too engrossed in her train of thought to do anything about it.

'Hot water bottle?'

Lauren lowered the magazine. Daniel was on his feet and heading for the kitchen. 'Fancy a cuppa as well?' He spoke over his shoulder, then stopped and turned around. 'Why are you looking at me like that?'

'Like what?' Lord, she hoped he couldn't read faces as well as he seemed to read her mind at times.

'As if you'd forgotten I was here.'

Unlikely.

'I'm impressed, actually, that you knew I'd love a hot water bottle.'

Daniel turned back towards the kitchen, filling the kettle and digging out the bottle before answering. 'I could tell from the way you were sitting you were uncomfortable.'

Lauren sighed. He was such a considerate and caring man, it really wasn't helping her heart.

–

Something woke Lauren in the early hours, and she yelped in pain.

'Gah!' Grasping her right calf, she eased out of the covers, swinging her legs out, to press her toes hard against the wooden floor.

The pain was excruciating, her toes feeling as though the bones were crossing over each other, and her calf was so taut she felt it might burst.

'Are you okay?'

Startled, Lauren peered through the gloom towards the voice. Daniel's silhouette moved into the room, lit by the light on the landing behind him.

'I heard a shout.'

'Sorry.' Lauren grasped her calf again as the pain intensified. 'Bloody cramp again. Getting worse.' She spoke through gritted teeth, barely noticing as Daniel tapped the bedside light, casting a dim glow over her legs.

Damn it, she knew she should have shaved them!

Tugging at the silky shorts, wishing she'd donned her full winter pyjama armour, Lauren tugged the sheet over her thighs as another wave of pain gripped her foot.

'Oh my God! *Why* does it hurt so much?'

'Here, let me.'

Trying not to notice his bare chest, Lauren drew in a sharp breath as Daniel lifted her leg and pressed her foot against his palm, flexing her toes back and forth.

It hurt, but it was worth the pain to feel the warmth of his skin against hers, albeit a base of one's foot could hardly be considered intimate!

Thank heavens it's so dark in here. If he could see the colour in my cheeks, he'd be calling for an ambulance.

–

The following morning, Lauren made her way downstairs, hoping not to bump into Daniel. She'd slept extremely well after he'd finished massaging her calves, but it had led to more rather interesting dreams, and she wasn't sure she could quite meet his eye just now.

There was no one in the kitchen, and she was about to take her mug of tea into the study when a message popped up. Anna.

Can you come over?

On my way.

Chapter Twenty-Two

Bored Walk

Lauren hurried as fast as her condition would allow down the hill. Was this to do with Anna's brother and, if so, was that message a good or bad omen?

'Lauren, it's him! The man they found is Alistair.' Anna's eyes were wide as she opened the door. 'When he was adopted, he became Matthew Locksley. They now have to see if he's prepared to meet me.' All colour drained from her face as they reached the kitchen. 'What if he won't? What if Ali— Matthew doesn't want to know me?'

'We've been down this road, love. What is it you say to me? One step at a time. Look, it will be what it will be. Besides, if he does agree to meet you, there's always the risk he won't be someone you get on with, or even like. Relatives can be like that.'

Anna nodded. 'Yes, you're right. Sorry for dragging you down here, just needed you with me. Got time for a cuppa?'

'Yes, but don't let me near your delicious cakes.' Lauren followed Anna over to the kitchen island.

'Trying to watch what you put inside your body?'

Lauren smirked. 'Should have been more careful with that about seven months ago.'

Half an hour later, they'd been joined by Phoenix and Nicki, and Lauren flicked through the calendar on her phone as the ladies chatted. Then, as she puffed out a long breath, she became aware three pairs of curious eyes had landed on her.

'Missing out on a fantastic night this weekend.' She waved her phone. 'My favourite hangout has a big party on.'

'You should've gone back for it.' Anna'd had her ear bent about it earlier in the week.

'It's a long way to go just for a party, but I do miss dating. Running rings round men used to be my fave pastime.'

'Closely followed by dancing,' added Anna.

'Yes! Nights out with the girls. Clubs. Prosecco. Juvenile giggles about everything and nothing!'

A fleeting look passed between Anna and Nicki, but Lauren was distracted by Phoenix.

'Good job you have Daniel,' she said. 'Bet he's looking after you right proper.'

Lauren huffed. 'Did you know he insisted on coming to the antenatal clinic with me last time? I made the mistake of saying I'd been the only one on their own and wasn't sure I'd go again. I mean, just how difficult can it be to bathe a baby?'

'They cover a lot to do with the birth, though,' interjected Anna. 'Good for the other half to be there for that. Some people choose a close family member, like a sister.'

'There was plenty of that,' Lauren conceded. 'One girl had a female partner with her, another had her mum there.'

Nicki eyed Lauren over the rim of her mug. 'So how did Daniel find it? Has it put him off going again?'

With a delicate snort, Lauren picked up her glass. 'Unfortunately not. He knew the answer to every question, left sporting the badge.' The others laughed. 'Why do men have to be so competitive?'

'No idea,' Phoenix pronounced. Then, she leaned in conspiratorially. 'But talking of men, how're they urges, then?'

Lauren blinked, unsure which particular one she had in mind.

'Phee needed to pee all the time,' Nicki said, reaching for a biscuit. 'Even before Verity Blue grew to a size when she would be pressing on her bladder.'

'Ah. I see.' Struggling with how horny being pregnant made her feel, Lauren didn't feel able to share, but Nicki giggled.

'I was randy as hell. Freaked Hamish out with the first pregnancy. Think he thought I wouldn't be interested for nine months.'

Lauren couldn't help but laugh. 'I assumed it was just me.' She pretended not to see Anna's look. She knew where her friend's mind had gone.

'Not at all. You should've heard some of the stories the ladies told at my classes.' Nicki wagged a finger at Lauren. 'And you've probably been told, no sex until six weeks after the birth.'

'There was this one maid,' Phoenix added. 'Turned up dreckly at post-natal clinic, already carrying another.'

Lauren sipped her tea with relief. At least she was more normal than she'd feared. Daniel was drawing her lustful interest because of hormones. Nothing else.

Lauren scrolled through her diary the following Monday. How could the year be flying by so fast? She could hardly believe she was still in Cornwall so long after she'd been due to leave.

Now thirty-one weeks pregnant, she'd just had her routine check-up with Pauline, who'd been pleased with the kick-counting Lauren relayed but hadn't been so happy at her blood pressure being slightly raised. Advised to rest as much as she could, Lauren had no idea how to achieve that when she had so much work to do.

Arching her aching back, Lauren closed her laptop on the plethora of photos on her friends' Instagram accounts – the past weekend would have been another gem: a hen party in Barcelona – and she wasn't even sure she'd get to her friend's wedding as it fell close to her due date.

She hadn't seen Daniel since breakfast, and she grabbed her latest read and stepped out of the bi-fold doors onto the extensive patio laid to the rear of The Lookout and sank onto a seat, enjoying the vista of sea and sky, the water teeming with rippling white sails as pleasure craft streamed from the harbour.

Summer was in full swing in Polkerran Point. The small fringe arts and literature festival had kicked off the night before, and the streets were clogged with people, performers and traffic. The weather remained as forecast, a mix of this and that, but the temperature was normal for the season, and Lauren leaned back, closing her eyes and enjoying the heat of the sun on her face.

Her hand rested briefly on her bump.

'We're over three-quarters there now, sweetie. Not long until we meet in person.' Her heart almost clenched in anticipation. 'Don't tell anyone, but I'm more excited about that than any date I ever went on.'

The sun-bathing was all very well, but having little success at concentrating on the psychological thriller – chosen on the assumption it wouldn't have any arousing content – Lauren tossed it aside. She was bored. Time to stretch her legs and then find some company.

A half-hour walk on the coast path helped blow away some of her frustration, and Lauren turned her steps down a track leading to the lane to Westerleigh. She had almost reached the bottom when a few familiar figures trooped past, oblivious to her approach.

Stepping into the lane, Lauren's gaze followed Mrs Lovelace, Jeannie and Mrs Clegg as they made their way towards the few shops on the eastern strip of the cove, nestled either side of the Lugger. Jeannie carried bags for life which looked rather heavy.

She checked her phone. Definitely afternoon. To her surprise, Daniel's Jeep was in the driveway, and Lauren entered the house through the boot room, expecting to find him in the kitchen with Anna, but only her friend was in sight.

'Hey,' Lauren greeted Anna. 'What's up with the usual crowd? Don't often see them over here this time of day.'

Anna looked a tad flustered as she turned from the sink.

'Oh, just had a few things to sort out.' She waved an airy hand, but Lauren knew her well enough to recognise its evasiveness.

Her mobile rang. Kit.

'Sorry, I'd best take this.' She walked over to the window and connected the call.

Kit seemed to have latched onto Lauren's mum's reassurances that her daughter wasn't having to go through everything alone. Not only was her best friend to hand, but she was now living with Daniel Tremayne.

'It helps knowing you're with someone.'

'Does it?'

Kit made a small sound. 'It hurts, but I can take it. I don't deserve otherwise.'

'I'm sorry.' She ought to tell him the truth, Lauren wasn't fond of hurting people. 'Look, Kit—'

'No, let's be done with apologies. Look, I think I know what would help me feel better.'

'Go for it.' She was full of curiosity, but a minute later, she stared at the phone in disbelief.

'Lauren? You there?'

'Yes. Yes, sorry.' She put a hand to her head, then huffed on a laugh. 'Wasn't expecting that. I loved living in your flat.'

'I can hardly take it with me. You can stay there rent-free.'

She shook her head. 'It's too much, you must let me—'

'No. If you want to help *me*, then let me do this for you. If you don't end up back in the north, then at least have it as a base when you come to see family. It would mean a lot to me, Lauren.'

Lauren's tone softened. 'It means a lot to me too, Kit.'

The call ended, and Lauren turned around only to meet Daniel's confused expression across the room.

'Tea, anyone?' Anna raised the kettle. 'Did you manage to fix it, Daniel?'

'What? Oh, yes.' Daniel gave his head a small shake. 'Yes, all done. It was a loose washer. No charge.'

'You're an angel. You've earned yourself a slice of cake as well as a cuppa.'

With Anna busying herself in the kitchen, Lauren joined Daniel in the centre of the room. 'Wasn't expecting to see you.'

He waved his spanner. 'Anna called me, said there was a leaking tap in one of the bathrooms. You okay?'

'Me? Yes. Why?'

A fleeting glance went to the phone in her hand. 'Nothing. I— er, the production people are coming next week. Gerry, wants to talk through the process. Is that okay?'

'Absolutely.' Her gaze dropped to her very obvious bump. 'I'll see what I can dig out to conceal the damage.'

Daniel shook his head. 'No need. They all know I'm not with Claudia now.'

Maybe not physically, mused Lauren as he walked over to take a tray from Anna, but I suspect she still holds sway.

—

A few days passed, with Lauren busy with work and Daniel likewise. In fact, so much so they barely saw each other beyond the evenings, but on the Friday they both had a few hours free at the same time and agreed, as the weather was hardly suitable for a walk on the beach, they'd resume the game they'd been playing the previous week.

When the doorbell rang, Daniel went to answer it as Lauren picked up the remote, but then she froze as a familiar voice reached her.

What on *earth* was her mother doing at The Lookout?

Chapter Twenty-Three

Mamma Here

Mrs Kirkham's decision to surprise her daughter by coming down to meet her new man was a resounding success. At least, in Lauren's mum's eyes.

Once over the shock, Lauren enquired as to where her mum was staying, but Linda Kirkham shrugged. She'd hoped to stay at Anna's but the B&B was full other than for the odd random night, and the hotel was booked by a coach party and summer visitors.

'Daniel did say I was welcome to come and visit.'

Lauren frowned, but Daniel good-naturedly took the lady's bag. 'I did say that. Come on, I'll show you to one of the spare bedrooms and you can settle in.'

Lauren remained downstairs, pacing to and fro in the kitchen.

'How am I going to send her packing, but happy?' She pounced on Daniel as soon as he came downstairs.

She put a hand to her head. At the risk of sounding like a heroine from one of Anna's historical novels, she felt faint.

'Hey.' Daniel came over and put his arms around her from behind, and Lauren leaned against him for a moment, then realised it wasn't helping the faintness.

He cleared his throat as she stepped away. 'Sorry. Instinct.'

'It's fine.' Lauren summoned a smile. 'Not your fault. It's just really getting to me.'

'Look, we've been playing a role to keep your mum happy. It's as simple as that. We've done it over distance, now we have to up our game. It's only for a few days.'

'But she'll assume we share a room!'

Daniel shrugged. 'I'll put a mattress in the dressing room. Once the bedroom door is shut, she'll never know.'

'I can't take your bed!'

'I think you're going to have to.'

They changed the sheets together, and when Linda professed tiredness from the journey and went for a lie down, Daniel man-handled the mattress off Lauren's bed into the dressing room, throwing a spare duvet and some pillows after it and closing the sliding doors on the sight.

Lauren ferried her toiletries into his bathroom, riddled with guilt at the deception and hoping they were doing right by her mum. She eyed her wary expression in the mirror over the sink.

This will put Mum's mind at rest, won't it, until I go home?

Lauren felt more at peace during the evening. Daniel was charm personified, and she could see her mum's approval shining from every pore. To be honest, she didn't pay that much attention, her mind consumed by how the night would go.

Daniel stayed downstairs when Lauren went up, taking her mother with her and ensuring she had everything she needed in her room.

'Oh, love.' Linda cupped Lauren's cheek gently. 'You do throw your dad and I some curve balls, but you always land on your feet. Daniel's such a sweetie!'

'Yes, he is. But don't assume this will end in wedding bells, Mum.'

Linda shook her head at her daughter and pulled back the duvet. 'This is such a beautiful room. Did you really furnish the house?'

'I chose a lot of things, and Daniel said yay or nay.' The memory of them pouring over catalogues and websites filled Lauren with joy for a second, and her mother came over to stand before her. They shared the same petite frame, and Linda fixed Lauren with a meaningful look.

'I can tell from your face that you're well and truly smitten. I'm so happy for you, love. I know you believed you'd found the right man in Kit, but I can see Daniel makes you so much happier.'

'Mum. You've only been here a matter of hours.'

'You can deny it all you like, young lady.' Linda wagged a finger at her youngest and walked over to extract a nightdress from the drawer of the dresser. 'I know you better than you know yourself. All that gadding about, date after date and never finding anyone good enough. I said to your dad—'

'*Mum.*' Lauren spoke firmly as Linda headed for the bathroom, toilet bag and nightdress in hand. 'It wasn't that they weren't good enough. I just didn't gel with them, there wasn't the spark I'd hoped for. Not enough to see them again, anyway.'

Linda paused on the threshold. 'Until Kit. He changed you.'

She disappeared inside the bathroom and Lauren wandered over to the window and stared out into the darkness. There was a light out at sea, probably a fishing boat heading home.

'I'm changed in many ways,' Lauren whispered, stroking the cocoon cradling her baby. 'Kit has been an unexpected influence, hasn't he, Mia?'

When her mum emerged, Lauren gave her a hug.

'I'll see you in the morning. We'll go out and explore before you head back to Dad.'

'Night, love.' Linda kissed her daughter's cheek and headed to the bed. 'Don't you worry about Dad or me. I've got a few days off and all the time in the world. I just want to see that my baby is well looked after. Then I'll be happy, too.'

–

Lauren wasn't sure how she got through the night sleeping in Daniel's bed, knowing he was just a short distance away. She'd feigned sleep when he came upstairs, lying still and willing herself not to fidget, even when her back ached and her legs twitched with cramp.

He'd left the sliding doors ajar, and she could hear him breathing, was conscious of him tossing and turning at one point, and when she'd eased off the bed for the usual early hours pee, he'd stirred, flopping over onto his back, the covers askew.

In the faint glow from the sensor light, she could tell he had some sort of clothing on. She'd tugged on a soft pair of loose leggings and a body, though she'd pondered what all the precaution was about. They were hardly in a position to jump on each other's bones!

She must have fallen into a deep sleep at some point, because next time Lauren opened her eyes, dawn had broken, and a haze of pale light filtered through the blinds.

'Morning.'

Lauren's head turned on the pillow. Daniel lay on his front, hugging a pillow, his hair sticking up in all directions as he eyed her in the dim light from his position on the mattress.

'Hey. Were you comfy enough?' Lauren eased up on her elbows, tugging at the strap of her body as it slipped off her shoulder.

'Fine, though I'm not sure I've slept this near the floor since my uni days.'

Lauren laughed, but it caught in her throat: tap, tappety tap.

Her frantic gaze shot to Daniel's.

'Shit!'

'Morning,' Linda's voice trilled through the door. 'Ready for a cup of tea?'

'Didn't you lock it?' Lauren whispered as Daniel shot up from the mattress.

'Er, hold on a minute, Mrs… er, Linda!' Daniel called as he and Lauren exchanged a look.

'Get in the bed,' Lauren said quietly, then hid her smile at his expression. 'Come on, you pillock! You said we had to play our role. And close those doors!'

Daniel slid the doors across, concealing the mattress and sped around the bed, slipping under the duvet, and Lauren tried not to quiver at his closeness.

He whipped off his T-shirt, and Lauren swallowed quickly.

'Come in, Linda!'

With a yelp, Lauren tugged the duvet up to her chin as her mum came in bearing two mugs and a beaming smile.

'I knew I could hear you talking. Here we are.'

She placed a mug on the table beside Lauren, cupping a hand to her daughter's cheek. 'You're flushed, my love. That bedding must be too warm for you.'

Or I'm just plain embarrassed…

'There, Daniel. I hope I remembered how you like it.' Linda placed the second mug on the table beside him and thankfully refrained from giving him a stroke, although Lauren almost wished she had, just to see his reaction.

'Now.' Her mother walked briskly to the window and raised the blind, before turning to face them. 'What shall we do today?'

–

By Sunday evening, Lauren was torn between wishing her mother would just pat her on the head like a well-behaved dog and head back up north, and hoping she'd stay a bit longer. Daniel was playing the role of a devoted partner to the hilt, and she'd rather taken to letting her hand rest in his as they'd walked some of the north coast path, enjoyed a pub lunch in Padstow and then hired some bikes to enjoy the estuary views on the Camel Trail.

Linda was a very active member of her local cycle club up in Pateley Bridge and spent most of the time saying how pleasant it was to ride on the flat and not have to tackle the strenuous Dales' lanes. Lauren refrained from suggesting the Dales would be missing her mother, but did mention that her dad must be, and Linda had sighed as they'd returned the bikes and got back into the BMW.

'He misses you too, my love.'

'I'll be back home before you know it, Mum.'

'But what about Daniel?' Linda leaned between the seats. 'Don't you want to be there for the birth?'

'I'll come up to Yorkshire,' Daniel reassured her, taking Lauren's hand once again to squeeze it. She appreciated the vagueness of the statement, hoping it would be enough to appease her mum.

Daniel had to go up to Bristol the following day, and trying not to think about whether he was meeting up with Claudia, Lauren took her mum to Anna's, where they had a morning with the locals. Linda did a class job of thoroughly convincing them the rumours were more than true, especially when she went into great detail on how fabulous the master suite was when she'd taken them a morning cuppa.

Lauren had ignored Anna's wide-eyed look, and after enjoying a tasty lunch, she'd tucked her arm in her mother's as they walked back up to The Lookout.

'Mum, please don't bring us tea in bed. It's really sweet but… awkward.'

'Oh. I'm so sorry, love.' Linda raised a finger and tapped her own nose. 'I understand. Special time. You are being careful, aren't you?'

Was it worth protesting? Lauren huffed on a smile. 'Well, I can hardly get pregnant again.'

'Now love, don't be flippant. It doesn't become you. I meant with the baby. I mean Daniel's got quite long—'

'*Mum!*'

'Feet, love. We all know what they say about that. I've had three boys, and I've seen the evidence myself.' She shook her head. 'Except for poor Luke. Still,' Linda brightened, 'Sarah seems perfectly content. I'm sure he makes up for it in other ways.'

Shaking her head, Lauren ushered her mother up the driveway to the front door. Sometimes, there were simply no words…

The evening passed pleasantly enough. Lauren and Daniel cooked and Linda enjoyed being waited on, heading up to bed at ten, after which they decamped to the snug to lose themselves in the fantasy of a PlayStation game.

Daniel left Lauren to go and get ready for bed before following her up, but she didn't feign sleep this time, and as he emerged from the bathroom he glanced over.

'Sleep well, Lauren.'

'You too,' she whispered, rolling onto her side and tucking her face into the pillow. He was wearing boxers and a close-fitting roundneck tee, and she closed her eyes. She was going to dream about him again, wasn't she?

They both lay awake, talking much more quietly the next morning, but then Daniel said, 'Do you think we're going to get another cuppa?'

'I have asked her not to, but probably.' Lauren pursed her lips in memory. 'She did it once before. I took a boyfriend home from uni, but I was nineteen then and her protective instinct was much more fierce.'

'He must have impressed you, to go and meet the parents and get to stay over.'

'I had my moments.'

'I'm sure you did.'

'What's that supposed to mean?' Lauren picked up the spare pillow and flung it at him. It was a pathetic throw and fell short.

'Hah! Not one of your finest.' He scrabbled up out of the bedding and Lauren's eyes were immediately drawn to his bare feet.

'Oomph!' With a gasp of laughter, she fell back against her own pillows as the spare one landed square in her face.

'Oh my God! Are you okay?'

Before she could push the pillow aside, Lauren felt warm hands grasp her own and pull her upwards. As the pillow toppled aside, Daniel swept her into his embrace, and she found her nose pressed up against his chest.

Heart thumping, Lauren willed her breathing to stabilise. 'M'ky,' she muttered into the fabric of his tee as he slowly released his hold.

It didn't help the heart rate when her eyes met his – just inches from her own – warm, brown and full of concern.

'I didn't think, I'm so sorry. I avoided throwing it at the baby but didn't mean to hit you in the face. Are you alright? You're out of breath.'

Tell me about it!

Daniel released her hand to brush hair from Lauren's forehead.

Not *helping*… she really wanted to kiss him…

Tap, tappety tap.

With a soft moan, Lauren fell back against the pillow.

'Lauren, Daniel? I'll just leave the tea out here in case you're… busy.'

A giggle rose in Lauren's throat, and she put a hand over her mouth at Daniel's incredulous expression.

It really was time her mother went home!

Chapter Twenty-Four

Spar Day

The next day, Lauren eyed her appearance critically. She'd applied what Anna used to call her pulling make up, albeit slightly toned down to suit the hour of the day, and tousled her layered hair. She turned to and fro, narrowing her gaze so she could pretend the bump wasn't protruding so much. The multi-shaded peacock-toned dress had a deep V-neck, which enhanced her newly developing cleavage without revealing too much, skimmed over the baby and fell in closely pleated folds above her knee. The empire-line nature would make the outfit useable even after the birth, and Lauren lifted her arms to examine the fall of the wispy sleeves. They made her feel like a butterfly, and she flapped them gently, then pulled a face at her reflection.

'Pillock. No wings are going to lift this weight any time soon.'

Still, not too shabby, even if she said so herself. Would Daniel like it?

'Forget it,' Lauren intoned as she slid her feet into heels and scooped up the production notes Daniel had given her the night before. 'Off limits is off limits and don't forget it.'

Daniel was in the kitchen prepping the coffee machine, but he turned around as she reached the bottom stair. His gaze sped from head to foot, colour washing his cheeks.

'Will I do?'

She held out her arms again, conscious by doing so the dress rose a few inches, then bit down on a smile as Daniel swiftly raised his eyes from her legs to her face.

'You look—' He cleared his throat. 'Great.'

'It's not too much? Gerry did harp on about being photogenic, and I need all the help I can get whilst I'm carrying a puppy.'

Daniel laughed, turning back to the machine and adding milk to the container. 'Gerry doesn't give a damn about the pregnancy. As far as she's concerned, it adds to the human element. The anonymous viewer isn't going to question whose baby it is.'

Lauren peeped at him under her lashes as she joined him. The colour had faded from his cheeks, and she nudged his arm.

'I don't want to let you down. The baby is enough of a complication.'

About to add beans to the machine, Daniel glanced at her, then said, 'You'd wow them in a bin liner.'

Lauren's heart did a skip. 'Aww, thanks, mate!' She nudged his arm again, but as he was in mid pour, beans scattered everywhere. 'Oh no! I'm sorry!'

'Sit on a stool; I'll fetch the dustpan.' Daniel glanced over his shoulder on his way to the utility. 'You'd have to wear the liner like a nappy though, to make the most of those pins.'

Warmed by his words, Lauren eased onto the stool he'd lowered to suit her height, examining said pins as she did so. She may not have Anna's length of leg but hers were shapely and slim, and her ankles had played ball and put in an appearance this morning.

Daniel cleared up the mess, just as the doorbell sounded.

'I'll get it, dears!'

Linda's sing-song voice reached them from the outer hall, and Lauren stared at Daniel in dismay.

'Didn't Mum say she was going out?'

Daniel headed for the hallway. 'She didn't say when, though.'

Hearing her mother greeting Gerry like an old friend, Lauren's shoulders sagged briefly, but then she laughed. If the company wanted the human touch, they were about to get it in spades!

–

'Well, Danny-boy.' Gerry flashed her toothy smile as the meeting drew to a close. 'A lot's happened since we were last here. House is finished – and what a beauty – and you've clearly brought Laura up to speed on the background of the build.' She turned her bright gaze on Lauren's bump. 'And this is just *perfect* for the segment.'

'It's *not* Laura,' Daniel muttered, and Lauren hid her smile.

'I wish I could say I'd done it just for you, Gerry.'

The lady laughed. 'Right, should warn you, there's a lot of down time, sitting around, and we're dependent on the right light for the externals.'

Lauren patted her stool. 'Sitting is good.'

'Excellent. Should take no more than a few hours for the wide shots – we'll be using a drone too; perhaps half a day for the interviews. As I mentioned, we don't use all the footage, but it does help to relax people if we record longer either side than we need.' Gerry bared her teeth. 'Great chemistry, by the way. Caught it well in the test shots. So, we'll see you early September.'

'Fine by me.' Lauren glanced at Daniel, disconcerted to find his thoughtful gaze on her. 'Daniel?'

'Oh, yes. Great.'

'Are you all finished?' Linda's beaming face appeared round the door from the hallway.

'Yes, all done.'

'It's all very exciting,' she gushed as Gerry gathered her belongings. 'Lauren always loved the camera, since she was a little girl. Loved to pose, and there was this one day when she stripped off her—'

'*Mum!*'

'The camera certainly loves Laura,' Gerry reaffirmed. 'The test footage was superb.'

Lauren watched as Daniel tried – and failed – to escort Gerry to the door without her mum in tow. Then, she checked her phone and hurried to the stairs.

Time to get into something a little more suitable for her Zoom meeting with a team from the Devere Corporation and hope in the meantime her mum wouldn't say anything too embarrassing in her absence.

–

On Linda's final evening, they went out to dinner with Anna and Oliver. Daniel had booked the bistro rather than the pub, thinking there would be fewer locals in there, but about twenty minutes into the meal, his aunt and uncle from Tremayne Manor came in and came over to be introduced.

Lauren was conscious of Mrs Tremayne's scrutiny, though she was pleasant enough and almost flirtatious with Oliver, who brushed off her attentions as though she were a persistent fly.

Once home again, Lauren went to sit in her mum's room while she packed and parted with as much advice as she could about the coming few weeks.

'There, my love,' Linda smiled as she fastened her case and turned to face her only daughter. 'It's been such a comfort to see you in this lovely home and with such a darling man. I hope Daniel won't mind you coming home for the birth? I just want to care for you for a bit.' She walked over to hug Lauren, where she sat perched on the end of the bed. 'You're my baby girl, after all.'

A frisson of guilt swept through Lauren again. Little did her mother know she wouldn't be returning to Cornwall straight afterwards – or Daniel and his lovely home.

But what if he and Claudia never made up?

The hope whispered through Lauren's mind, and she tried to push it away. Could she give Claudia a run for her money? Did she want to?

Enough, idiot, Lauren cautioned herself as she followed her mum from the room. *Your life can never be in a tiny place like Polkerran.*

–

A few days later – with Lauren ensconced back in her own room and pretending she was pleased about it – things had reverted to normal at The Lookout.

Daniel had some DIY jobs to finish off for Colin the Cod – a new fascia board outside the shop and some replacement tiles in the kitchen – and Lauren lost herself in work, finally closing the laptop around four and stretching her arms to ease her aching back. A quick inspection of the cupboards and fridge, and she headed out to the car. Time for a visit to the farm shop at Pengillis.

She was eyeing up the vegetables, debating over doing a healthy stir fry or grabbing one of the delicious-looking homemade creamy lasagnes when a voice came from behind. 'Excuse me? It's Lauren, isn't it? Do you have a minute?'

Lauren looked over her shoulder, and her tummy quivered: they may not have met in person, but the lady was unmistakable – and sporting a rich burgundy Mulberry bag Lauren tried not to covet.

'Hi.' Claudia held out a slender hand, and Lauren shook it firmly. 'We haven't met but I'm—'

'I know who you are, but I'm curious as to how you know me.'

Claudia gave a self-deprecating smile. 'I've got a friend at the TV station… saw some of the test footage.'

Assuming a coolness she was far from feeling, Lauren followed her out of the shop. The photo Claudia had given to Daniel was very like her, but Lauren frowned. Where was it now? She couldn't recall seeing it since she'd moved in…

'Shall we grab a seat?' Claudia waved a hand towards the cafe, and they headed for an outside table as Lauren's mind spun over what she might want. Why was it she felt a little nauseous, her insides in knots?

Lauren placed a comforting arm on Amelia as Claudia sank gracefully into her chair, before taking hers with slightly less elegance.

'Why did you want to talk to me?'

Claudia raised her chin a little. 'I keep being bombarded by the news Daniel's moved on. Just the goss from home at first. I'll be honest, I didn't believe the rumour mill. It's rarely on point. I know how Daniel feels about me. Then, Gerry told Dean – my friend at the TV channel – he wasn't just dating, you were living together. I still wasn't sure, but then his aunt saw you together the other day, she and my mum are old friends, said your mum was visiting. It all sounded a bit... serious.'

Lauren stirred in her seat. 'I'm not sure I follow.' She couldn't think what Mrs Tremayne could have discerned from the brief moment. All they were doing was having a meal. What on earth was it with people and their assumptions?

Claudia raised both hands, palm up, briefly. 'I thought perhaps Daniel was trying to get back at me, make me jealous, by dating someone, but moving in together. That was a shock. It's a huge step.'

'Tell me about it,' Lauren intoned silently.

'And then his aunt told me about...' For the first time, there was some hesitation in Claudia's manner as her eyes skimmed over Lauren's bump. 'I haven't been down for ages, and Daniel never said when we had a couple of calls, but I know it's not his baby.'

Lauren almost admired Claudia's confidence that no one would cheat on her, but even she knew enough about Daniel to understand he'd never do it. Still, she wasn't going to make things easy. She'd witnessed Daniel's despair over this woman far too often.

Claudia flashed her neatly aligned, vividly white teeth. 'I know him better than he thinks. We go way back.'

'But not forward. Daniel says you only dated for a few months, so it won't be long before it'll have been off longer than it was on.' Lauren's heart was racing, her shoulders rigid with tension, but she strove to speak evenly.

Claudia's gaze drifted to Lauren's bump again, then flicked upwards to meet her enquiring look.

'I just don't—'

'Understand?' Lauren raised both hands. 'I get it. I'm carrying a baby.' Instinctively, her hand went to her bump. 'But it doesn't stop me finding someone attractive.' She shook her head as Claudia went to speak. 'Or Daniel finding me attractive by return.' Under cover of the table, Lauren crossed her fingers. 'Pregnancy is a short-term condition. It doesn't define me or my capacity to love someone or be loved in return.'

If only, her heart whispered, but Lauren forced the idea aside, holding Claudia's earnest gaze.

'Hey, ladies.' They both looked around as a young chap carrying a tray went past. 'This ain't a meetin' room. You wanna seat, you order sommat.' His accent marked him as an incomer.

Lauren looked at Claudia. 'Aren't you technically his boss?'

Claudia's lips curved. 'Indirectly. I'm so rarely home, the part-timers don't recognise me. What do you want? Coffee?'

'In my dreams.' Lauren patted her bump. 'I'll have a decaff tea, please. English Breakfast.'

Lauren tried not to envy Claudia's catwalk sashay inside to the counter as her mobile pinged.

A WhatsApp from Daniel:

> What d'you want for dinner? I can call at
> the Spar if you've got any particular
> craving.

Probably best not to say.

Will have a think, she hastily replied. *Currently with your ex!!!!*

That would give Daniel something to chew on other than dinner.

Chapter Twenty-Five

Glove Island

Pocketing the phone, Lauren glanced around. Most of the tables were taken, a mixture of holidaymakers and young women with babies in strollers. It was a calm, rural scene, yet inside Lauren was churning. Why was this getting to her so much? What would Daniel want her to say? Should she continue to remain ambiguous in the way they'd done with her mum and Kit, or reveal the truth?

Lauren started as Claudia returned, placing the drinks on the table and resuming her seat.

'I know I've no right to ask anything.' Claudia stirred her coffee, her gaze on Lauren. 'But I'd like to understand how serious Daniel is about you.'

'Why?' Lauren cocked her head to one side. 'Forgive me if I'm a bit confused, but weren't you the one who decided on the break?'

Claudia waved a dismissive hand. 'I get bored. I'm an alley cat, always on the prowl. I've never stuck to a steady relationship since I started dating.' She sent Lauren a mischievous peek over the rim of her cup. 'And that was age four.'

Lauren raised a brow. Who'd have thought they'd have anything in common?

'Anna used to call me the serial dater of Harrogate. She wasn't wrong, either.'

Claudia put her cup down and leaned forward. 'Look, I *know* Daniel. He's kind to everyone.'

Not if you park in the wrong space, Lauren mused, recalling with affection their first meeting.

'He's always there for people in need. Supportive, loyal. Until this damn build took over his life, Daniel treated me in a way no man ever has. The sort that won't let a lady down, and I think—'

'He sees me as a lame duck, a damsel in distress?'

With a shrug, Claudia reclaimed her cup and took a sip. Lauren felt like grabbing it and tipping the remnants over her glossy head.

'Daniel's not the walking type.'

'And if I don't, then he'll be stuck with me? Is that your take on things?'

Lauren's patience was at its end. This woman had tossed Daniel aside without a moment's regret. If she truly understood his worth, knew his qualities, how could she do that?

'It's like I said. Daniel and I go back a long way. I care for him. I can tell from your expression you don't believe me. I hurt him, but he must have been on the rebound. I suppose I can't work out how you got him under your spell so quickly, especially in the circumstances.'

'You're wrong there. We met before you and Daniel split. I may not have known him long, but I believe Daniel's one of those men who needs to be with someone. It's part of his make up.' Where the hell was all this wisdom coming from? Lauren shook the thought aside. 'We're happy living together.'

That certainly wasn't a lie.

'I think you underestimate Daniel's feelings where I'm concerned.' Claudia drained her cup.

As it happened, Lauren didn't. She was beginning to realise she cared enough about Daniel to be fiercely protective, and in her heart she knew Claudia wasn't good for him. Hell, even Daniel admitted it!

Lauren's insides twisted in concern and with something else she struggled to identify.

'He needs time and space. How much, I've no idea. For now, though, we're together at The Lookout.'

There was no response at first, but then Claudia inclined her head. 'I get it. I need to find a way to persuade him I'm worth another try and soon.' They got to their feet. 'It looks like the gloves are off.'

Really? 'I'll keep mine on for now.'

With that, they parted company, and Lauren watched Claudia head to her sports car, her sense of unease deepening. Was she serious about actively trying to win Daniel around? Flooded with uncertainty, she picked up her bag, walking over to the low wall bounding the terrace but seeing nothing of the charming rural outlook.

Daniel may have seemed happier of late, but he'd made it clear he was far from over his passion for Claudia. He was of a more naturally forgiving nature than Lauren, his heart was vulnerable... would it withstand an assault? With a frustrated sigh, she shook her head, then turned away, heading for the car park.

The assumed relationship was supposed to appease Kit and keep her mum satisfied that Lauren wasn't going through her pregnancy alone. Had the ruse reaped an unexpected benefit for Daniel, in that Claudia had realised Daniel actually meant something to her?

Let it go, Lauren intoned as she reached the Mini. *It's not your problem to solve.*

Unanswerable questions weren't generally Lauren's thing, but her mind spun such a web around her thoughts as she made her way back to Polkerran, she was pulling into the driveway, before she recalled her reason for going to the farm shop in the first place: dinner.

Dropping her bag and keys onto the kitchen island, she looked around for evidence of where Daniel might be. Both the car and the Jeep were outside, but then she heard his voice coming from the study – a client call, by the sound of things.

Lauren opened the drawer where they kept the takeaway leaflets. It would have to be that or going out to eat.

It was another hour before Daniel emerged from the study, and Lauren had been upstairs to change into her comfiest loungewear. If the decision was in favour of the pub, she could soon get dressed again.

'Hey, that was a cryptic message earlier.'

Lauren had been debating with herself since she'd got back over whether it had been wise to mention Claudia, but as he'd raised it, she may as well explain.

'Claudia's down for a few days. One too many rumours abounding for her to resist checking out the lay of the land.'

Daniel said nothing for a moment, coming to sit on the stool next to Lauren at the island.

'I'm sorry you had to deal with that. I hope you didn't feel too bad.'

Lauren threw him a puzzled look. 'About what?'

'Being economical with the truth.' His eyes widened as a hand landed on her arm. 'You didn't tell her, did you?'

Shaking her head, Lauren picked up one of the takeaway menus, pretending nonchalance, though her heart had picked up its usual pace and was tapping out a rhythm beneath her breast.

'I confirmed we lived together and left her to make the assumption everyone else has. I think the rumours had reached her but she'd dismissed them. Until your aunt saw me – and my mum visiting – that is.'

'Ah.' Daniel's hand slipped from her arm and he ran it through his hair. 'Sorry. My bloody family.'

'There's something you need to know, though.'

Come on Kirkham. Courage.

'Our… situation appears to have reaped an unexpected bonus. For you.'

Daniel leaned against the backrest of the stool, his brown gaze fixed on Lauren, the edges of his mouth lifting. 'I know. It's a bit unexpected.'

Lauren's skin prickled as he rested his hand on her arm again and gave it a light squeeze. Was he leaning closer? If he was, she would, too…

'Having someone to game with has been the tops.'

She huffed out a breath. *Stupid woman.*

'Pillock. I mean Claudia seems rather interested in you again. Don't be surprised if she expresses some interest in getting back together.'

There, it was out there. She waited for delight to infuse Daniel's features, but he looked frozen in place.

Okay, so perhaps it was a shock.

'Honestly.' Lauren placed her hand on his arm this time. Lord, how she loved the warmth of his skin against hers! 'I wouldn't tease you about this. She seems fully convinced we're the couple the whole village has bought into. It'd be easy to reveal the true state of things. I can go back home any time so I'm out of the way.'

To her surprise, Daniel lifted his other hand and tucked a wayward tress of hair behind Lauren's ear, before briefly resting the back of his hand against her cheek.

Unable to stop herself, Lauren's eyes closed. Lord, she wished he was hers! She'd never treat him the way Claudia had.

'It's irrelevant.'

Lauren's eyes flew open as the hand was removed, and she dropped her hold on his arm.

'You're staying here until you're ready to go home to your parents. Even if...' Daniel's voice tailed away, and his eyes clouded.

'Hey?' Lauren nudged his arm.

'Sorry. Look, Claudia has no desire to move in here. If anything changes, it will merely be a resumption of being... whatever we were. Now...' Daniel pointed at the leaflets spread across the island, then took in Lauren's attire. 'What delight are we going to indulge in this evening?'

Lauren peeped at him covertly as he perused the curry house menu. She could think of several answers to that, none of which Daniel would be expecting, but thankfully her stomach intervened, giving an ominous growl.

'Mia says bring on the spice!'

Chapter Twenty-Six

Party Like it's 1984

As July drifted into August and Lauren approached her eighth month of pregnancy, she'd eyed her once petite figure with interest. Amelia had continued to grow into a neat ball of a bump on her front. Anna had even said the other day, when Lauren was wearing her maternity dungarees, that you couldn't tell she was pregnant from behind.

The same couldn't be said for how she felt. Her breasts were noticeably fuller, her back protested against the additional weight she bore and even the simple act of getting out of a low chair had become a challenge.

Lauren also found more things changing than her physical appearance. Daniel didn't mention Claudia much, but telling him about their meeting must have triggered a chance of a reconciliation. Even if he was still ignoring messages, Lauren knew they talked on the phone, having walked in on the tail end of too many conversations. She wondered how Claudia had progressed in her intention of getting back together with him, then dismissed it. If that had been so, it would have happened in an instant.

Although they continued to get on well when together, Daniel was preoccupied most of the time and used his consultancy work as an excuse, just as much as Lauren did. Her interest in him showed no signs of lessening, and Daniel didn't help by being continually thoughtful, considerate and... oh yes, damned gorgeous!

Things were changing, however. Blowing hot and cold, much like the typical English summer weather. Sometimes, they seemed on their old footing, challenging each other to a game on the PlayStation, eating takeaways off their lap in the snug in between rounds, or going for walks down to the beach below The Lookout, skimming stones and debating which sort of rescue dog Daniel should adopt.

At others – usually during the working day – they barely communicated. Lauren spent most of her time in the study, striving to complete projects before the enforced down time around Amelia's birth. Daniel seemed to have almost stopped doing DIY jobs around the cove and travelled up to London frequently, leaving before Lauren came downstairs in the morning and sometimes not returning for a few days. He'd mentioned being in Bristol a couple of times but Claudia's name wasn't brought up, and with the old easiness out of her grasp, Lauren didn't feel able to ask.

If she were honest, she didn't really want to know. Claudia had implied she was prepared to fight for Daniel. Little did she know, there wasn't a battle to be had when Lauren was merely his friend and lodger. Besides, she'd be leaving in a matter of weeks.

The only thing that continued was the so-called date night at the Lugger, a regular haunt for them on a Thursday, so Lauren could legitimately tell her mum about it on her weekly call and, missing a social life as well as Daniel's presence in the house, Lauren's anticipation had only intensified over time.

It was also her one chance to dress up, and it had become a thing at the pub, where she put up with the gentle ribbing of the landlords and the locals over each outfit. Lauren didn't care. She loved a bit of glam and had carefully curated a selection of outfits that would adapt or suit alteration afterwards. She refused to think about how much she enjoyed holding Daniel's hand, being able to gaze into his eyes without feeling she was overstepping a boundary. It was her own secret indulgence.

This week, Lauren wore a new dress she'd found online – designer maternity lines were a godsend – and she turned from side to side, admiring the simple elegance of the chiffon layers as they skimmed over her bump and swished against her calves. Her style choices had become strikingly more feminine since falling pregnant.

Stepping into her favourite sandals, thankfully slip-ons, as she couldn't bend down to fasten anything in the region of her feet these days, Lauren admired her pedicure. Nicki had a new product she wanted to test out and had asked her to be a guinea pig, applying the same to her finger-nails. Scooping up her Coach clutch, Lauren checked her tousled bob, pulling tendrils into place.

'You ready, Lauren?'

Daniel's voice, calling from the landing.

'Coming.' Lauren snatched up her shawl. 'Oh!'

Daniel leaned against the opposite wall, his eyes fixed on the bedroom door as it swung aside.

'You okay?' He stepped forward, so close there was only a slither of air between his shirt and the bump. 'You don't seem yourself lately.'

Nor do you.

Lauren summoned a light laugh from somewhere. 'I'm hungry! Get me to yonder pub, young'un!'

He didn't seem convinced, but moved aside so she could emerge onto the landing, but as Lauren grasped the handrail, Daniel's hand landed upon hers.

'Lauren, look at me.'

Why couldn't she turn her head? Lauren stared at Daniel's hand on hers, a myriad of sensations coursing through her veins. The old Daniel – corporate, ambitious, driven – would have been right up her street, at least for a few dates and some great sex. How come *this* version – kind, thoughtful, taking one day at a time – appealed so much, she wanted to throw herself in his arms and smother him with kisses?

Daniel eased Lauren's grip from the bannister and turned her around. She peeped up at him. Lord, she wanted him even more when he tilted his head like that.

'Sorry. Just in a hurry to feed the sprog.'

Daniel released her hand. 'You're not being honest with me.'

'I know. Forgive me? It's something…' She waved a pointless hand in the air. 'Or nothing. I don't know.'

'Okay. I'm as bad.' Daniel ran his fingers through his hair, the hand landing on the back of his neck. 'I'm concerned about you. It's not the baby?'

'No. Truly. It's me, being an idiot.' Lauren tried to smile, but he didn't return it. 'Come on. At least if I get fed that'll be one less complaint my body's making!'

The pub was almost empty when they walked in, and as Sebastian grabbed his phone to take a photo of her, she struck a pose.

'For the socials, darling. You don't mind?' He blew Lauren a kiss and she reciprocated.

'Anything for you, Seb.'

Lauren turned towards their usual table, but Daniel stayed her with a hand on her arm.

'This way.'

There was a door to one side of the bar, one she'd never really noticed before.

'What's in here?'

'It's the back room.'

'That's not an answer.'

Daniel merely smiled, then knocked firmly three times. A responding three knocks came from inside, and he pulled the door open to reveal a small, prettily lit room.

'Happy Surprise Shower!' Anna rushed forward, and Lauren sent Daniel a pleading glance as he backed out of the room and closed the door.

Please don't go! I hardly see you…

'I said I didn't need a baby shower,' Lauren spoke quietly to Anna as she took in the familiar faces of Nicki, Phoenix, Mrs Lovelace, Jeannie and Mrs Clegg.

'It's not what you think,' said Anna smugly. 'This is a "mummy" shower. This evening is for *you*! Take a look.'

Despite her conflicted emotions over Daniel, Lauren summoned a smile, taking in everyone's expectant faces. The room replicated the charm and character of the main pub, although its low beams were adorned with fairy lights, a glitterball suspended from the centre, and a long table was laid out with a plentiful buffet. There were copious strings of bunting suspended from the wall lights, some of which sported phrasing such as 'Happy 60th Birthday' and 'Welcome Home, Ted'.

'Looks like someone vomited party heaven in here,' Lauren whispered to Anna.

'Recycled, most of it,' Anna replied, sotto voce. 'You don't mind, do you? They really wanted to do this for you.'

Lauren squeezed her friend's arm, genuinely touched. 'It's lovely. Honestly.'

'You miss going out,' piped up Phoenix. 'So for one night only, we bring you the cove's latest offering, the *Crab Pot Club*.'

A small blackboard above a serving hatch proclaimed the name, and Lauren's breath hitched in her throat as she looked at their eager faces. They'd all dressed to the nines: Phoenix's skirt was all the colours of the rainbow, Nicki had almost out-glammed herself, Jean was wearing a dress for the first time since Lauren had met her, and the knitting ladies sported sparkly cardigans and paste tiaras.

''Phee had the idea of giving you a club night out.' Nicki waved a hand to where Gavin leaned through the hatch, ready to take drink orders.

Anna relieved Lauren of her shawl and bag. 'Time to flex those dance moves, Kirkham, and sample the best mocktails in town. Come on.'

Phoenix browsed the tunes on offer. 'It's all a bit sixties meets the eighties,' she warned before setting the jukebox going.

A few hours later, a tired but happy Lauren sank onto a banquette, a glass of water in her hand. She and Anna had danced to track after track, like the old days. Phee and Nicki had joined them, with Jeannie keeping the jukebox going and Mrs Lovelace and Mrs Clegg rocking from side to side to the music.

There had been gifts for Lauren too, including a small watercolour of the cove done by Phoenix, a fine silver bracelet, adorned with two shards of glass from the beach by the lighthouse, skilfully made by Jeannie, and a voucher from Anna and Oliver for a spa day.

Sebastian and Gavin handed over a bottle of Veuve Clicquot (for when the baby was born), and presented her with the glitterball.

'For the dance moves, babes,' Gavin said, dropping a kiss on Lauren's flushed cheek, and she'd thanked them all, choked with emotion as she looked around the room at their shining faces. All she needed to make this complete was…

The door opened and Daniel peered in, Oliver looking over his shoulder. 'Is it safe to come in?'

Chapter Twenty-Seven

All the Pregnant Ladies, All the Pregnant Ladies... Uh, Uh, Oh

Lauren's heart leapt, and she made a perfunctory effort to clamp down on her delight.

'Hey, how was it?' Daniel sat beside her. 'Bloody hell, you're warm.' He put the back of his hand against her slightly sweaty forehead. 'What have they been doing to you?'

'Nothing,' Lauren laughed. 'I did it to myself. Haven't danced in months, but I've had a blast. Feet are killing me, though.' She gestured at the discarded heels.

Several locals had filed through the door, most making for the ample remains of the buffet, but Tommy the Boat headed for the jukebox, putting on a jive, and he and Old Patrick soon had the knitting ladies on their feet.

When the tune came to an end, Mrs Lovelace sank onto the banquette next to Lauren, red in the face and struggling to breathe.

Daniel eyed her with some alarm. 'You okay, Mrs L?'

'Aye, young'un.' She gasped, her hands dropping to the tops of her legs. 'Oooh, haven't felt they inner thighs vibrating like that since Mr L passed.'

Lauren watched Daniel chatting to Seb through the hatch as he collected some water, willing her heart to behave. She had to find a way to curb this interest in the man. Hankering after him wasn't doing Lauren any favours.

Despite her inner caution, Lauren admired Daniel covertly as he brought water for Mrs Lovelace, then held a hand out to her.

'Dance with me.'

As her insides were already doing a jig, there didn't seem any point in turning down the opportunity, and to seal the deal, Mrs Lovelace leaned towards her.

'That's right, my lovely. Given enough time to us old 'uns, you have.'

Daniel took Lauren's hand firmly as soon as she'd slipped her feet back into the heels and he hauled her to her feet.

'Come on,' he said quietly. 'It's expected. It's your party, and – allegedly – I'm your man.'

I wish.

'Sounds like a cue for Wham.'

With a half-smile, Daniel led her the few steps into the centre of the room. 'Hey, Nic! Any nice slow George Michael tracks in there for an expectant lady?'

Nicki gave a thumbs up from by the jukebox, and as the opening notes of 'Careless Whisper' floated across the room, Daniel placed a hand on Lauren's absent waistline and took hold of hers with the other.

Suppressing a tumult of emotion, the like of which she didn't fully understand, Lauren swallowed quickly. Somehow, she had to regain her normal jokey self.

'I'm usually a bit more into Beyoncé, but I do love me a bit of George Michael.'

'I think this pace is better for your health right now than a rendition of "Single Ladies". Hey,' he added as they swayed to the music, 'you weren't even born when this came out.'

'My mum played his music all the time. I was weaned to this tune.' Her lips twitched. 'And "Club Tropicana". The sound of cicadas always makes me feel like a toddler again. Don't you love George Michael?'

'I'm not a fan, to be honest.'

Lauren tried not to notice the way Daniel rubbed his thumb soothingly over her clasped fingers. Her heart was all over the place, but she willed herself to drift into the moment. Hell, this man smelled delicious. Would he notice if she pressed her nose to his neck and had a good sniff?

Her shoulders rippled with poorly stifled amusement, and he lowered his head to catch her eye.

'This is supposed to be romantic.'

'Sorry,' she whispered.

'You okay?' Daniel spoke softly into her ear as they moved to the music. 'I know you've worn yourself out. I think the song's only five minutes long.'

Despite her fluttering emotions at their proximity, Lauren's lips twitched. 'That's very precise for not being a fan.'

'I may have been evasive with the truth.' He drew her close, and she started to giggle again.

'Stop it!' he hissed. 'The rumours are we're potty for each other.'

'I'm sorry, it's just that we must be a hilarious sight, with my bump in between us. I'm trying to tuck my bum in, but it's just not happening. You'll have to stick yours out.'

Daniel's chest vibrated, but he adjusted her position so that she was almost sideways on to him, altering his grasp on her hand as he swept an arm around her back. 'Better?'

It was heavenly. Lauren loved the protective way Daniel held her and the melody swirling around them.

'I could stay like this forever,' she whispered.

'Until you get hungry.'

'Rude.'

'They say the truth hurts.'

Lauren merely smiled. 'Shhh. I'm losing myself in the music.'

'Rest against me,' Daniel murmured, and she leaned her head against his shoulder, closing her eyes. She didn't want to see people's faces. She wanted to pretend this was real, that Daniel fancied her as much as she fancied him.

'Oh Lord.'

'What is it?' Lauren said softly, trying to cling onto her dream. 'I'm not looking.'

'Just Billy Two Feet and Charlie the Crab – you don't know them – attempting a tango. I fear for the safety of the buffet table.'

A small laugh escaped her, and Daniel's arms tightened around her as he lowered his head.

'How's Mia's evening going?'

'Enjoying this track more than the earlier ones.'

'We'll have to remember that. She's clearly got taste.'

Lauren smiled, but a brief sadness swept through her. Daniel spoke as though he'd be around as her child grew up… She reluctantly opened her eyes, visited immediately by the memory of the beautiful Claudia, confident in her ability to reclaim Daniel. Then, Lauren caught herself. Daniel wasn't even hers to lose… She drew in a hiccupping breath.

'Hey, what's up?'

'Sorry. Just thinking ahead.'

'Try not to for now. Most of them think we're madly in love. They don't want to see you looking sad. You need to up your game, Primrose.'

Fine. Time to go rogue.

Lauren raised her head as they continued to circle slowly to the music, then sent Daniel a mischievous smile, before going on tiptoes to plant a kiss on his cheek.

'Take that.'

'Ah, a definite favourite group of mine when I was a school-kid.'

Lauren chuckled. 'Mine too, though I loved the earlier ones. I'm such a nineties baby.' Then, she sobered at the look in his eyes.

'Never forget, Lauren, you can rule the world,' he said softly, but before Lauren could summon a Take That pun in return, he lifted his free hand and brushed the hair from her cheek, resting his palm against her skin.

They were barely moving now, and Lauren was oblivious to where they were and what they were doing as Daniel lowered his head and – to her surprise – kissed her.

It lasted barely a few seconds, but she could feel the lingering pressure of his mouth against hers, a sudden rush of heat coursing through her body, as he straightened. Lauren's heart was pounding so fiercely, she was surprised Amelia didn't respond with a kick.

'I win that one,' Daniel smirked, and she swatted his arm, aching at how little affected he seemed.

'Don't tempt me into another round. You know you'll lose.'

Daniel, however, merely smiled as the dance ended. 'Never challenge a competitive man.'

Lauren, suppressing the urge to throw 'Why Can't I Wake Up With You?' in there, was more concerned he'd detect the heat flooding her skin at his touch, and couldn't care less about being the champion of their silly game. She'd come to a gradual realisation over the evening, an all-consuming insight, and sending Daniel a cautious smile, she hurried over to Anna. Her emotions were in turmoil. Somehow, this silly hormonal urge was escalating into something more permanent.

'We'll take these out to the car.' Oliver picked up a couple of gift bags and Daniel scooped up the rest.

Lauren's eyes followed Daniel's back as he left the room, almost shaking with suppressed emotion. She had found him a bit of a dish almost from the moment they met, but that was normal for Lauren. She'd always had a visceral appreciation of men's looks, so much so it often led her astray, hence her inability to commit to relationships. Handsome men did not always have other traits she valued.

Kit had been the first to buck the trend, but even his looks had blinded her to the fact their bond came from their similarities of ambition and business acumen.

Somehow, Daniel had become so much more than any of those things. Yes, he had Kit's intelligence and a mind for business – when he chose to apply it – and the looks to catch Lauren's eye, but he also had a sense of humour, was a compassionate, kind and considerate man, and to be loved by him would truly be something.

Claudia was an imbecile, but Daniel loved her. It didn't matter whose gloves were on or off, there was no fight to be had.

'Ready?' Anna said brightly as she fetched up in front of Lauren, carrying bags filled with bunting, unused napkins and the glitterball trophy.

'Here, let me.' Oliver and Daniel were back, and as the former relieved Anna of her burden, the latter handed something to Lauren.

'I assumed you might want these.'

Despite her inner turmoil, Lauren laughed as she took the slippers from him. 'You are one of life's angels, Daniel Tremayne.'

Rolling his eyes, Daniel picked up her sandals and shawl as she slipped her feet into the soft fabric and grabbed her bag from the banquette. 'Robbie Williams' tracks don't count.'

They filed out of the back room into the main part of the pub, and Lauren cast a regretful glance at the *Crab Pot Club* sign. She couldn't bear to look at Daniel right now for fear of blurting out something she – and he – would regret.

They emerged from the pub to the lapping of water against the harbour slip and the clink of sails against masts. The hoot of an owl came from the trees above the village, and Lauren inhaled the now familiar tang of salty air, a hand resting on Amelia.

'I brought the car.' Daniel took her elbow before she realised he was there, and Lauren's fickle heart picked up its beat. 'Expected you to be too tired to climb the hill, even in your slippers.'

Anna and Oliver refused the offer of a lift, opting to stroll back at their own pace, and as Daniel closed the door and walked round to the driver's side, Lauren breathed in and out, much as she'd been instructed at the antenatal class. Why did she feel so out of sorts, so tied up in knots, elated but despondent all at once?

It was only a short drive, and then she'd escape to her room to try and process the jumble of sensations fighting for precedence in her small frame.

Daniel didn't speak as he drove back to The Lookout, and Lauren didn't question the silence as it suited her. She peeped at him, admiring his profile in the lamp light as the car slowed to take the turn into the lane leading up to the clifftop, but when he drew to a halt on the drive, he got out of the car, then leaned back in as Lauren unfastened her seatbelt. 'Stay there.'

Coming round to open the door for her, he offered his arm, and she took it reluctantly but out of necessity, then waited as he retrieved her gifts from the back seat.

Daniel placed the bags onto the table in the hall, and Lauren tried not to stare at his close-fitting shirt as she followed reluctantly behind.

'Fancy one before bed?'

Sometimes there are no words...

Daniel waved the kettle, and Lauren tried to assume her normal manner.

'All good for tea, thank you. Need my bed. 'Night, Daniel.'

Lauren cast him a swift look, but as the sight of him was all she needed for her insides to ripple and sway like sheets drying in a stiff breeze, she left the room and started up the stairs. Surely that wasn't disappointment in his face?

'Hey!'

Pausing halfway up the stairs, Lauren looked back into the hall. Daniel had shoved his hands into his pockets but all that did was emphasise how well fitting his chinos were, and she swallowed hard.

'Is something wrong?'

'No, not at all.' Summoning her brightest smile, Lauren waved a hand towards the landing. 'Just worn out. All that dancing!'

Daniel didn't seem convinced, but the edges of his mouth lifted. 'Sleep well, then. Hope Mia doesn't keep you awake practising her moves.'

Lauren closed the door to her room and leaned back against it, exhaling slowly. She may have a penchant for problem-solving, but how could she apply it to herself?

She walked over to the window and stared out into the darkness. There were no lights out to sea, at least, none she could detect without her glasses on. All she could perceive was her own reflection, shadowed and still.

How was she to extract herself from this dilemma?

A dilemma of your own making.

'Whatever.' Lauren spun around, her heart clenching in her chest as she walked over to the bed. 'Oh, Daniel. How has this happened?'

Then, she crumpled as exhaustion and emotional strain took its toll, sinking heavily onto the bed, her head in her hands.

Lauren had finally fallen properly for someone – a beautiful person, both inside and out – a man she adored with all her being, and sadly one convinced he was in love with someone else.

Chapter Twenty-Eight

Over and Out-Out

The weekend was soon upon them and although, Lauren wasn't quite sure how, it passed quickly. Her consciousness around Daniel overshadowed everything. She struggled to find the easy banter they'd shared, and found continued avoidance the best defence, citing an overdue project and shutting herself in the study.

On Monday, Daniel disappeared early – yet another trip to Bristol – and not wanting to think about what that might mean, Lauren worked until about three, after which she prowled around the house, fed up with her own company.

Everything reminded her of Daniel now: the sofa he'd pulled her down onto one day when he'd been watching a football game, saying she couldn't leave the room as she was his lucky charm. Apparently, his team, who never won anything, had just scored in a vital game.

At the time, Lauren had laughed and curled up next to him, reading a magazine, happy and content and not aware she was falling in love.

The snug was where they'd laughed and fought over numerous spats on a range of computer games.

The kitchen was the heart of the house and their relationship: cooking together, eating at the island, Daniel helping her complete the forms to set up her limited company and Lauren showing him the brochures when choosing decor for his home.

'Enough!' she exclaimed as her gaze fell on the chairs in the vast bay window, hers adorned with the throw she'd insisted on covering it with, Daniel's bearing the latest copy of *Easy Parenting* magazine.

She had to get out of here!

Ten minutes later, Lauren settled at Anna's table, skim reading through a job website as her friend brewed a pot of tea.

'Will you go for any of them?'

Lauren lowered the cover of the laptop and took the mug gratefully. 'Probably, although I'm still hoping something will come of the Devere connection.'

Anna took a seat, pushing a plate of biscuits towards Lauren. 'Is that the one with the Leeds operation?'

Taking a sip of her drink, Lauren savoured the heat on her tongue. 'Yep. Not city centre this time, but that's probably a good thing.'

Her gaze drifted to the stunning view through the window. She may not have Anna's longstanding attachment to Polkerran, but she had fallen under its spell, nonetheless. It would be an idyllic place for a child to grow up, certainly in the early years. Lauren had watched the children on their way to the village school, happy and chattering, surrounded by all this beauty – they probably had no idea how lucky they were.

Then, she shoved the thought away. Idyllic it may be, but there was no career for Lauren tucked away in this Cornish haven.

'Why can't you just continue as a consultant? It seems to pay well.'

Lauren sighed. 'Maybe if I had a role that meant I had to be on site. I don't think I'm cut out for full-time home working. It has its good points, but I find it isolating with the lack of personal contact with colleagues.' She smiled faintly. 'Miss being part of a corporate structure too. I know I have to consider the baby, but if I get a job commutable from Leeds, I've got Kit's flat at my disposal, and it's in a nice area.'

Anna poured more tea. 'Have you given any more thought to how you'll explain to your parents – about Daniel?'

Thinking of Daniel caused the ache in Lauren's breast to intensify, and she lowered her gaze to the baby bump. If only they'd met another time, when she wasn't as she was and his heart wasn't compromised…

'Hey.' Anna leaned forward, resting a hand on Lauren's arm. 'Come back!'

With a faint smile, Lauren patted her friend's hand before she removed it. 'I'll fess up, explain it was so they wouldn't worry. I'm not prepared to paint Daniel as a villain and the reason we're no longer a supposed couple.' Lauren stretched her back, but it didn't relieve the discomfort. 'Nor am I going to let Mum and Dad think I'm still being the commitment phobic daughter.'

'And Mia?' Anna spoke softly, as though the baby could hear, and Lauren sent her an affectionate glance.

'Mum's all up for looking after her on days off, rather than a child minder, but that will only work if I get a job back in Yorkshire. I wish you were still up there. You'd be the perfect auntie to do it.'

Anna's eyes shone. 'How I'd love to.' Then, she smirked knowingly. 'Of course, if you stay here with Daniel, then I can get to do that anyway.'

The words were a jolt, and Lauren stared at her friend. 'Don't be daft. He's still obsessed with Claudia!'

Anna shrugged, taking a sip from her mug. 'I was obsessed with Alex. For years. Doesn't mean it'll work out. I think you like Daniel more than you're admitting.'

Unlikely…

'He-he's…' Lauren swallowed hard. She didn't even know how to say it. 'I don't have the words. I can't explain what's happened to me. My thing was finding men attractive, not falling for them.'

'What makes you feel Daniel is something else?'

Where to begin?

'It's not just that I fancy him.' Understatement. 'I'm not saying I don't think about what it would be like, you know, with him. I love hanging out with him. We get on so well, we laugh. He listens to me. I want to be the one who makes him smile, and when I do, it's like I've won the lottery. He's the most decent man I've ever known. All I want is to make him happy, and I'm worried that the best I can do for him is get out of his life, let him be with Claudia.'

'Wow.' Anna said nothing for a moment, then added, 'Well, love, you may have taken your time, but you sure as heck have fallen hard.'

Lauren's breath hitched in her throat. 'I suppose it's fantastic if you both feel the same.'

She didn't want to think about it, because the reality hurt. Her expression was mulish, and Anna rolled her eyes. 'I've renamed Daniel lately, to Denial. What am I going to call you?'

'Please tell me it's not Loser.'

Anna smiled. 'I hope you realise that running away to the other end of the country won't stop you feeling how you do.'

Lauren sighed. 'I know. It's just...' She raised her eyes to Anna's kind ones. 'I can't stay here.'

Emotion gripped Lauren's throat at the thought of leaving; saying goodbye to Polkerran, not able to call on her best friend whenever she wanted, never seeing Daniel again, being under his warm brown gaze, holding his hand, pretending...

Anna leaned over again and hugged Lauren's shoulders. 'One step at a time, remember? Let's meet the baby first.'

Being alone with Daniel at The Lookout had changed for Lauren, so much so, she withdrew from him. It was a case of self-preservation.

Despite no longer reading the raunchy romance novels she loved, her imagination took over, leaving her desperate to avoid any touch from him. Lauren had the kettle on for her hot water bottle before he could offer, and when the leg cramps attacked in the early hours, she clamped down on her gasps and did her best to follow Daniel's practice of rubbing her calves. It was harder than ever to reach them, though, and sometimes she simply cried quietly until the pain subsided.

If only the ache inside would pass...

By mid-week, Lauren had reached the thirty-fifth week of her pregnancy and needed to be in Bristol for a meeting, so decided to head to Bath for a stop over to do some last-minute shopping for the baby. As it happened, Kit messaged her.

He'd been in Cardiff and suggested meeting her in Bath, and they'd had dinner, discussing his looming departure to the States – scheduled for the early autumn – and Lauren's plans to restart her career. She updated him on progress with her job applications, talking very little about the baby, and they parted – still with some regret on Kit's part, but none on Lauren's – on the footing of friendship.

A week later, Lauren's exhaustion got the better of her, not aided by the rarity of a heatwave. Struggling to sleep, what with the constant heartburn and her back aching from the strain of the weight she now carried, Lauren finally accepted the nagging from Anna, Daniel, Nicki and her midwife, Pauline, and stopped working. She had about four weeks until her due date, and most of her projects were complete, the final one being at a stage whereby she could pause her side of things.

Aside from the filming taking up two days the following week, all she had to do now was rest and pack, ready for the long drive north.

The weather remained set in, although there was the threat of it breaking with a massive thunderstorm soon, and she took to lounging on the terrace in her soft maternity shorts and a floaty strappy top, topping up her tan and trying to concentrate on the latest thriller novel. The hardest thing was trying to pretend she wasn't bored rigid, especially with Daniel keeping his distance.

Adjusting her position, Lauren picked up a wide-brimmed sun hat and popped it on, her arms behind her head. The baby was, apparently, the size of a lion cub now (or candy floss, according to Anna's latest preference) and certainly felt it. She looked over the prominent bump to the sea beyond.

'It's like you're a hillock, Mia,' she said softly, resting a hand on her precious cargo. 'I hope you're cosy in there, and not too warm. Thank heavens there's a breeze up here.'

Lauren fanned her sweaty cheeks with her book, then tossed it aside.

'Hey!'

With a start, Lauren looked up as Anna plonked herself on a patio chair. Struggling to sit up, she swung her legs to the ground and adjusted the hat.

'You should've pinged me. I'd have got the kettle on! Anna?' Lauren reached forward as best she could to touch her friend's hand. Anna was almost quivering, emotion playing across her features.

'He's agreed to the contact. Ali— Matthew.' Her voice cracked, and she drew in a breath which turned into a sob, and Lauren rose inelegantly from the recliner to put an arm around Anna's shoulders.

'Oh my God! That's fantastic news!'

Anna nodded, digging in her pocket for a tissue. 'I was going to call, but Oliver said I should come and tell you in person.' She sniffed, then laughed, wiping her eyes on the tissue. 'I think he'd been sobbed over enough and decided it was someone else's turn.'

Calmer now, Anna outlined what the ongoing process was, which basically meant she'd given permission for her contact details to be passed over to her brother. Then, all she had to do was wait for him to get in touch.

Delighted for her friend, Lauren gestured inside. 'Come on, this calls for a cider zero and some fizz!'

They took their glasses back out onto the terrace, sitting at the table this time in the shade, Anna talking animatedly, and Lauren letting her speak, asking the occasional question, her heart full on seeing how happy the news made her.

Lauren's phone started to ring. Kit.

'Sorry,' she mouthed at Anna. 'I'd better take this. I know Kit's got meetings in the States next week.'

Kit was in great spirits. After their meet-up in Bath the previous week, he'd been busy making the arrangements for Lauren to have the keys to his flat in Leeds, which would be left in the care of the concierge.

Lauren was touched and delighted, determined now to centre her job search in Yorkshire, and comforted because it meant Ameilia could be cared for mostly by her mum.

'Kit, you darling man!'

'It's good to hear you so happy!'

She smiled into the phone. 'Yes, yes I am. Safe travels, and I'll see you soon. Bye.'

Lauren ended the call, but looked up to see someone stood behind Anna.

Daniel.

'Sorry to interrupt.' He had been gone since breakfast, Lauren wasn't sure where. 'Can I have a word?'

Surprised, Lauren looked towards Anna, but she was on her feet, smiling widely at Daniel. 'I'm just leaving. I'll call you later, Lauren.'

She waved a hand and almost skipped as she left the terrace, and Lauren squinted up at Daniel.

'What's up?'

He looked uncomfortable, and Lauren's insides twisted with anxiety. 'Ready for some lunch?'

'If you'll give me a hand up.' She held out her hand, holding tightly to his as he helped her.

As Lauren laid out cutlery on the table, Daniel filled a pitcher with water and carried it over, returning to collect a couple of glasses.

'How are the ankles?'

Lauren glanced down, then realised she couldn't see them anyway. 'Present and correct, I think. Lord, I'll be glad when this is over!'

Pouring water into glasses, Daniel turned towards the fridge. 'Lunch, the birth or living with me?'

How to answer?

'Haha. You're so funny.' Lauren sent him a small smile as she accepted the tomatoes and cucumber, wishing she couldn't see his cute expression or find him deliciously attractive in his open-necked shirt and chinos. 'No offence to my baby, but I'll be so much happier when she's in my arms and not the embrace of my gut muscles.'

'I'm sorry it's making you so uncomfortable. What with the leg cramps, the backache and the heartburn, it's no wonder you wish it over.' He looked uncertain, then gave an almost imperceptible shake of his head. Retrieving a quiche, he headed back to the table, and Lauren eyed him thoughtfully.

'Is something up?'

He didn't answer as he pulled plates out of a cupboard, but Lauren stopped chopping the salad.

'Daniel?' It came out as a croak, and Lauren strove to clear her throat. 'Come on. I don't know what it is, but you can tell me.'

With a huff of breath, he turned around. 'I keep putting off talking to you because I know you don't feel great, and I know you're only down here for another week, but... argh.'

He shoved his hands in his pockets, walking over to the windows facing the terrace, his gaze on the horizon, and Lauren – having an ominous feeling about what this meant, her insides taking up their usual dance – eyed his broad shoulders and the way his hair brushed the collar of his shirt.

Then, Daniel turned around.

'It's Claudia. She— I... we're going to give it another try.'

Chapter Twenty-Nine

Spice Girl

Lauren's heart thudded against her rib cage, but she plastered a wide smile on her face as she placed the knife carefully on the worktop. Appetite? What appetite?

'That's wonderful, Daniel!' The words came out of her mouth instinctively, her insides churned.

'We've met up a few times when I've been in Bristol or London lately, just for a chat or a drink.' He gave a self-deprecating smile. 'Feel now like I was being interviewed and I finally got the role – except I might be out of my depth.'

There was no denying the crushing ache in her chest, just above where her child lay snuggled, oblivious to her mother's turmoil.

Lauren summoned a hard-won smile. 'We did it!'

She went to high five him, but his hands remained steadfastly in his pockets, his face wary. 'You don't appear to be...' What could she say? What *should* she say? 'Hey, go us! We got an unexpected result, and that's great. Everyone's happy: Kit, my mum, now you and Claudia.'

'And you?'

'I'm fine.' She waved an airy hand and picked up the knife again, concentrating on slicing the rest of the tomatoes. She really ought to consider retraining for a role in theatre. 'I've had an amazing summer, living in this gorgeous house, spending bonus time with my bestie, establishing my consultancy. What's not to like?'

Daniel said nothing, resuming his search for plates, but something struck Lauren as she dropped the salad into a bowl and took it over to the table.

'Does Claudia know it was just a ruse?'

'No. I didn't know how to tell her.' Daniel shrugged as he placed the plates on the table and met Lauren's gaze. 'I can't explain it.'

They settled down to their lunch, but the food was tasteless to Lauren. Any happiness Daniel might feel about the rapprochement appeared overshadowed by his concern for what Lauren would do next.

'I'll see if Anna's got a room into next week. It's not like I wasn't leaving soon anyway.'

There was a clatter as Daniel's fork slipped from his fingers onto the floor. 'Damn.' He leaned down to retrieve it. 'Claudia's not moving in. We're just going to have another go at the dating. Now the house is done, the filming all but finished, I'll have more time to... well.' He frowned. 'Why do you have to go to Anna's?'

Despite her inner sadness, Lauren couldn't help but smile at his expression, and she spoke gently. 'If you truly want to give yourselves a chance, you don't want Claudia thinking you're still living with an ex.'

Daniel stood up so fast, his chair rocked as colour flooded his cheeks. 'I'm an idiot. I hadn't seen it like that. God.' He strode over to the window, hands on his hips, and Lauren eased up from her chair and padded over to stand beside him.

It was a sunny day with a light breeze, and the sails of several boats shimmied on the sea as they dipped and swayed to the dance of the waves.

'I'll explain to Claud. It's not fair for you to have to leave early. Besides,' he turned to Lauren. 'What if Anna doesn't have room? You'll have to head straight home, and—'

'Daniel,' Lauren interrupted gently. 'Don't do any explaining to Claudia. This is the unexpected bonus payout from our joint venture.' She didn't approve of them as a couple – how could she – but it was likely Daniel's last chance to make it work with Claudia. Removing that would jeopardise things for Daniel, and that Lauren was not prepared to do.

'Hey,' she nudged Daniel's arm, 'Claudia can be here for the filming now, too. That's what was meant to happen. She knows all about the planning, the costings, etc. It would be bizarre for me to do it now, especially as you'll be together when the show airs.'

A bitter taste filled her mouth at the thought, but Lauren ignored it as Daniel ran a hand through his hair.

'Look, be proud of all we achieved. I freed up one of Anna's B&B rooms for the main season, my mum and Kit stopped fretting about me, and Claudia came to realise she *does* want to be with you.'

Daniel took both Lauren's hands in his. *His* hands clearly hadn't received the memo about Claudia's imminent return. They were as warm, firm and comforting as they'd been for the past few months. Only now, Lauren didn't feel she could allow it.

'I'll go—' Her voice stuck in her throat, and she tried to clear it, freeing herself from Daniel's hold. 'Call Anna.'

She didn't dare look over her shoulder as she hurried towards the stairs.

—

By some form of serendipity, Anna had a room free, a last-minute cancellation, which meant Lauren could stay until her original departure date the following week. She relayed the information to Daniel by WhatsApp, as he'd gone out after lunch, and then began a desultory attempt at packing. Of Daniel and Claudia she refused to think, battening the door shut on such thoughts and mentally throwing away the key.

Thankfully, a long call with the Devere Corporation had taken her mind off things. Everything looked hopeful for a job in the near future, and Lauren tried to absorb herself with that rather than the complications of loving a man who was smitten with someone else and whom she'd probably see nothing of once she left Polkerran.

By evening, Lauren's back was aching more than ever, Amelia was kicking as if in frustration at not yet being out in the world and her once slim ankles were non-existent again.

'Bad one?'

Daniel was in the kitchen when she came downstairs to see what to have for dinner, surveying the contents of the fridge.

'There don't appear to be any good ones at the moment.' Lauren wriggled awkwardly onto one of the high leather stools at the island and closed her eyes. She didn't want them on Daniel. It hurt too much. She hated leaving his house.

Own up to it, girl. You hate leaving him, *not the house.*

'Hey.'

Lauren's eyes flew open. Daniel had come to stand beside her, placing a comforting hand on her shoulder.

'Blimey, you're tense. This is stressing you out.'

Lauren swallowed hard. How she longed for Daniel to keep his warm, firm hand on her shoulder, perhaps place the other one there, take her in his arms—

Amelia gave her a resounding kick, and she released a reluctant laugh.

'Sorry, baby making its presence known.' Lauren patted her bump. 'Calm down. I'll feed you shortly.' She smiled at Daniel. 'I'm fine. Anna's chuffed to have me back for a few days before I head home.'

Daniel returned to his study of the fridge contents. 'What do you fancy?'

You, Lauren's mind whispered.

When she didn't answer, he turned around. 'Takeaway?'

Lauren shook her head. 'That fridge is bulging with food again, and so is your freezer.'

He closed the fridge door and came to lean on the island opposite her. Lauren drew in a short breath. He had such gorgeous, brown eyes, with small gold flecks in them. She'd drown in them if he'd let her.

Lauren blinked as Daniel waved a hand at her. 'Hey, come back from wherever you are.'

'I'm at Thai Dai's mentally perusing the menu.'

'Ha! I knew you'd go for it.'

By the time Lauren had been for a soak – no one needed to know how inelegantly she'd climbed out after getting onto all fours first; thank goodness it was an over-sized bath – changed into loose, comfortable clothing and donned her slippers, the doorbell had rung and the tempting smell of food drifted up the stairs.

'I never fail to be amazed at your ability to eat spicy food.' Daniel shook his head as he opened the cartons and placed a spoon by each one, the heady aroma filled Lauren's nostrils.

'Pauline says I should moderate my intake, but I've got this far without a problem. I get acid reflux after bland food, so I may as well eat what I enjoy.'

They tucked into their supper, Lauren sipping on a glass of alcohol-free wine as Daniel enjoyed a cold beer, making desultory conversation, and she tried not to think about how life would be if they were staying together in this amazing house.

'Argh.' Lauren stretched as they laid their cutlery on their empty plates. 'I need a hot water bottle.'

'I'll do it.' Daniel flicked the switch on the water heater and started to load the dishwasher. 'Go and sit down.'

Lauren padded over to the sitting area at the far end of the room. The nights were slowly drawing in, though the horizon remained bright as the sun set. Staring out across the dappled sea as dusk fell, Lauren was gripped by a fleeting sadness.

'Here you go.'

With a start, she swung around and took the bottle from Daniel.

'This is not what I call sitting.'

Lauren gave a rueful smile. 'Distracted by the view, as always.' She sank into the chair she'd pretty much claimed as her own. Would this be the last time she curled up here, in this beautiful room, alone with this lovely man?

Let it go, girl. Time to move on, make a fresh start, a new life.

'When is Claudia due back in Polkerran?' There, keep it real.

Daniel didn't respond at first. His gaze was fixed on the ever-darkening sky, a bottle of beer clenched in his hand.

Lauren shifted in her seat, trying to position the water bottle more comfortably behind her, but it was a futile effort. There was no 'comfortable' anymore.

'Sorry. Did you say something?' Daniel turned his warm gaze on Lauren.

'I was just wondering if Claudia would be down this weekend. I've only got a small tote to pack in the morning, so I'll head up to Anna's after breakfast.'

It was hard to read Daniel's expression in the dim light of a solitary lamp, but she had a feeling he'd muttered something to himself.

'She's due down after work tomorrow.' He shrugged. 'Usual Friday thing.'

So that was that. Claudia would be back in Polkerran at weekends, Daniel would continue to believe he was in love with her and his happiness would continue to drain from him.

Sadness settled on Lauren's shoulders like a heavy cloak. She tried to shake it off, but it felt as though it had been sewn into place. Daniel had resumed his study of the window, though it was now so dark there was little to be seen other than a distorted reflection of them both.

Should she speak out, tell Daniel about her feelings?

The baby kicked her. Did Amelia agree, or was it a warning to restrain her habitual impulsivity?

Eyeing her indistinct image in the tall glass pane, there was no denying the bump. This was no time for such foolishness. She was weeks from giving birth to this life within her, and Daniel was finally back on track with the love of his life. He didn't need the complication of Lauren, or the awkwardness she might invite by revealing how she felt about him. Besides, this charming fishing village on the south-west coast was never going to be home.

'How shall we tell the locals?'

Daniel let out a huff of breath. 'Just tell Mrs L, she'll do the rest. I think we'll explain – as we've tried to several times already – that we've been good friends, that's all.'

He was right. That's all they had been, or could ever be.

Pretending her heart wasn't splintering into a thousand pieces, Lauren straightened her legs and eased forward in her seat.

'I'm off to bed, Daniel. Can't get comfortable.'

He'd leapt from his seat before she could stop him.

'Here.' He held out both hands. 'You'll never get out of there without help.'

He was right, but Lauren reluctantly placed her hands in his. Feeling the warmth of his skin, the firm hold he had upon her as he eased her to her feet and the kindness in his face as he reached behind her to retrieve the hot water bottle all threatened to overwhelm her, and she muttered a rushed goodnight and hurried to the stairs.

Lauren's departure couldn't come soon enough, before she thoroughly embarrassed them both with a declaration that could never end well.

Chapter Thirty

Mini Mini Bang Bang

A few clouds had bubbled up the next morning, and after clearing the patio table, her heart heavy, Lauren stacked the dishwasher as Daniel went upstairs to fetch her things.

Although it was late summer, Anna was delighted to welcome her again. She'd moved a booking into Anna's old room, freeing up Aunt Meg's for Lauren.

Her heart clenched in her chest as Daniel came down the stairs with the bags. Leaving would be painful, even though they'd be bound to meet to say goodbye before she left properly.

Lauren went into the study to gather up her laptop bag and check she'd not left anything else on the desk, but when she came out, she realised Daniel had gone out to the terrace, his mobile to his ear. The clouds had thickened, and the air had become muggy.

Turning on her heel, Lauren surveyed the open-plan interior, memories washing over her, from pouring over brochures at the island with Daniel, to arguing in favour of how many cushions to have on the sofas. It had been an adventure, so much fun, until she'd stopped just finding him easy on the eye and realised how deeply she loved him.

Shoving away the thought, Lauren looked over as Daniel came into the house.

'I'll book a table for eight.' There was a pause. 'Yes, I'll see you later. Bye.'

Lauren drew in a short breath.

Please don't let Claudia break his heart again…

Daniel looked up. 'Are you going now?'

'Yup. All packed.' Lauren tried to stifle her misgivings, scooping up her laptop bag and keys as Daniel grabbed her roller case and holdall, and she followed him out to the car. Lord, she'd miss living with this lovely man!

Lauren tossed the bag onto the passenger seat, then thought, 'to hell with it' and leaned up to kiss Daniel's cheek. 'Don't you dare forget to come and say goodbye before I leave.'

How was she even breathing? Her chest felt so tight, surely she had lost the ability?

'Are you okay?'

Daniel eyed Lauren with concern. 'You're white as can be. Come in and sit down for a minute. You shouldn't drive if—'

'I'm *fine!*' Her voice sounded as strangled as her throat felt, but keeping face was all important right now. Pinning the smile in place, much as she used to after an unsuccessful meeting at work, Lauren held out her hand.

Daniel stared at her extended arm, then raised puzzled eyes to her. 'What—'

'We had an agreement, didn't we?' Lauren's voice almost gave out as she spoke the words, but she essayed a smile only for it to fade the moment Daniel grasped her hand in his.

Oh, dear Lord. This man's touch did things to her she couldn't suppress, even in her condition! And he didn't let go.

Heat rising in her body, Lauren tugged at her hand. Daniel's brown eyes held their usual warmth, but was there something else?

'I'd best go,' she said, but the words were so faint, she barely heard them.

Were they just going to stand there forever, holding hands as the warm Cornish breeze caressed their skin, toyed with their hair, tugged at their clothing?

Shot through with emotion, Lauren almost gasped as Daniel let her go, shoving his hand into his pocket. He wasn't smiling now, and he took a step back.

'So, see you later.'

Her throat so tight, she could barely swallow, Lauren nodded. What was this constriction around her eyes? Turning away, she grasped the door handle and shot into the seat with a speed that belied her large belly.

She sped out of the driveway, her driving glasses forgotten, the tyres spurting gravel as she went.

'You damn, foolish idiot. How could you be so bloody *stupid*?' Lauren dashed fingers across her eyes.

She'd reached the bottom of the lane now, and regrets battling with relief, she turned onto the slightly less narrow road leading away from Polkerran. She couldn't face Anna just now, or holing up in the B&B. She'd drive to the next car park and take a walk on a beach and give herself a good talking to at the same time.

'Oh, Daniel. Why didn't you come into my life a year ago? If only I'd accepted Anna's invite to visit her at Westerleigh before I committed to moving in with Kit…'

Then, her gaze drifted to the bump. 'But then I wouldn't have you, little one, whoever you might turn out to be.'

There was a sharp bend coming up, but her sight blurred by the droplets forming on her lashes, she didn't see the oncoming van until it was too late.

With a shriek, she veered to the left, only for the Mini to scrape the stone walling, coming to a screeching stop.

'You okay, love?'

The man opened the door, and Lauren eyed him hazily, heart pounding fiercely, a protective arm across her bump.

'Miss?'

'Yes. Sorry.' She swallowed back on her shock over what had happened. 'Can you give me a hand?'

The young man helped her from the car, and she walked unsteadily across the road to lean against a tree, eyeing the Mini warily.

'Is yours unscathed?'

'Yeah. I'll reverse down the lane. There's a driveway there, and I'll wait for you to go past.' The young man returned to his van, and Lauren, her heart calming, rested her hand on the baby.

'Sorry, sweetie. My fault. Not concentrating. We were lucky it's only a prang.'

Not wanting to think about what could've happened, Lauren drew in a few breaths of air. It was cooler in the lane, with the high hedgerows shielding the road from light, and she shivered.

It looked like just a bit of damage to her car's near side. She'd get it into the garage once back in Yorkshire.

That was when the tractor came round the corner, and the Mini didn't stand a chance.

Chapter Thirty-One

Big Matt and Cries

The tractor was relatively unscathed, and George, the shocked young farmhand driving – once reassured there was no one inside the car – towed the stricken Mini into an opening in the hedgerow which gave access to a field.

A police motorbike came out from Port Wenneth, but as there were no injuries, insurance details had already been exchanged and Sam the Spanner – who ran the local garage just outside Polkerran Point – was on his way with a small tow truck to pick up the car, there was little else to be done.

The young man with the van gave Lauren a lift to Westerleigh Cottage with her bags, where Anna greeted her with hugs, a consoling mug of tea and a freshly baked brownie.

The rest of the morning passed in a whirl for Lauren, leaving her little time to think about how the reunion between Daniel and Claudia would go later. She spent most of it newly installed in her old room, on the phone in lengthy conversations with the insurance company, the garage, talking to her mum and reconnecting with her original midwife in Yorkshire over her imminent return.

Ending the final call, Lauren drained her glass of water and wandered over to the window, pushing it wide and leaning on the sill. The air was oppressive, the clouds a seamless grey mantle hanging over the dark waters rippling below.

There were no gigs in the harbour today, and very few pleasure craft out on the open sea. A few canoeists paddled past the foot of the cliff below Harbourwatch, and a solitary fishing boat could be seen chugging across from the harbour to the boatyard, from which emanated the sound of welding.

Closing the window, Lauren checked the battery on her phone, and seeing it was low, popped it on charge, smiling at the familiar creak of the floorboard by the bed. She picked up her laptop and headed down the stairs, aware of voices and entered the kitchen to find the usual crowd at Anna's table.

'Here comes the maid.' Mrs Lovelace beamed at Lauren. 'Now sit y'onself down, my lovely. 'Tis a vast mound you'm carrying, and all to the fore. I'd have known it for a girl, never you mind them fancy scan things.'

Nicki laughed. 'You told me Liam was a girl because I carried him all up front, Mrs L. Could've been a bit of a shock if I hadn't had my gender scan.' She turned to Lauren. 'Did you decide whether to join the NCT classes?'

'Pah!' Phoenix turned up her nose. 'Too posh. You're best going down the village hall, to the Mums and Babies group.'

'How're you feeling, Lauren?' Jean looked concerned. 'Anna says you had a bit of a knock in your car.'

'I'm fine, honestly.' Lauren took the seat beside Mrs Lovelace, who patted her on the arm before resuming her knitting. 'My poor car is the casualty. I'm not sure it's repairable.'

'Where's it to, then?' Phoenix dunked a biscuit into her mug, then popped the morsel in her mouth. 'Ummm, Anna. These biscuits are lush.'

'Someone called Sam collected it. He just called to say it's at the garage, but he's pretty certain it's a write-off.'

To Lauren's relief, she had joined the locals just as they had begun to discuss the upcoming harvest festival, and none of them seemed to have heard about Lauren moving out of The Lookout, so she sipped her tea, letting the conversation roll around her until they decided it was time to make a move. Somehow, she and Daniel would need to come clean and reassure the ladies that it had been friendship all along – at least, for Daniel…

'How did your calls go?' Anna closed the door on the departing visitors and walked back to where Lauren had begun to clear the table. 'Leave that. Go and sit down.'

Doing as she was bid, Lauren picked up a magazine and lowered herself onto the sofa. 'Okay. There's insurance forms to complete. All a bit of a faff, but can't be helped.'

At least the kerfuffle had taken her mind off the pain of leaving The Lookout. Lauren stared morosely at the unopened glossy, conscious Anna was approaching.

'Hey.'

Lauren looked up to meet her friend's contemplative gaze.

'Daniel's not indifferent to you. Anyone can see that.'

She sighed. 'It was a pretence, Anna.'

'Watch out for your invite to the BAFTAs, then. *Both* of you.' Her friend chuckled as Lauren rolled her eyes, then Anna's phone pinged, and she grabbed it from the table. 'Email notification. Oh!'

A hand shot to Anna's throat, and Lauren eased herself forward to the edge of her seat, concerned. 'What is it? You've gone white.'

Easy tears filled Anna's eyes, and Lauren pushed herself to her feet and went over to place a protective arm around her friend.

'Look,' Anna's voice wobbled. 'It's from Ali— Matthew. My brother.' The last word was barely audible as she thrust the phone at Lauren, a tear sliding down each cheek.

Lauren scanned the message, then smiled at Anna. 'It's what you wanted. He can't wait to meet you! Go on, call him.' She persuaded her out of the chair and wiping her face with her hand, Anna took the phone and headed for the hallway.

Delighted at the outcome of Anna's long wait for family, Lauren wrapped her arms around her bump and walked over to stare out to sea, wondering how the call was going. She didn't have long to wait, as Anna soon returned, her skin now flushed with excitement, eyes shining.

'I can't believe I spoke to him! He wants to meet on Sunday. He's in Hampshire, suggested meeting halfway between us.' Anna's face fell. 'I've got breakfasts to do, and—'

'I'll take care of your guests, and Nicki will help me with the beds and so on. Go and tell Oliver, get it sorted.'

With a tremulous smile, Anna hugged Lauren, then fled from the room, the phone grasped in her hand, but within moments of the boot room door closing behind her, it was thrust open with a bang, and a white-faced Daniel burst into the room.

Lauren grasped the back of Oliver's armchair as he let out an expletive, then stormed across the room and gripped her by the shoulders.

'I've been going out of my mind! Why aren't you answering your bloody phone? Anna's was engaged. The car—' His voice was hoarse with emotion. 'I saw what's left of the Mini on Sam's low loader. I thought...' He stopped and swallowed visibly. 'I had visions of the worst.'

Lauren supposed his reaction could be understood. They had, after all, grown close in recent months.

'I'm sorry,' Lauren sighed. 'It was a silly prang on the front end, and we were safely out of the car before it made the acquaintance of the tractor.'

'I'm supposed to be in Truro this afternoon.' Daniel ran a hand through his hair and took a step back. 'When I saw the Mini, I almost ran into the car in front of me. I tried calling but there was no answer, and Anna's phone was busy, so I hightailed it here.' Daniel drew in a short breath. 'What will you do? How will you drive back to Yorkshire?'

'I'm still sorting things out.' Lauren waved an airy hand. 'I only need a two-day car hire, because then I'll have Kit's car.'

Daniel shoved his hands in his jacket pockets. 'Oh, I see.'

He probably didn't, but Lauren felt weary and sad. She didn't want to leave Daniel, but she had no choice. She'd already been through the pain of leaving his home earlier, and the subsequent incident and its aftermath had been a useful distraction. Seeing him again only reinforced how deep her feelings ran.

'But you've still got to get home. I can rearrange some things, drive you back.'

'You're so sweet, Daniel.' Lauren desperately wanted to step closer to him, but didn't dare. 'But it's a minimum two-day trip there and back, and your attention needs to be on Claudia.'

His expression darkened, and she longed to reach out to him, but Lauren's focus was returning.

'I'll sort something out. You'd better dash if you're off to Truro.'

Daniel held her gaze, seemed about to speak, but the door opened again and Anna came in, Oliver following behind, and with a hasty goodbye, Daniel scooted past them and left.

'What was that all about?' Anna frowned as she joined Lauren in the middle of the room.

'Nothing. He'd just heard about the car, came to check I was okay.'

Anna sent Lauren a knowing look, but as her attention was really on her recent contact with Matthew – or Matt, as he preferred – the subject of Daniel was easily dropped.

–

The weather broke overnight, and Lauren was awoken by thunder overhead and, when she padded over to the window, splashes of lightning flickering over the dark waters like paparazzi flashlights.

It continued to rain all of Saturday, the clouds finally parting on Sunday morning, and Lauren waved Anna and Oliver off and returned to the kitchen, ready to serve breakfast as soon as the guests emerged from their rooms.

Her energy levels were as low as her mood, and she didn't feel up to doing much. Was it going to be like this for the next few weeks? Shutting out any thought of Daniel, The Lookout or Polkerran, Lauren relocated to the study at the back of the house. Here, there was no view, only the driveway, currently bereft of cars, to distract her, and she re-read the email she'd received on Friday afternoon.

It was an offer of a face-to-face interview following on from a video call the previous week, currently scheduled in ten days' time. The company had headquarters in Sheffield and a site in Europe, and although it was a much smaller company than she'd hoped for, the location meant she couldn't afford to pass the chance up.

Time to immerse herself in preparation. Lauren glanced at her watch. Anna and Oliver would be arriving in Shaftesbury any time soon, and she chewed thoughtfully on her lip. She couldn't imagine how her friend was feeling, but she prayed in her heart it would be the answer to her dreams.

A few hours later, Lauren moved her back warily. The chair and desk in the study were definitely more conducive to working than the pine table, but even so, she felt her inactivity.

Her phone rang, and seeing the name, she snatched it up.

'How was it? Anna? You there?'

'Sorry.' Anna's voice was strained. 'I— it was—' She seemed to be struggling to clear her throat. 'Oh, Lauren. It was...' Anna choked on a sob, and Lauren's throat tightened.

'Do you want to talk when you get home?'

'No! No, don't go.' Anna drew in a shuddering breath. 'It was... Lauren, it was amazing. We have the same colouring, the same eyes even. Our mum's, we assume, from the photos.'

Relief flooded through Lauren, and she sank onto the sofa, a hand resting on her bump.

'Are you okay?'

There was silence, then a shuddering breath. 'I can barely speak.' Then, a watery laugh. 'I think we both talked so long, our voices gave up on us. I'm so happy...' Anna began to weep, and then Oliver's voice came on the phone.

'Don't worry about her. She's a sopping mess right now, but a very happy one.'

'Oh my God.' Unable to help it, Lauren's own voice was breaking. 'Tell her I love her, and I can't wait to hear all about it when you're back.'

'Don't you start as well!' She could picture Oliver rolling his eyes, but Lauren shook her head.

'It would take a lot to make me cry, trust me. I'm just so happy for her.'

'So am I.' The love Oliver had for Anna throbbed in his deep voice, and Lauren smiled, despite the emotion of the moment.

The call ended and she sat for a few seconds, holding the phone and stroking her distended belly.

Anna's desire to feel she belonged, to be part of a family, had haunted her. Finding Oliver had been a huge step towards the dream she'd always held, but to have flesh and blood, a brother in her life, would finally make her complete.

Struggling to her feet, Lauren pocketed her phone and walked over to take her coat from the hook by the door. She needed fresh air and exercise. Would Amelia make her own life complete?

Daniel's face swam before her eyes, and she resolutely pushed it away.

'Don't pine for what you can't have, Kirkham.' Lauren spoke firmly, then opened the door. A brisk walk – at least, as brisk as she could manage – would send these pointless longings where they belonged.

It was time to apply herself to life after the baby's birth, and that would be a long way from Polkerran.

Chapter Thirty-Two

Kelp!

Sunday was a late night, with Anna and Oliver arriving back early evening and then dinner to cook and so much to talk about.

Bizarrely, Matt had heard of Polkerran. Apparently, there was a tidal creek up river from the village with an unusual claim to fame, being home to a large house with a recording studio beneath it. So popular had it become – its isolation perfect for creative types – big name bands from the eighties and nineties had flocked there to record some iconic albums.

'Also known as Cannabis Creek,' Oliver intoned dryly as they made their way upstairs around midnight.

Lauren couldn't settle to sleep, despite a hot water bottle and the Gaviscon. The heartburn seemed as permanent as her raised blood pressure lately, and she swung her feet out of bed on Monday morning feeling disgruntled, uncomfortable and far from rested.

The floorboard creaked loudly as she stood, and she sent it a wry look. 'Sorry. Appreciate you're having to put up with a lot more weight from me than when I first moved in.'

Then, shaking her head as she realised she was talking to a piece of wood, Lauren picked up the glass on her bedside table and sipped some water, a hand resting on her aching lower back.

The walk yesterday had done her some good, and she'd managed to sleep during the afternoon. Perhaps that was the answer today? After all, she had a long drive ahead of her tomorrow.

With all the guests checked out and the B&B empty for the next few nights, Oliver persuaded Anna to go for a walk on Bodmin Moor. They'd invited Lauren to join them, assuring her it was a fairly level route, but she knew how much they relished their alone time, especially with Oliver about to head to Dubai soon, where he needed to sort out some matters relating to his father's residence there.

After they'd gone, taking Dougal with them, Lauren called her mum to reassure her she was fine, that she'd break the journey if she became too tired to continue, then looked out the window to check on the weather.

The weekend's storm had long passed over, and blue skies reigned above Polkerran, dotted with a few powder-puff clouds batted along by a strong breeze.

Lauren huffed and puffed as she tried to don her walking boots, bending to tie the laces was beyond her, so she settled for a pair of slip-on Skechers.

'We just have to get through the next few weeks, sweetie,' she whispered as she headed along the cliff path, deliberately keeping her gaze averted from the chimney of The Lookout, currently the only visible part of the house now the trees were in such full leaf, before coming to the steps down to her favourite beach.

Lauren hesitated, wondering if it was sensible to go down. Her promise to Daniel had only been about running, not a sensible descent, and she had time to kill, the tide was out and the sea air would hopefully do its work and help her grab a few hours' sleep on her return to the house.

Carefully making her way down the steps, Lauren grasped the handrail with determination, her mind busy as her heart lay heavy in her breast.

'It's a good job we're getting away soon, little one,' she muttered as she dodged some wet seaweed on the bottom steps and picked her way across the sand, avoiding the area where she and Daniel had previously sat. 'Away from here, away from *him*.'

This job would be the answer, of course, if she could secure it. Kit's offer of the flat was a lifeline and it had three bedrooms, which meant her mum could come and stay for a while. Mrs Kirkham had been through this four times and wouldn't be daunted by the baby's frailties, its tiny fingers, trying to interpret what each cry meant. And Lauren would learn more quickly with her mum's guidance.

Lauren had reached the shoreline now. The tide was out, the waves rolling and dipping in the distance, only ripples of shallow water rolling across the wet sand towards her feet. She watched them, mesmerised for a moment, concentrating on breathing evenly after the brisk walk. Her back was niggling again; she'd best not linger too long.

About Daniel, she strove not to think. Her mind could not be allowed to go there. A seagull's lone call high above her drew Lauren's attention, and she watched as it wheeled against the sky before disappearing over the clifftop.

Lauren glanced at her watch, trying to keep the hair from her eyes, but the wind was persistent. Her gaze drifted back out to sea, but memories of Daniel were impossible to avoid on this beach and, throat tight with unspoken words, head a whirlwind of unformed thoughts, Lauren began to retrace her steps.

She kept her eyes on her Skechers as they made dents in the firmer sand, pausing when she reached the bottom step to take her back up the cliff. It looked a long way up all of a sudden. Perhaps she shouldn't have come.

'But I had to…' she whispered softly, the words whipped from her lips as soon as they formed.

She looked over her shoulder, taking in the sweep of beach visible only at low tide, the outcrop of rocks where she and Daniel had sat on the day she'd realised she was beginning to have feelings for him. They would disappear beneath the incoming tide in a few hours, as though they no longer existed.

'Goodbye,' she whispered, her voice hitching in her throat.

Lauren grasped the handrail and took the first step, then the second, but her heel landed on some seaweed and she lost her footing, tumbling back onto the sand with a shriek, accompanied by a small splash.

Struggling for breath, Lauren lay where she'd fallen for a moment. A sharp pain had lanced her side, and she rolled away, glaring at the small protruding rock, feeling the dampness seeping through her trousers from the wet sand after the recent storm.

'Okay, not your best move.' Lauren lay on the sand on her back, staring at the blue sky. A few more gulls had appeared, soaring in an arc against the heavens. The sounds of the sea felt distant, as though she was in a dreamlike place, but then a pain gripped her entire middle and she yelped, grasping her belly. A jolt of fear swept through her for her unborn baby. She drew in a steadying breath; this was no time for hysterics.

'Right, we need to get out of here, sweetie.'

With a bit of rocking, Lauren managed to sit upright, thankful the pain had receded into a dull ache. She'd probably bruised herself, but she'd call Pauline as soon as she got to the top of the steps and see if she could check her over.

'Yow!' To Lauren's dismay, she couldn't put her left foot down. 'Damn it.'

Had she broken it? Tentatively, she tried to place it on the floor but the pain was excruciating, and she hovered on one leg, wondering how long her balance would last.

With a determined hop or two, she managed to reach the bottom of the steps again, which at least gave her something to hold onto, but she looked up at their steepness and knew there was no way she could risk hopping her way up them. If she fell from even higher, the baby would be in danger.

She eyed the lower steps, then lowered herself gingerly onto the second one, trying to keep her left foot from touching anything and wincing when it did. Digging in her pocket, she frowned. She could have sworn her phone was in the right hand one. She tucked her hand into the left, but no phone.

It didn't take long to locate it. There was a small rock pool at the foot of the steps, and lying in its watery depths was Lauren's phone.

Muttering an expletive, she struggled onto her one steady foot again and hopped over but she couldn't bend in the middle to reach it. 'If I'd needed a workout, I'd have gone to the gym.'

Lowering herself as carefully as she could, but unable to avoid her stricken foot touching the ground, which brought with it a wave of nausea, Lauren dipped her hand into the water and retrieved her sodden phone. She gave it a perfunctory shake, then rubbed it against her coat, sending up a silent prayer as she touched the screen.

Nothing.

For a moment, she simply stared at it, trying to ignore the dull ache around her middle.

One thing at a time, okay. Let's get some help.

She rubbed the phone between her hands, gave it another shake, trying not to notice the drops of water still seeping from its casing. Then, she tried the screen again. Nothing.

'Damn it!' She thrust it into her pocket, then repeated her awkward manoeuvre to get to her one solid foot, banging the other on the floor again and yelping with pain.

The dull ache in her back was intensifying again, and spurred Lauren on. She couldn't call for help. No one knew she was here, if anyone tried her phone, they'd assume she'd switched it off to nap.

'It's just you and me, Mia. I have to get us out of this; I have to help *you*.' The pain was becoming more apparent, but Lauren knew if she let her fear take hold, she'd never be able to do what she had to.

Going very slowly, and thankful the tide remained well out, she hopped back to the relative safety of the handrail.

'One step at a time,' she intoned, suppressing a laugh at the reality. 'One step— ouch, at a time.'

Holding onto the handrail with all her might, refusing to look down or back, Lauren made her way up the stone steps with excruciating slowness, managing to avoid banging her painful foot too often. She paused now and again to regain her breath, striving to ignore for now the persistent pulsing of pain in her lower back. The baby had to be okay; she just had to be.

Chapter Thirty-Three

Life Boy

'Be thankful,' gasped Lauren as she neared the top of the steps. 'Be thankful it's not getting dark, or raining. And those bloody gulls,' she threw them a baleful look, 'haven't dropped a load on your head. They've clearly got you earmarked as a potential target.'

The sheer relief of reaching the clifftop threatened to overwhelm her, and she collapsed onto the grassy verge, her eyes tight with unshed tears, her hands clutching her belly. There was nothing for her to hold onto along the path back towards civilisation. If only there was a long stick to hand, but there were no trees on the clifftop to oblige with a discarded branch.

Bending forward seemed to ease the ache a little, but bending of itself was a challenge. At least her foot didn't throb so much – unless it was the distraction of her back pain…

Lauren closed her eyes, waiting for the pain to recede, then drew in several shallow breaths.

Suddenly, she heard a voice – a child, and her eyes flew open. A young boy in a bright red anorak had stopped some distance away, staring at her. She supposed she was quite a sight.

Lauren raised a hand. 'Hey there. Can you help me?'

The little boy turned and ran, and Lauren sighed resignedly. At least this was the South West Coast Path. Surely there'd be some walkers along sooner or later? And the boy had been too young to be out alone…

Weary now, Lauren closed her eyes again, almost insensible to the discomfort of her position slumped on the verge. Her legs were shaking and felt strangely hot around her groin. The throbbing from her foot seemed to have receded now she wasn't active, but the aches around her middle weren't going away. Getting to a phone and speaking to Pauline was a priority.

'What the hell… Lauren!'

The relief of hearing a voice would have been sufficient to fill Lauren with emotion, but she knew it was Daniel before she raised her weary lids.

Her breath hitched in her throat as he reached her, and Daniel wrapped his arms around her, and she let him cradle her for a moment, savouring the feel of his body next to hers.

Involuntarily she let out a hiss of breath as the sharp pain lanced her side, much as it had done when she fell, and he released her, sitting back on his haunches.

'What happened? Why are you sitting here?'

'I needed a rest.' She waved a hand towards the steps. 'I went for a walk and—'

Daniel's face, which had seemed pale when he reached her, turned to stone. Then, he got to his feet, glaring at her.

'You went down to the beach, on your own, in your condition? Are you *mad*? You could have fallen.'

Lauren had never seen Daniel angry, and she wasn't sure she liked it.

'I'm pregnant, that's all. I'm perfectly able to make my own decisions, and if I want to walk somewhere, I will.'

It sounded all very well, but her breath hitched in her throat at the pain, and the futility of her argument was plain to see.

'What's wrong with your foot?'

'Nothing. I banged it, that's all.'

'Then why is it the size of melon?'

It was?

Lauren looked down at her throbbing foot. He was right, the ankle was horribly swollen – probably from her exertions in scaling the steps, and now that he'd drawn her attention to it, the Skecher had become extremely tight, which probably meant her foot was swelling up too.

'How did you bang it?' Daniel had returned to examine her ankle, crouching down beside her, and she brushed a hand across her eyes. This was ridiculous. Lauren didn't cry.

'Lauren?' He raised his eyes to meet hers, but there was no denying the firmness in his tone or his gaze.

'I fell. Only a little,' she hastened to add. 'I had only just started up the steps, and I landed awkwardly. My phone fell in some water, I couldn't call anyone, so I had to get back up.'

'You're cold and incredibly pale.' Daniel placed the back of his hand against her damp cheek. 'We need to get you to the hospital. Are you in pain, other than this foot?'

The relief of having someone there making decisions, taking care of her, was too much. Lauren nodded, but then her face fell.

'I'm scared, Daniel. What if the baby's hurt? I'm in pain.'

His gaze narrowed and he put an arm around her. 'Not just the foot?'

She shook her head, unable to say more as a wave of pain shook her.

Daniel fished his phone out of his pocket. She vaguely heard him speaking to someone as she breathed through the pain.

'I have to leave you for a few minutes, okay?'

'What? You can't leave me here!'

'I'm not, but I can't carry you all the way back to the house from here.' His lips twitched. 'I could try, but you do realise they make it look easy in films and take several shots?' His features softened and he took her hand in both of hers. 'I've called an ambulance; it will meet us at The Lookout. I daren't try carrying you in case I trip or I drop you, which would make things even worse. I'll be back in a few minutes.'

Before she could respond, he was off, back down the cliff path at a sprint, and Lauren dug into her pocket for a tissue and attempted to clean up her face. No doubt her mascara was becoming closely acquainted with her lipstick.

At least the ache in her heart was getting close competition from everywhere else in her body today. Lauren's hand went protectively to her belly.

'I'm so sorry, Mia. We'll get you some help, and then I'll rest.' She eyed her swollen foot warily.

A low rumbling noise drew her attention, and she stared down the cliff path, trying to breathe through a new wave of pain as her gaze narrowed on the sight before her.

'Here we go.' Daniel fetched up in front of her.

'I'm not getting in that.'

Lauren stared at Daniel's trusty wheelbarrow.

'You are. Look, I've lined it nicely with a blanket. You won't get dirty.'

'Daniel, I'm sitting on a muddy cliff path. I don't think it's the time to worry about soiling my clothes. I'm concerned about the buffeting of the baby.'

'Well, we need to get you to the house. It's that or sit it out and wait for the paramedics to get you on a stretcher.'

'Fine.'

With Daniel's assistance, Lauren managed to move herself to rest against the up-ended wheelbarrow.

'Now hold on and don't shriek. You'll frighten the birds.'

Lauren closed her eyes, gripping the sides of the wheelbarrow as Daniel slowly raised the handles so that she was lying back in it. Please, Lord, don't let the glamourous Claudia see me like this!

'This has to be the most inglorious way to travel. Ouch!'

'Sorry. I'm trying to avoid the bumps as best I can.'

It was a slow ride back to the house, but Lauren was so thankful, she didn't care. Daniel eased her from it when they reached The Lookout and let her lean on his arm as she hopped to the porch, where he lowered her onto the seat and went to fetch some water for her.

Barely had she taken a few sips, however, when the ambulance appeared, and within minutes she was on the way to the nearest hospital, thankful for the comfort of medical support and trying not to think about Daniel's despondent countenance when she'd said there was no need for him to come with her.

-

It turned out Lauren's damp trousers had nothing to do with the previous weekend's weather and more to do with the fact her waters had broken.

'You're in the early stages of labour, my lovely.' The young medic, who had assessed Lauren on her arrival at hospital, had a warm, West Country burr to her voice, and she gave Lauren a reassuring pat on the arm.

'But I'm not due for a few weeks yet.'

'Sometimes, babies decide they want to arrive earlier. We're moving you to the neonatal unit, but first we need to strap up y'on foot. The midwife will be along just now, and she'll assess where your progress is to.'

'What about Pauline?' Lauren gasped as a wave of pain came. 'She's my community midwife.'

'We'll let her know. She'll come to see you afterwards to arrange post-natal care.'

The relief, after a quick scan and check of the baby's heartbeat, was immense, but Lauren was grappling with the fact that the moment she'd both dreaded and dreamed of was upon her. There would be no more weeks when it would be just herself to think about. There was no time to get her mum down, or sort the job interview; no time to pack up and leave.

Amelia had decided to be born in Cornwall. Her child would forever be connected to Polkerran Point, wherever Lauren decided to settle.

Somehow, this comforted Lauren, but as the pain was coming in fairly regular waves now, it was no difficulty to push these thoughts aside and become consumed by the here and now. A kindly maternity care assistant contacted Anna on Lauren's behalf to explain the situation and her lack of phone, passing on the request to also let her mum know. As the lady made the call, Lauren was contrarily consumed by a desperate desire for Daniel's calming presence, but before she could make such a foolish request, a wave of pain swept the temptation aside.

Several hours later, drained but elated, Lauren stared down at the tiny face poking out of the muslin wrap. Amelia was here.

Her beautiful daughter had arrived and Lauren was awash with love and full of gratitude for being so blessed.

–

There was a woodpecker in the tree outside Lauren's window. She could hear it tapping the wood, then pausing to speak.

'Hey.'

Lauren's eyes snapped open, then squinted against the bright overhead light in her hospital room.

'Sorry. Were you sleeping?'

She turned her head on the pillow, then beamed at Daniel, hesitating on the threshold.

'Is it okay? For me to come in, I mean?'

'Yes. Please do. I'm sorry about earlier. I wasn't thinking very straight by the time the ambulance came. It seemed wrong to have you come to the hospital. I mean, we're not…' Words failed her.

Daniel shook his head, then produced the hand he had behind his back. 'I got you these.'

'They're beautiful.' Lauren loved roses. 'Would you like to meet my little gift?'

Placing the flowers on a side table, Daniel edged nearer to the bed, his gaze fixed on the mobile cot on Lauren's other side.

'How are you? Is she… okay?' The concern on his face was endearing.

'You can take a peek.'

Lauren bit her lip as Daniel tiptoed round the end of the bed and neared the cot, clearly trying not to make a sound.

He leaned over the bundle of white wrapping.

'Is she asleep? I don't want to disturb her,' he whispered.

'Just pull the cover back a bit.'

Gingerly, he leaned forward and did so, then leaped back with an exclamation. Lauren found it impossible not to laugh at his resigned expression.

'Sorry.' She couldn't stop giggling. 'Couldn't resist.'

Daniel reached into the cot and pulled out Mrs Lovelace's knitted creature, Twiddler. 'Gave me the shock of my life.'

'Amelia's in an incubator as she's a bit early. She's a good weight for thirty-six weeks, though, and they don't think she'll need extra help for long. The cot was in here when Anna dropped off my stuff – she put Twiddler in for a laugh. Sorry.' She tried to ignore the tremble within her insides as Daniel ran a hand through his hair in an adorably familiar way.

He dropped into the chair by the bed. 'Bloody hell, Lauren. My heart's still pounding!'

So's mine, but probably not for the same reason.

'I'm sorry, honestly.' She longed to reach out and hold his hand, but it wasn't right to be sitting in a bed wearing nothing but a hospital gown, which was far from decent and having *in*decent thoughts about the gorgeous man who was no longer single. Damn it.

Lauren hitched the shoulder of her gown up a bit and ran a hand through her own dishevelled hair.

'I need a shower, but I can't stand easily and the staff are lovely but crazy busy. Until then, I have to live in this.' She swept a hand in the air to indicate her attire. 'Geometric and salmon were never my style choice.'

'You'd look stunning in anything.'

Lauren bit her lip as colour (not remotely salmon-tinted) flooded Daniel's cheeks.

'Sorry. Inappropriate.'

'No, it's nice. Truly.' She smiled, leaning forward to grasp the hand she'd been eyeing. 'It's also nice to be able to bend a little after all these months.'

She gave his hand a quick squeeze and released it just as the door opened and a nursing assistant returned with a wheelchair. Relieved at the interruption, Lauren beamed at Daniel.

'Time for proper introductions, I think. Can you push me? The staff are rushed off their feet.'

Chapter Thirty-Four

Boy Banned

The baby's unanticipated arrival meant Lauren's time in Cornwall would be extended, especially as she wanted to stay under Pauline's care and guidance.

Ameila remained in hospital for a week, but made such good progress, Lauren was able to take her back to Polkerran on the day the filming had been due to commence up at The Lookout.

As it happened, a severe thunderstorm the night before, knocked out a lot of the power locally, and the glowering skies and wet conditions continued into the week. Anna relayed the news that the production team were going to have to postpone until the end of the month, down to the crew being booked into other commitments in the interim.

Lauren barely had time to reflect on how frustrated Daniel must feel. He'd wanted to draw a line under the filming experience and obviously he'd want it out the way so that Claudia no longer saw it as taking attention from her.

As it was, the initial weeks after Amelia's birth were all-consuming. Lauren's fear on first leaving hospital with her precious bundle was intense, despite her mum arriving to spend the week with her. Even with Anna also on hand, it had dawned on Lauren that she alone was responsible for the safety and well-being of her baby.

Much as she missed Daniel, Lauren welcomed the distraction Amelia brought, and being at Westerleigh with Anna and her mum on hand was a godsend. To be fair, Daniel didn't seem to be around much, spending a lot of time – according to the rumour mill – in London and, Lauren supposed, Bristol. There was certainly no sign of him or Claudia in the cove, and though she missed seeing his face so much it physically hurt, Lauren felt relief there was no chance of coming across them.

Daniel had sent a couple of WhatsApps, just saying he hoped everything was going okay, but Lauren hadn't responded. In Claudia's eyes, she was the ex, and it just didn't feel right to be messaging someone else's boyfriend.

Linda took the news Lauren was no longer with Daniel badly until her daughter went on to explain the truth and why she'd let her assume more than there was. Linda had accepted it, appreciating the intention and admitting it had served its purpose, and even fell to teasing her daughter about them having to get in the same bed.

A similar, but less intimate conversation had taken place with the ladies around Anna's table as, with her friend and her mum's support, Lauren explained that she and Daniel had always been telling the truth when they said they were just friends. As it was widely known that he and Claudia were an item again, and Lauren was so genuinely insistent, they'd finally accepted the truth of the matter and all said how happy they were that no one was suffering any hurt feelings.

Anna had squeezed her friend's shoulder as she went to boil the kettle again, and Lauren had choked back the lump rising in her throat at finally putting to bed any hint of there being something between her and Daniel. It was nothing more than the stuff of Cornish legend.

A further unwelcome anxiety was how much Lauren struggled to feed the baby herself. She felt a failure, but with Pauline's help, she weaned Amelia onto bottle feeding and took on board the midwife's reassurances about breastfeeding not being for everyone.

Satisfied Lauren was coping and in good hands – and with her holiday allowance used up – her mum returned home after a week, intent on ensuring everything was ready for the baby's arrival in Yorkshire, although Lauren assured her that she'd be moving into Kit's flat as soon as she felt confident to do so.

There were moments when she was filled with trepidation, unsure how she'd ever be able to leave Amelia behind to spend a day in an office. How she would focus on work when her daughter wasn't just in the next room, she couldn't imagine.

Oliver was engrossed in dealing with a legal firm over probate for his father's estate and generally putting his matters in order, which meant returning to Dubai – the illness being so sudden, Mr Seymour Senior had pretty much upped and left on diagnosis. Anna had blocked out the guest rooms so that only existing bookings stood, meaning most of the time it was just the two friends and the tiny baby – a good thing, Lauren reflected to Anna as Amelia reached four weeks of age, and her original due date – for her daughter had a powerful pair of lungs on her and was particularly fond of expressing her thoughts with them in the middle of the night.

Anna's theory was that she was her mother's daughter, and that Lauren's late-night lifestyle had caught up on her.

She still hadn't seen Daniel since the hospital, but Anna had heard from him. Claudia had suggested they go away until the rearranged filming could take place. Her friend's theory was that Claudia felt Daniel owed her some one-on-one attention. Lauren's was that Claudia wanted to ensure she had a good tan for when the cameras came back.

Resolutely clamping down on her feelings, and shying away from thinking about the pair enjoying themselves on a beach somewhere, Lauren buried herself in preparations for the move back to Yorkshire, grateful to Kit for his offer of a home. With the Mini out of action, she appreciated his car too, and he also offered to come down to collect them, saying he could fit it in in late September, before his relocation to New Jersey in early October.

–

Lauren approached the village hall with a surprising level of trepidation. How was it she'd walked into boardrooms, conferences and introduced herself to many a stranger in the past, yet the prospect of her first Mums and Babies group filled her with trepidation?

She dropped a kiss on Amelia's head as she reached the door. There was an assortment of buggies and pushchairs to the left of the door, along with a small scooter.

'Goodness, Mia, there must be some very advanced babies in there. Don't let them intimidate you.'

Two hours later, Amelia securely fastened into her carrier, Lauren walked briskly down the lane towards the centre of Polkerran. With a small smile, she accepted it had been a far less intimidating ordeal than her first presentation or leading her own initial team meeting.

Her gaze took in the harbour as she reached the water-front before moving across to rest on Westerleigh. Unable to help herself, Lauren's focus drifted up above the treeline beyond the cottage, where the rooftops of The Lookout could be seen poking through the treetops.

Daniel had spoken to Anna on the phone, saying the film crew were due to return at the end of the following week, and she'd told him Lauren was leaving soon after. To Lauren, it felt like a line drawn under the whole experience. She'd come to Polkerran Point to escape for a while, to figure out what her unknown future ought to be. Who would've thought, six months on, she'd be viewing another new life full of uncertainties, that her escape had brought not just new life but a completely unanticipated heartbreak?

–

In between feeds and changes, whenever Ameila chose to sleep, Lauren worked feverishly to complete the project for the Devere Corporation and finally received what she'd hoped would come of it: a job offer based in their Leeds operation, which meant she could knock the interview with the other company on the head.

It was a great role, not a directorship, but senior management and with huge potential for the future. She would be able to resume her old way of life... up to a point.

'Hey, Lauren.'

Thankful for the interruption as Anna came in from the boot room, Lauren pointed to the kettle. 'Want one?'

'Where's Mia?' Anna whispered as she joined Lauren.

'Snoozing.' She pulled a face. 'I swear some days she sleeps more than Heathcliff.'

Anna grinned. 'Make the most of it. Don't you remember Nicki's advice? It isn't going to last forever.'

They both spoke more softly than normal. 'How was the Mums and Babies group?'

'I'm not really sure. I mean, it was better than I expected on one level, but on another, it was *everything* I expected.'

'Will you go again?'

Lauren hesitated. 'Not sure. I lost my identity on the way in. No Lauren, I just became Mia's mum.' She blew out a breath. 'Suppose I ought to keep going for her sake.'

There was a snort of laughter from her friend. 'She's less than a month old, mate. What do you think she's getting from it? First date with a playmate? Dinner plans?' Anna's smile softened. 'It's for the mums so they can share experiences, get advice and be reassured anything they're feeling or thinking is perfectly normal.'

Her mind instinctively fleeing to thoughts of Daniel, Lauren shook her head. 'I'm not so sure about that.' Then, she pulled herself together. 'I have some news. The Devere job is mine, Leeds based too. They've been incredibly accommodating, pushing the start date back so I can take some maternity leave.'

'That's fantastic. And we can celebrate with wine now!'

Lauren smiled, but somehow it didn't reach her eyes and Anna was quick to notice.

'I can't believe you're leaving soon.'

'I have to. I need time to establish a routine for Mia in our new home, and once I start the job, I'll have to be in the office three days a week. Mum's part time now, so she's going to come to the flat to be there for the baby when I'm at work.'

'Do you have any idea how flat your voice is?'

Lauren walked over to stare out of the window, taking in the stunning view she had grown to love. The idea of leaving was tearing her apart, but she could hardly commute from Cornwall and besides, there was Daniel…

A gentle hand was laid on her shoulder, and Lauren turned to face Anna.

'Daniel and Claudia are no doubt making sweet music together. Much as I love you, there's nothing for me here.'

'They're sure to be back soon. The new filming dates are next week.' Anna glanced out of the window at the threatening skies. 'Though the weather might scupper the outdoor stuff again.'

Anna leaned against the island as Lauren made the tea.

'I've got news, too. I had an email from Ali— Matt. He's got some time free and wants to see where I live, so he's coming over for a few days.'

'He shall forever be known as Ali-Matt. I'm so pleased for you, Anna.' Lauren walked over to hug her friend, then laughed. 'Couldn't have done that a few weeks ago.'

They both glanced at her much reduced midriff.

'I don't know how I would have coped without you here, Lauren.'

'Ditto, love. Although you do have Oliver.'

'I know, but he's been away so much, and he only has two ears. Sometimes I think I bend them backwards.'

The next few days sped by, and Lauren kept herself busy. She'd resumed her running at times when Anna could watch Amelia. She also liaised with HR at the Devere Corporation over a start date, and spent time on video chatting to her mum, with the baby on her lap and sometimes at Anna's table, listening to the locals doing their usual.

They'd all been so kind to her, but she still didn't know if they believed she and Daniel had been just friends. Still, they'd put the truth out there, and there wasn't much else she could do.

–

When Lauren arrived back at Westerleigh the following afternoon, after a walk with Mia, Oliver was just on his way out.

'Anna's on the terrace.' Oliver peered at Mia. 'I could take her with me to the library. They have a no talking rule, so she should be fine for a few months.'

Lauren laughed. 'Unfortunately, she has other ways of breaching their preference for silence.' She inclined her head towards the terrace. 'How is she?'

His gaze narrowing, Oliver opened the car door. 'You mean, how's the brother?'

'Obviously! All Anna's text said was "wait and see".'

Oliver shrugged. 'Jury's still out for me.'

With a frown, Lauren watched Oliver reverse the car through the gates before walking over to close them. What did he mean?

'Now be on your best behaviour, Mia.' Lauren stepped briskly onto the terrace, a smile pinned to her face.

Anna saw her immediately and waved, and the man sitting with his back to her got to his feet and turned around. He was tall and lean, with hair much like Anna's – brown and thick in texture, worn a little longer than the current fashion. He wore distressed jeans and a tightly fitting white T-shirt. A leather jacket hung on the back of his chair.

'Lauren, come and meet my brother.' Anna smiled at the man. 'Matt, this is my best mate, Lauren. We go back a long way.'

'Unlike me and Anna.' The man had a rich voice, well-modulated, and at closer range was extremely eye-catching with sparkling hazel eyes. He held out his hand to shake Lauren's.

'Pleased to meet you.' Lauren unfastened the carrier and lifted the baby out. 'This is Mia. She has a very limited acquaintance so far.'

'I'm honoured.'

'There's something familiar about you.' Lauren settled on a seat opposite the two siblings, Amelia in her arms. Then, she laughed. 'I suppose it's the family likeness.'

Matt looked amused. 'I still get recognised a lot, to be honest.'

Curious, Lauren looked to Anna for clarification.

'Matt used to be in a band. Do you remember Border-Line Beat?'

With a gasp, Lauren surveyed the man again. 'Remember? Oh my, I had a massive crush on your lead singer back in the day.'

Matt pulled a face then grinned. 'Occupational hazard. No-one really noticed the rest of us.'

With a smile, Lauren dropped a kiss on the blonde fuzz coating Amelia's little head. That wasn't entirely true. From what she recalled, Matt Locksley had been the real heartthrob in the young pop band – until they split and disappeared who knew where.

'Ready for some lunch, Lauren? Oliver won't be back until dinner.'

'Absolutely, it'll give me chance to grill Matt about life in a band in the late Noughties.'

Chapter Thirty-Five

The Pipes, the Pipes are Calling

The weekend flew by, with Anna intent on taking Matt to as many of her favourite haunts as possible, and Lauren – in between caring for Amelia – busy working on her final project, which she was keen to complete before the upheaval of the move.

Lauren had seen the TV vans crawling along the lane on the Monday, when walking back from the ferry with the buggy, but on Tuesday, it poured with rain which looked well set in. Had they managed to get the necessary shots before the weather broke?

Realising it was no longer anything to do with her, Lauren tried not to think about it, and she was suitably distracted that evening when a message popped in from Kit.

> Slight hitch. Can you be ready to leave this Friday? Can get to you Thursday night, but have to fly out on Monday now.

What difference did it make? In some ways, Lauren couldn't wait to escape.

I'll be ready. Will get Anna to reserve a
room for you.

The next day passed in a myriad of packing, seeing to
Amelia's needs and spending time with Anna, who had
reluctantly said goodbye to Matt after the weekend, but
was looking forward to visiting him when autumn fully
kicked in and B&B bookings were slower.

Lauren tried, but generally failed, to put any reflections
on Daniel aside, but being in Polkerran wasn't conducive
to relegating him to the past. He was too close now he
was back at The Lookout.

She avoided the beach where they'd had so many
conversations, and skirted past the Lugger where they'd
enjoyed so many fake date nights and exchanged their
only, very chaste, kiss, as though it were shrouded in sea
fog.

After yet another disturbed night, not entirely down to
a newborn baby, Lauren awoke to a myriad of feelings on
the day of her departure from Cornwall.

Rolling onto her side, she could see her sleeping
daughter – so adorable when it wasn't three a.m., her
face red from screaming – and, heavy-eyed, Lauren's lids
closed on the sight. At five weeks old, the little mite had
no idea she was about to have her first move from one
end of the country to another. How many others might
she experience in her life, if Lauren pursued the career she
dreamed of?

'Come on, Kirkham. Rise and shine.' Lauren spoke
softly, opening her eyes again. Time to get on with the
next phase of her life. Noticing the time, she stretched,
longing for the freedom to go for a morning run.

She managed a quick shower, an ear stretched in case of any sound from the cot, and by the time she'd dressed and sent a quick message to Anna, Mia was stirring.

When Lauren entered the kitchen, a half hour later, Anna was busy and she could see Kit out on the terrace tucking into his breakfast.

Anna indicated a plate on the island bearing a bacon bap before holding out her arms to take the baby.

'Can Auntie Anna have a cuddle?'

'Always, but let me eat this first. Don't want to dribble sauce on you.'

Anna rolled her eyes, relieving Lauren of Amelia in exchange for the plate. 'Your mummy thinks she's *so* funny.' She nuzzled the baby's neck. 'Does Mia have any idea how gorgeous she smells?'

Lauren paused with the bap to her mouth. 'Her fragrance wasn't quite so fine ten minutes ago.'

Walking away, cradling the baby against her shoulder, Anna made soothing noises, and Lauren stepped outside to join Kit at the stone table.

'Sorry if the noise kept you awake.'

Kit took a sip of juice, pointing to his earphones on the table. 'Didn't hear a thing.' He eyed Lauren uneasily. 'Looks like you were the one who suffered.'

'Rude.' Lauren smirked. 'Is that your way of saying I look like shit?'

Returning his attention to his breakfast, Kit shook his head. 'You're paler than usual, that's all. And your eyes are tired.'

'Not likely to change any time soon,' Lauren mused, then took a bite of her bap, chewing thoughtfully. 'I can't believe I still love brown sauce. Hated it before I got pregnant and assumed I'd revert to type after Mia was born.'

'I hate to say it, but standing on the outside looking in, I don't think it's the only thing you won't be able to revert to type on.'

What could one say to that? Never a truer word...

Wiping her fingers on her jeans, Lauren picked up a glass but Kit took it from her to top it up with juice.

'Thanks.' She took a sip, then cast a glance over her shoulder into the house. Anna stood by the far window, gently rocking Amelia to and fro. 'You didn't say much last night. What was it like, meeting your child for the first time? I'm not judging you,' Lauren added earnestly. 'I'm genuinely interested.'

Kit placed his knife and fork together on the plate, leaning back in his seat.

'Don't hate me, Lauren, but I didn't feel anything. She's a baby. Like all babies. Small, needy, cute... possibly. I'd still rather have a kitten.'

He turned in his seat to face her, and Lauren swallowed the morsel of bacon she'd just popped into her mouth as he took her hands in his.

'I love you. I'm haunted by the "what ifs". What we could have been together.'

Lauren tugged at her hands, but he didn't let go.

'You never said those words before.' Was she moved by it? Possibly. Did it alter anything? No.

'Nor did you.'

Because I never loved you. And I only realised that when I fell in love properly with another. Truly, madly, deeply, to quote the film.

'Listen, Lauren.' Kit rose to his feet, perforce, taking her with him.

She hoped she hadn't got crumbs round her mouth. Would it be cruel if she told Kit she'd rather listen to the gulls calling than what he had to say?

'I won't let Amelia go short of things. I'll support her financially whenever she needs it, I just can't be part of her life.' He let out a short breath. 'Makes me sound a right dick said out loud.'

Lauren huffed on a laugh. 'You are. But I get it. Parenthood isn't for everyone, and perhaps if more people owned it, there'd be less unhappy kids in the world. Besides,' she sent a fond look towards the house, though Anna and Mia were no longer visible, and she could detect voices, 'I've got more than enough love for Mia. She won't go short.'

'Come here.' Kit pulled Lauren towards him, and she stepped into the once familiar embrace, resting her head on his chest. The magic was gone. This wasn't the man for her, or the father Amelia needed. Kit wasn't a bad man, he just wasn't made to be a parent.

'I'll have to add you to my list of brothers,' she said into Kit's chest, and it rumbled as he laughed.

'I suspect they'd consider me the black sheep of the family.'

'Probably.'

Kit released his hold on her, but took her hands in his again, leaning down to place a firm kiss on her cheek. Then, he placed a hand on her face. 'So, I can still say I love you?'

Smiling, she placed a hand over his. 'And I love you, Kit, as a— oh!' Lauren's heart lurched in her breast. Daniel stood by the corner of the house.

'Hi.' Why couldn't she breathe? 'How— how are you? How did the filming go? I didn't realise you were here.'

Daniel's expression was non-committal. He and Kit exchanged nods, but then he addressed Lauren.

'Popped over to see Oliver about a few things. Sorry.' He gestured towards them, and Lauren realised she and Kit were still holding hands. 'Didn't mean to interrupt.'

Dropping Kit's hands, she shoved her own into her cardigan pockets, feeling like a kid caught with a hand in the cookie jar.

'You got time for a coffee?'

Daniel shook his head. 'Got to dash. The film crew just turned up. They couldn't do the outside shots on Tuesday.' He took a step towards Lauren. 'Anna just told me you're leaving today. I don't understand, it was supposed to be next Monday.'

Lauren's gaze was fixed hungrily on him, taking in every last detail, and Kit threw her a questioning look, then turned to Daniel.

'Need to get back tonight, I'm afraid.'

'Long journey for a baby.' Daniel's brow creased. 'Can't you break it?'

'We're calling on mutual friends in the Cotswolds this afternoon.' Kit smiled at Daniel. 'And making frequent use of service stations, I suspect.'

'I'll come and say goodbye.' Lauren's throat was tight with unspoken words.

Daniel said nothing for a moment. Then, he turned on his heel. 'Great. See you later.' He disappeared from sight, and Lauren sank into a chair, fighting a strange sensation around her eyes.

'You've made some good friends. You'll miss them.'

'Yes,' Lauren said softly, as her gaze took in Polkerran harbour, the run of colour-washed cottages and tree-clad hillsides to Harbourwatch, then the beach below and the rocks pointing out to sea, marked by the lighthouse on the tip. 'I'll miss all of it.'

—

Kit stowed Lauren's bags in his car, along with all of Amelia's paraphernalia.

'Why does she need all this stuff? She's only a few weeks old!'

Lauren laughed. 'This is just the start of it. Wait until I turn one of the bedrooms into a nursery.'

'I'd rather not,' Kit muttered nervously, as he closed the boot.

'Yoo-hoo!'

Lauren turned around. 'Morning.' She waved as Mrs Lovelace, Jean and Phoenix trapsed through the gate, followed quickly by Nicki, then stepped closer to Kit. 'It's Polkerran's own barmy army,' she said quietly. 'Hope you're ready for this.'

'This is the *cricket* team?'

With a laugh, Lauren shook her head. 'Not quite. Come on, time you were initiated.'

The locals were all bent on saying a final farewell to Lauren, and she watched them all take seats at the scrubbed table with a fondness she could never have anticipated six months ago. Cuddling Amelia against the weight she bore in her breast, Lauren tried to count her blessings. She may not have the man she loved, but she did have this beautiful being in her life. She wasn't leaving Polkerran empty-hearted at all.

As Anna produced toasted teacakes, buttered malt loaf and her melt-in-the-mouth signature brownies, washed down with plenty of tea, coffee and homemade lemonade, the conversation made its usual detour from topic to topic, and Lauren and Anna exchanged amused glances now and again at Kit's baffled expression.

'Where's that Old Patrick to, then?' Mrs Lovelace reached for a slice of malt loaf. 'Want a word with him, I does.'

'I think he's getting ready to cut the grass.' Anna gestured towards the garden. 'He was in the shed earlier.'

'Expect he'll be in for his cup of tea dreckly, Mum.' Jean handed a paper napkin to her mother, who promptly tucked it up her sleeve.

Mrs Lovelace made a derogatory noise, and Nicki snorted. 'What's he done now, Mrs L?'

'Hmph.' The elderly lady crossed her arms on her chest. 'Carried away, he was, beheading my peruvians.'

'Harsh,' intoned Lauren as Kit eyed Mrs Lovelace warily.

'Petunias, love,' Jean mouthed at him. 'Taking off the dead heads.'

Mia stirred in Lauren's arms, and she walked over to place her in the seat carrier, tucking a light blanket around her, rocking it to and fro until she slept, then returned to the table. Judging by Kit's face, he'd probably had enough of the full Mrs L effect. Probably time they made a move.

Receiving a hug from each of them, Lauren was touched by their kindness and surprised at how emotional she felt. She didn't want to think about the looming farewell with Daniel. Thank goodness there would be people around.

'Here, my lovely.' Mrs Lovelace pressed something soft into Lauren's hands before giving her a hug. 'In case you'm ever in need of a muff to twiddle.'

Seeing Kit's astonished face amidst the general laughter, Lauren took his arm as Anna carried the car seat bearing the baby across the room.

'I'll explain in the car.'

—

Lauren had barely recovered from saying goodbye to Anna and Oliver when Kit pulled the car into a space at The Lookout.

'Wow.'

He stepped from the car, staring at the stunning house as Lauren took in the filming paraphernalia, cables everywhere, sound men, cameras and there, being interviewed on screen, was Daniel.

He wore her favourite shirt, the blue one. A shirt she'd rested her cheek on at the dance, listening to the steady beat of his heart as they moved around the room to George Michael. It seemed a lifetime ago.

Lauren gave Kit a potted history of the build, speaking in a low voice, but then, Claudia emerged on the step and, seeing them, waved gaily and came over.

'Are you off?'

'Yes. Not the best timing.' Lauren nodded towards the mayhem.

Claudia flashed her fabulous smile. 'Daniel's being a bit of a grump, so Gerry's trying to warm him up. They only need a few more outdoor shots and they're done, but he's not being very obliging.' She turned to the man at Lauren's side. 'You must be Kit.'

'Yes, sorry! Forgetting my manners. Kit, this is Claudia.'

'Lovely to meet you.' Claudia glanced over her shoulder. 'Here he comes.'

Lauren drew in a sharp breath, averting her gaze as Daniel joined them.

'So, you're off then.'

'I'm told it's the optimal time to fit around the feeding, cleaning, sleeping schedule.' Kit explained, and Lauren raised her head.

Daniel's gaze was on her, his brown eyes guarded. 'Safe travels.' He swallowed visibly, and Lauren placed her hands behind her back to avoid launching herself into his arms. 'Let me know how Mia is after the journey.'

And me? What about me? she wanted to scream.

Lauren put out a hand to Claudia. 'Hope the programme goes down a storm. I won't get to see it as its regional.'

'It'll be up on YouTube at some point. I'll send Anna a link to forward.' Claudia's smile was warm as she turned to Kit. 'Drive carefully, precious cargo and all that.'

Lauren hesitated. Should she offer a hand to Daniel again, like she had when she left The Lookout last time? The cameras might have a field day if she dragged him into the house and up the stairs, begging him to make passionate love to her, to never let her go…

'Er, Lauren?' She started, looking at Kit. 'You okay? You've gone very pink.'

'Yes, yes. All good.' Lauren pinned a smile on her face. 'Goodbye, Daniel. So pleased the house all came together, and… well, you know…' She held out a hand, deeming it the safest option, but Daniel clearly hadn't seen the rushes.

He grasped the offered hand and pulled her into his embrace, wrapping both arms around her. Heart pounding, Lauren closed her eyes, pretending they weren't stood with Claudia and Kit, or surrounded by an entire camera crew who seemed particularly attached to their equipment. Never had she experienced such closeness to this man, the one who held her heart. Always, the baby had been between them, but now she could savour how well they fitted together.

'Hey, Danny-boy!' Gerry's voice pierced the moment, and Lauren reluctantly opened her eyes as Daniel's arms slowly released her.

Stepping back, she tried to clear her throat, which was taut with emotion, raising wide eyes to his. He took both her hands in his.

'Thank you,' he whispered, and she leaned forward to catch the words. 'For an amazing summer. Let's never forget.'

If emotion hadn't stolen Lauren's ability to speak, she might have found a Take That response, but the director's voice intruded.

'*Danny-boy!* We need to make use of this light.'

'Damn it.' He stroked his thumb across her palm. 'Be happy, Lauren.'

He leaned down and placed a soft kiss at the side of her mouth, then turned and walked back to the crew without a backward glance, Claudia hurrying in his wake.

Lauren's vision seemed blurry as she got into the car, oblivious to the drive down the lane to the bridge.

'Jeez, Lauren,' Kit said, throwing her a sideways glance as they drove along the harbour. 'Isn't it supposed to be babies that cry all the time?'

Through her tears, Lauren saw the parking sign she'd followed on her arrival, peering down the lane towards the cafe where she'd first met Daniel as they passed by. The ache in Lauren's chest almost took her breath.

Sometimes, dreams have to end.

Her escape to Polkerran Point was over. Time to revisit the real world.

Chapter Thirty-Six

Greatest Daze

When Amelia reached two and a half months of age, by which time she'd become adept at chewing fingers and waving her arms excitedly at the sight of her favourite toy, Lauren started her new job at the Devere Corporation's Leeds site, just a short drive from Kit's flat where she had set up home.

At first, her mum had stayed with them, but after a few weeks, she only came from Tuesday morning to Thursday evening, when Lauren had to be in the office. On Mondays and Fridays, she worked from home, managing to care for Amelia around her work and calls, though she had her camera off in some meetings, and occasionally the audio too, just listening in. No one knew she had the baby in her arms, soothing or feeding her a bottle.

Amelia had settled into a routine of sorts, though there were the occasional bad nights, but she had Lauren's talent for sleeping like a log once she'd gone off. It was just that she favoured not 'going off' until around one a.m. and then didn't want to wake up – other than for a bottle around four – until Lauren's work day was well under way.

'You're going to be a night-owl like your mum, aren't you, sweetie,' Lauren said as she rocked Amelia to and fro in her arms, one ear on the meeting taking place off camera.

Anna had been in touch frequently and was off to stay with Matt shortly. Oliver was waiting on probate before he could finally be done with his father's affairs, but the inheritance would enable him to set up a new business venture, which Daniel was to head up – though the latter had barely been in Polkerran, it seemed.

Anna never mentioned Claudia, and Lauren assumed Daniel, if he was so absent from Cornwall, was spending more time in Bristol. She didn't ask about how things were going between them. Anna would hardly know if they didn't come to Polkerran, but Lauren was pleased to hear Daniel had moved onto something else other than the consultancy work, which had seemed to be bringing him down towards the end.

Several times, she'd tapped a message into WhatsApp, but then she'd delete it. Yes, they'd been mates. Good ones, but the same thing stood: it wasn't right for her to message him as a supposed ex. She knew she wouldn't have liked it.

The moments of quiet were less obliging, and the loss of the first man she'd ever truly loved consumed her. She missed Daniel – and life at The Lookout – so much her body ached. Sessions down the gym whenever her mum stayed over and early morning runs were of no help. Besides, the streets of Leeds, even in the leafy Roundhay area, weren't the lanes of Polkerran Point or the cliff paths. She missed the views from the coast path, the ever-changing skies, the ceaseless call of the seabirds and the pounding waves, and wondered if she'd ever fully adjust to the city noises again. It all felt out of kilter for Amelia. Life couldn't just go on as it had before.

Although her days were busy, and it was easier to shut Daniel out, the ache in her breast never dissipated and the moment she was alone in the flat, he filled her mind. Precious moments haunted Lauren, as memory after memory flooded her non-working senses.

Becoming thin, her mother tried to feed her up, but Lauren's appetite was non-existent. Amelia was her saving grace, her love for her daughter knowing no bounds, and as she grew in confidence in her ability to care for the little one, she drew comfort from the bond she felt they'd already developed.

Anna had called recently too, full of her impending visit to the parents who had raised Matt. She was in two minds about how she'd feel about it all, but felt it important to meet them, and he was keen for her to do so.

–

Lauren was in an office meeting room the following Thursday, dictating a report, when a message came in from Anna.

> Check your email. Sent a large file over. xx

It was followed by an intriguing array of emojis, and Lauren smiled. She'd read it later. Amelia was having her first morning in the company creche, and Lauren tried to curb the urge to visit every hour, limiting herself to a couple of calls to check on her and spending her lunch break down there before her mum came to collect her charge.

Amelia, of course, was oblivious and perfectly content, and the two ladies running the creche were lovely.

It was evening before Lauren would have a moment to check personal emails, and she fed and winded Amelia first, spending a rewarding hour with her before lying her on the play mat with its overhead baby gym as her mum prepared dinner.

Anna's email was brief, simply saying, 'You need to watch this'. It was followed by another row of emojis and a great many hearts.

Curious, Lauren poured herself a small glass of wine and sat cross-legged on the massive leather sofa, the laptop perched on top of a box file on the coffee table to make it the right height for viewing.

Lauren's breath hitched in her throat as the short video opened with a soaring aerial shot, no doubt from a drone, of The Lookout and its stunning location on the clifftop, before panning round to show the cove. The familiar call of the seabirds drifted around the room as the image faded and became one of Daniel.

Wrapping her arms around her middle, Lauren's gaze fixed hungrily on his features. She realised it must have been from when Gerry had brought someone to do screen tests on Lauren, only she hadn't noticed they'd taken some of Daniel too, or that there was video footage as well as the stills they'd been shown.

The screen shimmered as the image faded, to be replaced by one of the two of them, laughing about something. Gerry had been right about the screen capturing their chemistry. Lauren couldn't recall what they'd been amused by, but probably Gerry's insistence on calling Lauren by the wrong name. There were several similar clips, and the sound of the waves in the distance had slowly faded into faint wisps of music which Lauren couldn't quite identify.

Then, the screen faded once more, before revealing footage of Daniel – a full-length shot of him frozen in place. It felt as though an invisible band tightened around Lauren's rib cage as the camera moved in, slowly roaming over his features. A light breeze lifted the edge of his dark blond hair as an expression filled his face – one she'd seen now and again when caught unawares, his warm brown eyes seeming to darken.

The image merged with another: Lauren, standing rigid, her gaze fixed on something immediately ahead, and then, in a succession of shots, the camera caught their movement towards each other, Lauren's outstretched hand and Daniel pulling her into his embrace.

With a gasp of breath, Lauren leaned closer, reaching out a hand to touch the screen as she noticed something she couldn't have seen on the day: a tear on Daniel's cheek as he cradled her and the way his hands trembled against her back.

The music grew louder, became recognisable, and as the lyrics became clearer, Lauren was swept up in the memory of how she'd felt at the time. A hand shot to her throat as the camera caught the anguish in her own eyes as they stepped away from each other.

The images faded to black, as did the last note of Take That's 'Everything Changes'. What on earth?!

Lauren wiped her cheeks.

'Lauren, love?'

Sniffing, she hastily closed the laptop.

'Is it ready?' Her voice sounded foreign to her ears. 'I—' She cleared her throat. 'I just need to have a quick call with Anna.'

'I can always keep yours warm. You go, I'll come and sit with Mia.'

Lauren checked on Amelia, who emitted a reassuring gurgle, eyes darting to and fro as she tried to swipe at the overhanging soft toys, and as her mum came into the room, Lauren hurried to the study and connected a video call with her friend. Her emotions were shot, what was Anna *doing* to her?

Niceties first.

'How're things in Cornwall? How'd it go with Matt's family?'

Anna waved a dismissive hand. 'I'll tell you another time.' She leaned forward. 'Did you watch it?'

'Yes.' Lauren's voice was hoarse with emotion. 'I had no idea anyone filmed us. Has Daniel seen it?'

'No. He came over and we watched the main recording of the show that will go out, but there was this other file and Daniel dismissed it, saying Gerry had sent it over, but he hadn't seen it yet. Outtakes and the like. I decided to have a peek and—' Anna held up her hands. 'Well, I felt you ought to see some of it. Matt's a whizz at editing, so he cut the boring stuff and put this together.' She smirked. 'Don't show it to anyone. It's probably infringing Gary Barlow's copyright.'

'But why that track? I mean, it does feel like we're a thousand miles apart, but...' Lauren desperately wanted to watch it again, but what did it matter? '*Nothing* has changed. Daniel's with Claudia. Besides, he's made no effort to be in touch.'

'He's not, and I'm pretty sure *that's* because he mistakenly assumed you were back with Kit.'

'*What?* When did they... But I'm not. I wasn't ever...' Lauren put a hand to her head, thoroughly confused.

Hope and despair were leaping and diving through her in equal measure and she grasped her middle in an attempt to head off a collision. 'Why would he think that?'

'He said he'd twice walked in on intimate conversations between the two of you – on the phone and in person. All the signs pointed to it. Daniel knew you were moving into Kit's flat, and his coming to fetch you both sealed the deal for him.' Anna shrugged. 'Two plus two equals seven?'

Lauren hung her head. It wasn't easy talking about Daniel, and after what she'd just seen, the agony had intensified.

'Lauren?' Anna's voice roused her and she looked back at the screen. 'If I'd known what he thought, I'd have put him right, but as you know, I've been off to meet the Locksley family, and Daniel's been away and then scooting all over Cornwall, so we hadn't seen him properly for ages.'

'But he knows now?' Lauren interjected. 'Though I don't see that it matters.' She still hadn't heard from him.

'As of last night, but he and Oliver went away early this morning and won't be back until late tomorrow.'

Lauren's brow furrowed. 'Why?'

'Part of this new venture of Oliver's, there's this auction for… never mind that now. They had to go.'

What should she do? Desperate to see Daniel, Lauren stared at her friend.

What if her friend was misinterpreting these clips? Anna was such a romantic at heart. Had her brother, unintentionally, manipulated the images to portray something that wasn't really there?

'What happened with Claudia?' Part of her wasn't surprised it hadn't worked out, but even if it was finally over, it didn't mean Daniel wasn't heartbroken all over again.

'I'm not sure entirely, but it sounds like the trip abroad wasn't exactly what it seemed.'

'How— and how is he? Is he… is Daniel okay?'

'No, he's not, but before you assume that's because it's over with Claudia, you need to know that he left here last night in a state of shock over you and Kit not being back together.'

'I need to contact him.'

'You need to come here, back to Polkerran Point.'

Polkerran…

'Daniel needs *you*, Lauren – not a WhatsApp message.'

It felt as though Lauren's heart stopped, then began racing. 'Is he unwell?'

'On the contrary,' Anna said dryly. 'He's a tad lovesick, possibly, but if you've watched those clips carefully enough, you'll know the reason why.'

Lauren's gaze was drawn to the window and the intense lights of Leeds city centre, the snaking rows of cars, the constantly changing traffic lights: red, amber, green, repeat. The buzz she used to feel working for a big corporation, the excitement of a vibrant city, remained there but it was muted, as though muffled by something Lauren couldn't determine.

The ache in her middle, one she'd carried with her ever since she'd left Cornwall – and Daniel – behind intensified. How could she bear the idea he was suffering, but how could she trust she was the cause? He'd never said anything, never tried anything beyond that kiss, which had been done as part of their silly competing… hadn't it? Was Anna really interpreting the video correctly?

'In case you're in any doubt, on the recording – this episode, which is due to air next month – you might be interested to know the caption describes Claudia as "A close family friend".'

'Oh!' Lauren stared at her hands, hope swirling through her uncertainty like the waves below The Lookout.

'Lauren?' Her attention snapped back to the screen.

'Sorry. Miles away.'

'You are, and it's time you did something about it.'

Chapter Thirty-Seven

Land's End

Friday was a day just to get through. Lauren finished work around four, loaded the car and set off with Amelia, stopping overnight in Gloucestershire to break the journey.

Late autumn had truly arrived as she drove down the winding hill into Polkerran the next morning. Those trees still in leaf were tipped with copper, but many were already bereft of much of their foliage, clinging on to a few trembling leaves as though stripped to their underwear. The light over the sea had altered to a steely grey, almost merging with the sky on the horizon. Plumes of smoke rose from cottage chimneys, and crows gathered in clusters on the telegraph poles. It seemed a lifetime since Lauren had first arrived in the village, and she eased Kit's much larger car along the lane to Anna's with her heart pounding in her chest.

A whimper came from the car seat behind, and Lauren glanced instinctively at the rear-view mirror.

'It's alright, little one. We're here now. Time for your next feed.' Lauren wrinkled her nose. 'And a change, and then Mummy has something to take care of.'

Anna was almost as delighted to see Lauren as she was Amelia. The baby was cuddled and exclaimed over, how she'd grown and changed, and as Lauren went through the feeding and changing process, Anna began to talk about Daniel.

'I'm so glad you decided to come and talk to him. This Wednesday evening was the only time I've seen him in ages, although we've had the odd text exchange, and he's not a happy man.'

Lauren walked to and fro, rubbing Amelia gently on her tiny back.

'You have no idea how hard it was not to drive straight to The Lookout, but I really think there's a conversation to be had that would be better done without Mia present.'

'I told him I didn't think you'd settled.'

Lauren stared at her friend. 'Why would you do that?'

'Because it's true. Look at you, Lauren. You're wasting away. Besides, one of you has to get off your backside and speak first. Honestly, for experienced execs, you're both ridiculous at communication.'

The reservations that had haunted Lauren through the long drive returned, and her troubled gaze met Anna's amused look.

'I've no idea what I'm doing. I had to come, because I adore that man. If there's any chance he's going to adore me back,' a rush of emotion gripped Lauren, and she swallowed hard on it as she held Amelia close, 'I'll take it. But I don't know where it will take *us*. My life isn't here, and Daniel's is.'

'Lauren.' Anna's voice was firm. 'Letting it go round and round in your head isn't going to solve anything. Surely the most important thing right now is to talk. It sounds like you've both made assumptions that have not been helped by Kit's presence in your life lately, I suspect.'

Anna was right, and Lauren knew it. *One step at a time…*

She glanced down at Amelia, whose lids had closed. 'Will you be alright with the baby for a short while?'

'Obviously! Go, and let me be the auntie I've longed to be.'

'But what about Ali-Matt? And his parents. You haven't told me anything yet.'

Joy emanated from her friend, and Lauren sniffed back a recalcitrant tear. Why was she so damned emotional lately?

'There's lots to tell. The parents… well, nothing's ever what it seems, is it? Anyway, Matt said he might come and stay in Cornwall for a while next year. I'll tell you everything, but not until you've sorted yourself out.'

—

Lauren pulled into a space at The Lookout, relieved to see the Jeep and BMW there. Her gaze roamed over the house as she emerged from the car, and she closed her eyes for a moment, having an almost visceral response to seeing it again.

Then, she looked around. The summer planting had long faded, and a tremor shot through Lauren at the memory of the day she'd said goodbye to Daniel, standing in this very spot.

She rang the doorbell, but no one came, and tentatively she tried the handle but the door was locked. Uncertain now, she walked around the outside of the house, peering into the windows. No sign of life.

Glancing at her watch, Lauren mulled on the likelihood Daniel's late night return home had led to a prolonged lie-in. Then, she dismissed it. He'd never shown any predilection for lying in before.

Her heart had resumed its pounding, but now she felt more anxious than anything. She couldn't have come all this way for nothing, yet there was no way she could have said what she wanted to over the phone. All the same, she put in a call to Daniel, but it went straight to voicemail.

Reluctantly, Lauren retraced her steps, but then a thought crossed her mind, and she followed the cliff path so she could survey the beach below.

Daniel sat on the rocks, staring out to sea. Her insides swirling much like the shallows as they embraced the small rocks on the beach, Lauren made her way down the steps, throwing the small pool which had claimed her old phone a stern look.

Why had her mind gone blank? Lauren had memorised presentations and talks for years, delivered without any notes, yet now, she couldn't recall the carefully rehearsed words she'd muttered to herself through the long hours of the drive south. Where had they gone?

Daniel still had his back to her, but barely had she taken two steps towards him when he turned around.

He rose slowly to his feet, and seeing him again almost took Lauren's breath. Today, he wore a thick sweater and jeans tucked into his Hunters, the breeze ruffling his short hair and stubble shadowing his cheeks.

'Hi.' Lauren croaked, but the word was whipped away by the wind as Daniel jumped down off the rock, striding across the sand towards her.

Filled with tension, Lauren tucked her hands into her jacket pockets as he reached her, and they both spoke at once.

'Anna said—'

'Anna says—'

They stopped.

'You go,' she urged him.

Daniel gave his head a faint shake. 'I don't understand. Anna told me you're not with Kit, but I heard you on the phone to him, and then he came all this way to fetch you both.' He ran a hand through his hair in the old familiar way, and Lauren's heart swelled with love as uncertainty filled his face. 'He's Mia's father. I assumed you'd reconciled. That last day… I felt terrible when I appeared at an awkward moment just as you were telling him—'

'I loved him?' Lauren shook her head. 'I didn't get a chance to finish with "as a friend". And Kit *is* a good friend. He collected me to make the journey easier, save me hiring a car with the Mini smashed up, but he's still child-averse. We're not together, haven't been since we split in February.'

'But I saw a photo. A selfie of you both.' Daniel looked a little sheepish. 'On Instagram. You were at Heathrow.'

'Saying goodbye, Daniel. He's moved to the States for at least the next three years, if not more.'

He took a step closer, his clenched hands by his side. 'What did Anna say?'

Lauren gave a small laugh. 'What didn't she? Most importantly to me, that you and Claudia are no longer together. Only no one told me… you never got in touch.'

Daniel edged closer, his fingers uncurling and voice softening. 'I had no reason to. You'd left for your new life, far away from here; the all-important career re-boot. Kit was on the scene – or so I thought.'

'And Claudia? You went away together until the filming. When did it…' Her voice tailed away as Daniel shook his head firmly.

'If I think on it, the relationship was over before we even met. Took me a while to understand why.' He took another step closer. 'When you came back from that talk with Claudia, I felt that something had changed – I just couldn't work out what.' He ran a hand through his hair. 'I ended it at the airport, before we got on the plane. We'll always be friends of some sort, Claud and I, but nothing more. She flew to Greece, as we'd planned, and I bought a ticket to Switzerland. Went and tried to lose myself, hiking in the Alps.'

'But why?'

'I like chocolate.'

Lauren rolled her eyes.

'I didn't know what to do, where to go, but Oliver's always going on about the Matterhorn.' The edges of his mouth twitched. 'I have to admit, I hadn't worked through the luggage implications in swapping a beach for mountains.'

'Idiot.'

Daniel's mouth twitched. 'So long as I'm your idiot, I'll take it.'

A smile tugged at Lauren's lips, and her heart pulsed at the implication, but she had to know. 'I meant, why did you finish it. Why then?'

'Because I knew something, categorically, that I'd been denying for weeks, months even. I'd no interest in attempting to rekindle my doomed relationship with Claud because I'd fallen in love with someone else, someone completely out of my reach. When I left Polkerran for the airport, knowing how close you would be to leaving forever when I got back, I realised where I truly wanted to be.' He lifted his shoulders in a helpless gesture. 'I stayed away for the sake of my sanity.'

Silence descended for a moment as Lauren absorbed Daniel's words. 'Anna was right. We're lousy communicators.'

'Then let's prove her wrong.'

Daniel closed what was left of the gap between them, claiming Lauren's mouth in a long, intense kiss, which she returned with delight, thankful to be able to finally express the pent-up passion she'd resisted for so long. Heat spread through her body as Daniel broke away to bury his face in her neck before trailing kisses along her chin, his mouth then reclaiming Lauren's. Senses swimming, the hands which had clung to Daniel's shoulders crept into his hair, and she was aware of his hand cupping the back of her head as his mouth moved sensuously over hers.

When they broke apart, Lauren put a hand to her lips.

'Oh. My. God,' she said in between breaths. 'You have no idea how long I've wanted that to happen.'

'Me too. I missed you so much.' Daniel's voice was hoarse, but his warm brown eyes were fixed intently upon Lauren as he secured her hand in his. 'I knew I had no right to try and interfere, with you back on track with your career, starting a new life. Then, when Anna came back yesterday and gave me hope, I just had to know if I had a chance. I planned to come to Leeds with no game plan other than seeing you, testing the water.'

Lauren raised a hand and touched his face, cradling his cheek in her hand.

'I don't know how to resolve the work thing, but I do know that I'm madly in love with you.'

'You have no idea how I've longed to hear those words. I didn't mean to fall in love with you, Lauren, and it felt so wrong when you were carrying another man's child. It was easier to lie to myself, pretend I was still crazy for

Claudia.' He gave a self-deprecating laugh. 'After all these years, it was easy to convince my stupid brain, despite the feelings I had for you being so different to an infatuation. I had no intention of telling you. Your career has been part of who you are ever since you sold that first lollipop at playgroup. I've no right to ask you to be something you don't want to be.'

Lauren had closed her eyes as Daniel spoke of loving her, and a tear slid down her cheek. How had this man come to mean so much to her?

She opened her eyes as he wiped the tear away. 'I fell in love you with so gradually, I hardly knew it was happening, but I've never felt like this in my life.'

Daniel kissed the tip of her nose. 'So, what do we do about it?'

'I honestly don't know. My career matters, but there's a new part of me now, and it's bigger than any of that. Mia has changed me, for the better, I hope. I'm never going to be content with staying at home, but there has to be a compromise.' She hesitated. 'I don't want to pressure you, but I feel if I have you by my side, I can achieve anything I want to.'

There was silence for a moment as Daniel's gaze raked her face. Then, a smile touched his lips, spread to his eyes and he swept her into another passionate embrace, only breaking off to tell her how much he loved her.

Lauren snuggled against his chest, loving how close they fitted now there was no bump between them. She raised her head.

'I must get back to Mia.'

'How long can you stay?'

'Only until tomorrow. I'm new to the role, so I've no holiday entitlement.'

'Let's go now. I can't wait to see her. Do you think she'll remember me?'

They set off across the sand, and Lauren tucked her arm through his. 'Of course she will. She has her mother's taste in men.'

—

Waking on Sunday morning, Lauren stretched languorously. November sunlight streamed through the vast window, with nothing but sea to be seen. For a second, she closed her eyes, her mouth curved as she reflected on the previous night with Daniel, then she began to laugh quietly.

The lovemaking had been as ardent and intense as Lauren had imagined but interspersed with bouts of resigned amusement. Neither of them had quite anticipated the frequency of interruptions from the baby in the adjacent dressing room.

Lauren's eyes flew open. Amelia! She shot out of the bed, snatching up her dressing gown and struggling into it as she reached the crib. It was empty, but before her momentary panic could manifest itself, she heard Daniel's voice.

'Let's go and see if Mummy is awake, shall we?'

Looking up, she was relieved to see him walk in, the baby nestled against his shoulder, and she held out her arms.

'You have to hug me first,' Daniel warned, and Lauren wrapped her arms around his firm body, wishing they could have a repeat of last night, then relieved him of Amelia.

'She's had half a bottle. I did as you showed me last night, but I think I failed with the nappy. It keeps coming undone.'

Lauren smirked. 'You'll learn. It's not like you won't get lots of practice.'

She cuddled Amelia, dropped a kiss on the fine down on her head. 'I'll give her a bath.'

Reaching up, she pressed a kiss on Daniel's mouth, and he placed an arm around her, returning the kiss with the promise of more later.

'I'll get breakfast ready. What time will you have to leave?'

Lauren's heart sank. She'd woken to such happiness, and now it was as though a cloud had smothered the sun. 'It's six to seven hours' drive, depending on traffic, and I'll have to make a few stops, so I'd best head off around midday.'

Daniel threw her a keen look, then turned away. 'I'll put the coffee on.'

Half an hour later, Lauren carried Amelia down the stairs, appreciating the aroma emanating from the kitchen. The baby was more obliging than she'd been overnight and went to sleep in her carrier by Lauren's feet as they tucked into bacon and eggs at the island.

'She had a disturbed night,' Lauren mused, casting the baby a fond look.

Daniel reached out and took her hand. 'So did we, for all the best reasons.' He raised her hand and pressed a kiss on the back, keeping his gaze on Lauren's, and warmth filled her cheeks at the memory.

'When can we do it again?' she whispered.

With a knowing look, Daniel released her hand and picked up his fork. 'Well now, I think you might be a bit tired tonight, with the journey here and back in two days, but Monday's looking good.'

Lauren pouted. 'Don't tease.' Her chest bore a heavy weight, contemplating leaving after so fleeting a reunion. Then, she brightened. 'Or were you thinking of sexting?'

Daniel glanced at the sleeping baby. 'Feels slightly wrong to talk like this in Mia's presence.'

'She's her mother's child. She sleeps deeply once she's off.'

They finished their breakfast and cleared the things away, and then walked over to the vast bay window and looked out over the open sea. It was a cold but sunny day, and the sky and water were no longer a dull grey.

Desperate for another kiss, Lauren tugged at Daniel's arm, and he looked down, then claimed her lips for a moment before holding her close.

'I meant what I said about Monday.' Lauren frowned into his chest, but he continued. 'I'm coming back with you today.'

Lauren pulled back in astonishment. 'But how?'

Letting her go, Daniel sat in the nearby armchair and pulled her down to sit on his lap, and she leaned back against his chest, conscious of the steady thump of his heart.

'I desperately want to be with you, and if you can't come to me,' she felt him shrug, 'it makes sense for me to come to you. I'll bring my car too, because I'll have to come and go, but there's nothing holding me here, Lauren.'

'But what about this role for Oliver?'

'We're going into partnership, with him as a sort of silent partner because he's so busy with his lecturing and writing. He's done what he can with his own funds, but now he's inherited his dad's property portfolio, he can really make a difference.' Anticipation fluttered through Lauren as Daniel's voice reverberated through her body. 'I'm to oversee it and also find other investments for the company – that's what Friday's auction was all about – but we've agreed we need to recruit a hands-on, local manager for the Cornish properties. The intention will be continuing to lease to locals at affordable rents. As Oliver says, it's a long-term investment. The properties will repay him whenever he sells, but that will only ever be with local residential occupancy restrictions in place. He's asked me to investigate how we put it in place.'

Lauren sat up, swivelling round in Daniel's lap. 'I can't believe it! You'd do this, for me?'

He raised a hand and tucked a strand of Lauren's hair behind her ear. 'For us. I love you so much, Lauren Primrose Kirkham. I'd do anything for you, but this is a no brainer. The house is finished, there's nothing to hold me here. I can do 90 per cent of the job from anywhere in the country, and when I need to come back, I've this house to stay in. We can holiday here too – you, me and Mia.'

Overwhelmed with happiness, Lauren threw her arms around Daniel, nestling her face into his neck and inhaling his scent. God, he smelled good!

She raised her head, placing a long kiss on his lips, feeling his mouth curve into a smile before it became mutually passionate. 'Do you think we could—'

A wail came from the carrier in the kitchen. Amelia had decided otherwise, but as she went to fetch her daughter and Daniel headed upstairs to pack a suitcase, Lauren scooped her daughter into her arms and walked back to drink in the stunning scenery.

'We're going to be so happy, little one,' Lauren whispered, rocking gently from side to side, Mia nuzzled against her shoulder. 'And we're going to love calling this our home from home as you grow up.'

Her heart full, Lauren stepped closer to the window as Amelia's eyelids drooped once more.

'Goodbye, little Cornish cove,' she whispered. 'Who knew my escape to Polkerran would bring me more happiness than I could ever have imagined.'

Amelia was fast asleep again, and Lauren softly stroked the baby's back, then took one last look at the view. It was a breezy day, and white caps flickered over the sea as gulls swooped low before soaring away against the pale blue sky. A lone fishing boat chugged towards the entrance to Polkerran, and Lauren's gaze fell upon the lighthouse on the rocks, just visible above the hedgerow bordering the house.

'We'll see you again soon. I promise.'

Acknowledgements

When I set out to write this story, I had no idea how complicated it would become.

Poor Lauren was so comfortably in control of her life throughout the first book in the series, I'm sure she's still trying to work out why I threw her so many curveballs in this second one.

As a result, I am excessively grateful to my fabulous editor, Emily Bedford, whose patience and wisdom prevented this book (several times) from ending up in my shredder! Emily, your guidance and feedback helped me to craft a complicated jumble of chapters into a story I now love with all my heart. I'd also like to say a huge thank you to Chere Tricot for the meticulous copy edit and Vicki Vrint for her eye for detail when proof-reading.

Special thanks go to the lovely Miranda Mapleton, for being so generous with her time, answering my many questions about the challenges of transitioning from a successful career with several high-profile multinationals to managing her own consultancy and working from home, with a little one in the wings. Miranda, your insights and experience on the blessings and downsides of such a transition were so helpful as I forged a new path for Lauren.

It's many years since I went through pregnancy, as both my children are now in their thirties, so I am full of gratitude and admiration for the lovely ladies who answered my plea and talked openly of their own, much more recent, experiences. There were many message exchanges and a few video chats, including the sharing of some very precious memories, both of the joys and the sad times: Eleanor Ray (Liz), Melanie Golding, Eleanor Pattison, Rebecca (Becs) Ryan, Lucy Ayrton and Andi Michael Forsythe, you are all absolute gems. Thank you so much.

Massive, heart-felt thanks go to all the lovely bloggers, who diligently support authors by taking the time to read and review their books. Your generosity of time and dedication to the reviewing craft are much appreciated.

The writing community is a solid one, and I'm fortunate to have made many friends over the years, but I'm keen to express my love and gratitude to two of my writing besties. They are both incredibly talented authors but also my very special friends: Kitty Wilson and Jane Cable aka Eva Glyn. They are always there for me, whenever I need a vent, encouragement or just a laugh. Kitty, thank you for helping me choose a romantic way to deliver a certain message near the end of this book, and Jane, thank you for understanding me better than I know myself!

Finally, my deepest love and thanks go to my husband, Julian. On a practical level, having lived with someone who's worked in supply chain for a multinational and watched him travel the world with them throughout his varied career, helped immensely in deciding what Lauren's work life would have been. On a more personal level, without Julian by my side, I wouldn't have the time, the support or the emotional inclination to write.

Plus, he never fails to make me laugh, even on a bad day (and mixes great drinks)! Love you forever xx